CRIME SKEIN

A Knitorious Murder Mystery

REAGAN DAVIS

D1319124

COPYRIGHT

ISBN: 978-1-7772359-4-9 (ebook)

ISBN: 978-1-7772359-5-6 (print)

ISBN: 978-1-990228-24-7 (hardcover)

ISBN: 978-1-990228-25-4 (large print paperback)

FOREWORD

Dear Reader,

Despite several layers of editing and proofreading, occasionally a typo or grammar mistake is so stubborn that it manages to thwart my editing efforts and camouflage itself amongst the words in the book.

If you encounter one of these obstinate typos or errors in this book, please let me know by contacting me at Hello@ReaganDavis.com.

Hopefully, together we can exterminate the annoying pests.

Thank you!

Reagan Davis

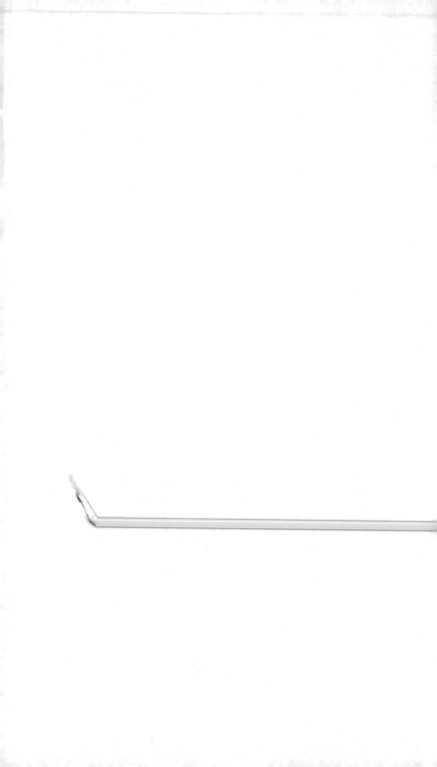

CONTENTS

CHAPTER 1

THURSDAY, January 14th

Tomorrow morning, Harmony Lake will either stay the cozy, sweet town I know and love, or become a soon-to-be tacky resort town on the cusp of a corporate coup.

I'm hoping for the former, not the latter.

Harmony Lake isn't like other towns. We have a big-box policy to protect us from corporate invasion. I support the big-box policy. I don't want big business to commercialize our lovely little lakeside sanctuary. Residents who *oppose* the big-box policy, and want to see our town overrun with drive-thrus and giant warehouse stores, are known as big-boxers. They are a loud minority, made up of residents who would benefit from selling land to the corporate invaders.

Our quaint, family-owned businesses and restaurants make Harmony Lake the intimate and cozy refuge we call home. There are no drive-thrus, no neon signs advertising corporate logos, and no multi-level parking structures. Our town is a blissful oasis, free from the corporate landscape found in most cities and suburbs. The reason tourists flock here is to escape the hustle and bustle of their day-to-day lives and immerse themselves in our small-town charm.

"Is that a cat toy for the Animal Centre?" Sheamus asks, pointing to my knitting.

"Yes," I reply, nodding. "Nothing like knitting for a worthy cause."

Sheamus isn't a knitter, so I'm surprised he knows about the cat toy initiative for the Animal Centre.

Our local charity knitting guild is collecting knitted cat toys to benefit The Vanity Fur Centre for Animal Health & Wellness—known to locals as the Animal Centre. It's our local, all-in-one animal shelter, veterinary hospital, animal sanctuary, and animal education centre. The donated cat toys will be sold in their gift shop and online store.

"No need to ask who you voted for, I take it?" Sheamus shouts over the buzz of the crowd, as he stands next to our booth at the Irish Embassy Pub.

"What gave it away?" I reply teasingly.

I brush aside my brown curls and point to the MARTEL FOR MAYOR button affixed to the front of my hand-knit sweater.

Today is election day in Harmony Lake's first ever mayoral by-election, a historic event in our tiny town.

Harmony Lake was a reliable hotbed of political rest, then our town's predictable political balance was thrown into upheaval by a scandal so shocking that the former mayor and police chief were forced to leave town in a cloud of corruption and disgrace.

Today, the residents of Harmony Lake will choose between two potential leaders, and the future of our cozy town hangs in the balance. Everything is on the line.

"What did Sheamus say?" April leans over and asks in my ear.

April is my best friend. We thought a quiet post-ballot dinner at the Irish Embassy Pub would be a nice way to commemorate the end of the mayoral campaign. Apparently, the rest of the town had the same idea, and the pub is packed. Standing room only.

"He asked me who I voted for," I reply directly into her ear.

April smiles and nods. Her blue eyes sparkle, and she tucks a few long, blonde strands of hair behind the ear I'm speaking into. Her year-round, sun-kissed glow gives her the appearance of someone who just returned from a sunny getaway down south. All winter long, people assume she's fresh off a plane from some sun-filled destination or other and are shocked when she tells them she has been nowhere. No one makes that mistake with me. My hazel eyes and fair, alabaster skin are more likely to elicit questions about what type of anemia I have. I don't have anemia; this is just how I look.

April leans forward and turns her head so her wife, Tamara, can yell into her ear next.

"He asked who Megan voted for," April shouts in response to her wife's question, while nudging her head toward me. Tamara nods and smiles, leans back in her seat, and gives us a thumbs-up.

Sheamus is leaning away from me now and speaking into Eric's ear. I don't know what he's saying, but his full head of shocking red hair bobs up and down as he speaks. Whatever he's saying, Eric isn't very enthusiastic about it. He replies with the occasional shrug and a few uncertain smiles.

Eric Sloane is my boyfriend. We met over a year ago when the Harmony Lake Police Department borrowed him from another police force to investigate the first murder in our town's history. He solved the case—and a few more since—and moved here after accepting a detective sergeant position with the Harmony Lake Police Department. Eric is also my tenant; he lives in the apartment above my yarn store, Knitorious. We've been dating for almost a year. In fact, the anniversary of our first date is next week. Eric is planning something special to celebrate it, but whenever I ask him for details, he tells me it's a surprise.

Sheamus leans toward me and jerks his thumb toward Eric. "Megan, convince yer man, here, to come by my place later for a bit of poker, will ya?" he yells with a hint of Irish brogue, flashing me a wide grin.

"I'll see what I can do," I shout back with a wink.

Sheamus is wearing a lovely hand-knit scarf. It looks like two strands of bulky weight yarn held together. One yarn looks to be a variegated combination of greens and rusts, and the other is a complimentary solid cream. I want to reach out and touch it, but over the years, I've learned that non-knitters think it's weird when knitters randomly reach out and pet their clothing. Or get within an inch to inspect the stitches. Or sniff it. When knitters spot hand knits in the wild, personal space protocols go out the window. I speak from experience.

I file away a mental image of the scarf and make a mental note to ask Sheamus about it when we find ourselves in circumstances more conducive to conversation. Sheamus finishes speaking to Eric and moves along to spread his unique brand of blarney to a group of tourists at the next booth.

Sheamus O'Brien is the second-generation owner of The Irish Embassy, known as The Pub, or The Embassy to us locals. The embassy is as close to a genuine Irish pub experience as you can get without hopping on a plane and flying to Ireland.

"Ready to go?" Eric mouths to me from across the table.

His phone buzzes and vibrates. When he picks it up to check it, I notice how tired he looks. His eyes are heavy, and his posture is more limp than normal, like he's wilting. Even the honey-coloured flecks in his brown eyes seem duller than normal.

"Sure," I say, nodding.

He puts down his phone, winks, and gives me a warm smile that makes the butterflies in my stomach wake up and start fluttering.

I lean over and tell April that Eric and I are heading out. She informs me that she and Tamara won't be far behind us.

We pay the bill and wrap ourselves in our winter woollies because it's freezing outside. The temperature is at least minus ten with the windchill, and we're supposed to have a snowstorm tonight. Environment Canada issued a snowfall warning saying we should expect up to fifteen centimetres before morning.

We're about to get up from the booth when Adam waves to me from the door. I gesture for him to come over. Adam Martel is my ex-husband and the mayor presumptive of Harmony Lake. By the time the residents of Harmony Lake wake up tomorrow morning to shovel their driveways, Adam will hopefully be our new mayor. Our big-box policy will remain securely in place for the duration of his term in office.

Adam and I were married for almost twenty years. We finalized our divorce in October. Our daughter, Hannah, is nineteen and goes to university in Toronto. We have a virtual brunch with her every Sunday. I'm proud of how Adam and I handled our divorce. We were careful to make sure the implosion of our marriage had a minimal effect on the people we love, and we redefined our relationship and learned how to be friends. We're not married anymore, but we're still family.

Adam is Harmony Lake's local lawyer. He's politically inclined and passionate about the small town where we live and raised our daughter; he'll be an amazing mayor.

"Good evening, Your Worship," I greet him playfully.

Your Worship is the appropriate way to address a mayor. He better not get used to it. I don't intend to call him Your Worship ever again.

"It might be premature for that," he chuckles, then bends down, and we exchange a double-cheek kiss.

Adam turns to Eric and asks him if he's going to Sheamus's place later to play cards. When Eric says he doubts he'll go, Adam tries to persuade him.

Yes, my ex-husband and boyfriend are friends. Good friends. Eric was new in town and didn't know anyone in Harmony Lake, and despite living here most of his adult life, Adam didn't have many close relationships in Harmony Lake either. Before opening his own practice, Adam was a workaholic senior partner at a law firm in the city. They bonded over a mutual love of golf, and the rest is history. Sometimes it's weird that they're friends, but no weirder than the friendship I have with Adam's new partner, Jess.

Jess and I kiss cheeks, and April and I shove over in the booth so she can slide in with us.

"I'm surprised you're here tonight," I say to Jess. "With the snowstorm coming, I didn't think you'd risk the drive."

Jess lives and works forty-five minutes away in Harmony Hills. She takes off her toque and shakes out her long, strawberry-blond hair.

"I wanted to be here tonight for Adam," she explains. "I won't stay long. I plan to get on the road before the worst of the snow starts."

"Full house tonight." Adam scans the pub, searching for an available table or booth.

"We're just leaving," Eric says. "Why don't you sit here?"

With that decided, Eric and I vacate the booth, giving Adam and Jess our seats.

Stepping into the cool night air is a relief. It took us at least ten minutes to get from the booth to the door. We stopped at almost every table and booth to say hi to friends and neighbours—one hazard of living in a small town where everyone knows everyone else. Stopping to chat while wearing two layers of clothes, a down-filled winter coat, a thick hand-knit ear warmer, cowl, and mittens is a recipe for overheating.

"Are you going to play cards with the guys?" I ask Eric as we walk up Water Street toward Knitorious.

"I don't think so," he replies. "I'm tired, and they

always play on a weeknight when I have to work the next day."

"Maybe you're tired because you're working two jobs," I suggest. "It's pretty much a done deal that Adam will win this election. Tomorrow, he'll appoint you as the permanent chief of police. You can't be police chief and Harmony Lake PD's only detective. It's too much. Have you given any more thought to hiring a detective to replace you?"

After the scandal that shook our town to its core, the deputy mayor asked Eric to step in as interim chief of police until the newly elected mayor could choose a permanent replacement. He's been doing two jobs for three months, and it's taking a toll.

When Adam was approached to run for mayor, he made it a condition that he would only enter the race if, upon his election, Eric agreed to become the chief of police permanently. Eric accepted because he knows the locals—who are skeptical of outsiders on a good day—will hesitate to accept a police chief recruited from elsewhere.

"I haven't had much time to think about it because I'm so busy." Eric gathers his scarf around his neck and takes my hand. From inside his coat pocket, his phone makes the notification sounds that have become the soundtrack to our lives lately. "I hope to promote someone from within because I don't think the town is ready to accept any new people, especially someone in a position of authority."

I keep my face down and look at my feet to avoid the sharp sting of the frigid January air on my face.

"Ms. Martel, Police Chief Sloane, so lovely to see you both."

I look up when I hear my name.

Saxon Renaud. Ugh! What an unpleasant way to end the day.

Eric looks up at the same time as me and utters a curse word under his breath, then plasters a fake smile on his handsome face.

"Mr. Renaud." I nod, intending to continue walking.

"Saxon," Eric nods, also still walking.

Saxon steps in front of us, forcing us to stop.

"Hi, Rick," I say with a smile to Saxon's hired henchman, Rick Ransan.

"H-hi, Megan," Rick smiles.

Rick is such a pleasant person. Why does he hang around with someone as insufferable as Saxon Renaud?

"Rick." Eric nods.

"H-h-i, Chief S-Sloane." Rick returns the nod.

In what qualifies as the weirdest thing I've seen today, Saxon uses the long metal tip of his whangee bamboo handle umbrella to draw a line in the snow that's beginning to accumulate on the sidewalk. A line between where Eric and I stand and where Saxon and Rick stand. Is it some kind of metaphorical or literal battle line?

Watching Saxon scrape the tip of his umbrella along the sidewalk, I notice that instead of wearing boots, which would be a practical footwear choice for a night like tonight, he's wearing his signature penny loafers. Complete with pennies, even though we haven't made pennies in this country for years, and rubber overshoes with no insulation value.

Saxon Renaud carrying an umbrella during a blizzard isn't strange to me. He carries his umbrella with him everywhere he goes, all the time, no matter the weather situation. It's like an extension of his right arm; the umbrella is Saxon's quirk.

Using it to draw a line in the snow, however, is new. At least it's new to me. I've never seen him do it before. He's also fond of using his umbrella as a cattle prod to protect his personal space and make people—women— jump out of his way. I've been on the receiving end of his prodding, and it's infuriating. Saxon Renaud is a hard person to like.

I sigh. "What's up, Saxon?" I ask, since he has made no attempt to tell us why he stopped us or to explain the weird line he drew in the snow.

I'm tempted to use the toe of my boot to erase his stupid line, but I resist the urge. The snow is falling faster now, and the line is already disappearing, anyway.

"Chief Sloane, I was hoping to run into you," Saxon says, ignoring me and my question, and looking up at Eric. "I'm willing to give you one more chance to change your mind and accept the permanent chief of police position when I'm confirmed as mayor tomorrow."

Eric shakes his head, rolls his eyes, and chuckles breathily. "No thank you, Saxon," he replies, still shaking his head. "I told you, I would *never* be police chief in a town that would have you as mayor."

"Are you sure?" Saxon asks again. "I suspect you might regret it tomorrow morning."

"A risk I'm willing to take." Eric grins. "Now if you'll excuse us, gentlemen, it's chilly out here." Eric tightens his grip on my hand and walks straight at them, forcing them to part and let us through.

I glance behind us to make sure Saxon and Rick are out of earshot, then quicken my pace to keep up with Eric. He's almost a foot taller than me, and his strides are longer than mine. "The only way Saxon Renaud might win this mayoral election is by cheating," I assert with confidence.

"He won't win," Eric agrees. "There's no way. I'd bet my life on it."

I know he wouldn't *literally* bet his life on it, but I wish he wouldn't tempt fate by saying that.

We both turn to check one more time and make sure the two men haven't doubled back and are walking behind us, listening to our conversation. We glimpse them disappearing into the pub.

"It looks like we left just in time," I remark.

"Yep," Eric concurs. "It might get pretty heated in the pub tonight with both candidates there."

CHAPTER 2

"REMIND me again why we vote today but don't get the results until tomorrow?" Eric asks as I unleash Sophie and take off her sweater after our walk.

Sophie is my corgi. She comes to work with me every day. If Eric and I go out after work, she hangs out in his apartment until we get home. Sophie has a full suite of toys, food, dishes, sweaters, and even a bed here. Knitorious and Eric's apartment are her homes away from home.

"Well," I start, "this year it's due to the weather. Because of the snowfall warning, voting hours were extended until 10 p.m. to give residents who commute enough time to get home to Harmony Lake and cast their votes."

"And in previous years?" he asks.

I shrug. "I don't know. Tradition, I guess? You know how much this town likes tradition."

It's snowing heavily now, and visibility is bad. A fresh layer of white covers everything like a blanket and makes our already-picturesque town look even more postcard worthy. The glow from the slivered fraction of the waxing moon, and the streetlights reflecting off the new-fallen snow, makes the light coming in the windows brighter than usual for a January night.

I hem and haw about whether to go home or stay at Eric's apartment for the night. He convinces me to stay by warming my favourite flannel pyjamas in the dryer and showing me his PVR full of mindless TV shows we like to watch.

There are advantages to dating my tenant; I sleep above the store when the weather is bad, and my morning commute is only thirty seconds.

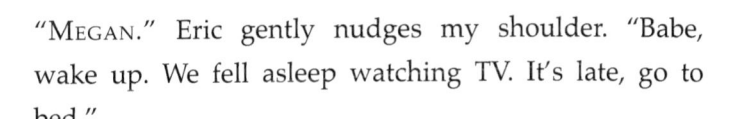

"MEGAN." Eric gently nudges my shoulder. "Babe, wake up. We fell asleep watching TV. It's late, go to bed."

Disoriented and groggy, I take a deep breath and force open my heavy eyes. Overwhelmed by the harsh glare of artificial light, I shut them again. The last thing I remember is knitting a mouse ear and trying to stay awake for the big reveal on the home renovation reality show we were watching. Eric fell asleep checking his email on his phone within ten minutes of the opening credits and was snoring softly on the sofa next to me. I felt myself being lulled to sleep by his rhythmic breathing and fought to stay awake. I guess I failed.

"Why are you dressed?" I ask, squinting while my eyes adjust to being awake. "Is everything OK?"

"I was called into work," he replies. "They called me to a hit and run out on Lake Access Road."

"In a snowstorm?" I asked, still confused, but better able to focus and take in my surroundings.

"Not everything shuts down because of terrible weather." Eric smiles and holds out his hands. "I'll be back as soon as I can."

I take his hands and let him pull me to my feet. I walk him to the door and wrap him in hand knits until I'm satisfied he's protected from the cold and wind, remind him to drive safely, and kiss him good night. After locking the door behind him, Sophie and I trudge off to bed.

SOPHIE'S SHRILL bark startles me awake, and I jolt upright to a sitting position.

"What's the matter, Soph? Do you need to go outside?"

Without looking at me, the corgi barks again and launches herself off the bed. Her paws don't touch the floor until she lands in the hallway outside the bedroom. She scampers off toward the apartment door.

Turning on lights as I go, I follow Sophie and find

her whining and scratching at the apartment door. Then I hear it. Someone is pounding on the outside door, downstairs. It's the middle of the night. I squint at the clock on the stove. 1:12 a.m. Eric hasn't been gone very long. I can't believe I fell asleep so fast. Who's knocking at this hour?

Sophie and I descend the stairs while the pounding continues. Sophie, having twice as many legs as me and being built for speed, gets to the bottom first and yelps, then scratches the back of the door. This is her friendly yelp, the one she uses for friends. She knows and likes whoever is on the other side of the door.

I'm about to pick up the brick we use to prop open the back door, just in case, when I hear a familiar voice.

"Sophie? Is that you? Meg? Are you there? It's me!"

Adam. What the heck is he doing here?

"Adam?" I ask through the closed door.

"Yes, it's me. Can you open the door, please?"

I open the door, and there stands Adam, his hands shoved in his pockets, the collar of his navy-blue pea coat turned up against the wind, and his hair and shoulders covered in a dusting of big, fluffy snowflakes. He blinks a few snowflakes from his eyelashes, and I step aside so he can come in.

"What's wrong?" I ask.

Adam kicks the brick wall next to the door to knock the excess snow off his boots, then steps inside.

"I'm stranded," Adam replies, using his bare hand to shake the snow from his salt-and-pepper hair.

"How are you stranded?" I ask, "You live ten minutes away." Dramatic much?

I use my bare hand to dust snow from the shoulders of his coat. He's not wearing a hat, a scarf, or mittens. He's inadequately dressed for regular January weather, never mind a blizzard.

"I can't find my keys," Adam explains. "I think they fell out of my coat pocket at Sheamus's house. I can't start my car, and my phone is dead. Even if I walk home, I can't unlock the door."

"Did you go back to Sheamus's house to see if your keys are there?"

He nods. "I searched around outside the house, and the path from the front door to my car, but nothing. For all I know, they fell in the snow. Sheamus isn't there. No one's there. The poker game ended abruptly, and we cleared out in a hurry. I lost my keys in the commotion. I was hoping Eric could drive me to your place, so I can get the spare set of keys, pick up my car, and go home."

"Eric's not here," I explain. "He went to work because of a car accident or something."

"Can you drive me to get the spare set of keys?" Adam asks.

I shake my head. "My car isn't here. I walked to work this morning—yesterday morning—whenever."

Adam huffs in frustration, rubs his hands together vigorously, and uses them to cup his red ears.

"Crash in the spare room." I jerk my head toward

the stairs. "It's too late and snowy to do anything tonight. We'll find your keys in the morning."

Adam agrees, and after lending him one of Eric's t-shirts and a pair of sweatpants, I set him up in the small spare room. When Sophie and I check the door to make sure it's locked, I notice Adam's dead phone on the breakfast bar. I plug it into the phone charger in the kitchen, then Sophie and I shuffle off to bed. Again.

Drifting off to sleep for the third time tonight, I replay my conversation with Adam in my head. Why did the poker game end abruptly? And why did they leave Sheamus's house in a hurry? What did he mean when he said he lost his keys in the commotion? What commotion? Between being dazed from waking up prematurely, and shocked at finding Adam on the doorstep in the middle of the night, it didn't occur to me to ask questions. As sleep takes over my brain, I make a mental list of questions I want to ask him in the morning.

FRIDAY, January 15th

I'm a morning person. This time of year, I'm awake before the sun is up. I know everyone isn't an early riser and try to be considerate.

That's why, after I shower and dress, I tiptoe around the small apartment, trying to make as little noise as possible. The door to the spare bedroom is still closed, and I don't want to wake Adam.

Eric isn't home yet from wherever he went in the middle of the night. He must be exhausted. Intending to text him and see how he's doing, I grab my phone, quietly close the apartment door, and sneak downstairs with Sophie to get ready for our morning walk.

"Which sweater do you want to wear today, Soph?" I ask, holding up a sweater in each hand.

If Sophie prefers one sweater over the other, she doesn't share it with me, so I choose for her. I bundle myself up, then help Sophie into her purple, cabled, turtleneck sweater and unlock the back door.

Walking through the park, I'm grateful the windchill has eased, and it's less frigid this morning. The world is still and silent, except for the occasional echo of a branch in the distance cracking under the weight of last night's snowfall, and the snow crunching beneath our feet and paws as we walk. The snow is smooth and untouched, shimmering in the pre-dawn light. Tree branches curve toward the ground, reaching lower than usual, yielding to the weight of the snow on top of them. My heart is bursting with gratitude because I live in the prettiest town on earth!

"I was just about to text you," I say when I see Eric getting out of his car in the parking lot behind Knitorious.

"How'd you sleep?" he asks, then kisses me hello.

"Interrupted and not long enough," I reply, walking through the back door he's holding for Sophie and me.

I unleash Sophie and take off her sweater, then take off my winter gear, and put everything away.

"I'm going upstairs to grab a quick shower, then I have to go back to work," Eric says, heading toward the stairs. "After my shower, I'll tell you about the hit and run I attended last night. It was a doozy."

"Adam slept in the spare room last night. Be quiet because I think he's still asleep," I warn him.

Eric stops and turns to me, his eyes narrow and focussed. Hot intensity emanates from him. "Adam's here?" He steps toward me and narrows his eyes even more. "Why? What time did he show up? Where's his car? It's not in the parking lot."

He's using his cop voice, and I feel like I'm being interrogated.

"Am I a witness or something?" I ask, confused.

"We've been looking for Adam for hours. He's not at home, he's not at his office, he's not with Jess, and his phone is off."

"*We*?" Are the police looking for Adam? Why?" I demand.

An anxious knot forms in my stomach. My heart pounds against my ribs. I feel panicky, and I'm not sure why.

Heavy shoulders, long arms, I remind myself and take a deep breath. Heavy shoulders, long arms is a mantra I learned in a yoga class once upon a time. It reminds me to let go of the tension in my neck and shoulders.

"Someone saw his car driving away from the hit and run," Eric replies. "His car isn't in his parking spot at the condo, it's not at his office, it's not anywhere."

"It's at Sheamus's house," I inform him. "But the witness must be mistaken," I insist, wondering who the witness is.

Eric mumbles something about already checking Sheamus's house while he unlocks his phone and starts typing with his thumbs.

"Adam showed up here after you left," I say. "He lost his keys. He couldn't have been driving on Lake Access Road."

Eric pauses his thumbs mid-type, looks up at me, and says, "LAWYRUP," then looks down at his phone again and resumes typing, presumably to dispatch a patrol car to Sheamus's house.

LAWYRUP is the lawyer-themed vanity license plate Adam bought himself years ago when he got the job at the firm in the city. Everyone in town knows his plate.

"The witness was close enough to read Adam's license plate in a blizzard?" I ask, dubious.

Adam drives the only late model maroon Jaguar sedan in town. But I'm sure lots of cars would resemble his car, right? Most sedans look the same to me, anyway, and at night, in a blizzard, one sedan must look like another.

Eric fights back a yawn, musses his short, dark hair

with one hand, and turns to climb the stairs. I follow him, and Sophie follows me, but she zooms past both of us and reaches the apartment door first.

"Adam's not here," Eric booms from the spare room. "What time did he leave?"

I shrug. "I'm not sure. I haven't seen him since he closed the bedroom door." I rack my brain, trying to remember if Adam's coat and boots were downstairs, when Sophie and I got ready for our morning walk. I can't remember. I turn toward the charger on the breakfast bar where I plugged in Adam's dead phone last night. Just a charging cable, no phone. Was his phone plugged in this morning after my shower? I didn't notice.

"He took his phone," I mutter. I look at Eric. "I'm sorry, I don't know when he left. I'm usually more observant than this. I don't know why I'm off my game today. He took his phone, and it's charged. Try texting him."

"It's not your job to be observant, babe, it's OK," he reassures me. "You had a long night, and you're tired."

Eric texts, then calls Adam's cell phone while he paces the living room.

He drops the hand with the phone in it to his side and exhales loudly. I assume Adam didn't answer.

I feed Sophie breakfast and drop a pod in the coffee maker.

Our phones ding in unison.

"He's acclaimed," Eric says, reading the text. "Adam is officially the mayor of Harmony Lake."

I got the same text. It's from Connie, my mother-friend. She sent it to the Modern Family group chat, a group text chat with me, Eric, Adam and his girlfriend, Jess, April and her wife, Tamara, Connie and her boyfriend, Archie, and Ryan and Lin who are Archie's son and his partner.

"I'm sure Saxon Renaud is already on his way to the town hall to contest the results and demand a recount," I remark.

"I doubt it," Eric says. "Saxon Renaud is dead."

CHAPTER 3

"DEAD? How? We just saw him last night walking into the pub. Was it a heart attack or something?" I ask, hopeful that Saxon's death was because of natural causes.

Eric leads me to the leather club chair in the living room and coaxes me to sit. I look up at him, stunned. He squats, making us close to eye level.

"Saxon was the victim of the hit and run I attended," he explains.

I slouch deeper into the chair. After taking a moment to process what he just said, I pull myself up and sit up straight.

"Was he wearing a seatbelt? And why was Saxon on Lake Access Road in the middle of the night?" I ask.

Saxon Renaud owned a lot of property in and around Harmony Lake. It's the reason he wanted to become mayor. If he could reverse the big-box policy, he stood to make a lot of money selling land to developers and corporations. As far as I know, though, he didn't own property near Lake Access Road, and he didn't live there; no one does. Lake Access Road is a secluded, dirt road on the far side of the lake that leads to a slipway boaters use to move their boats in and out of the water. It's deserted this time of year.

"He wasn't in a car," Eric clarifies. "As far as we can tell, he was in the middle of the road when the car hit him."

Eric retrieves my coffee from the coffee maker, adds the sweetener I like, and brings it to me.

"In a snowstorm?" I shake my head as if it will help this story make sense. It doesn't. "You're saying Saxon Renaud *walked* all the way to Lake Access Road in a blizzard, wearing his penny loafers, and was walking down the middle of the remote, poorly lit road when a car ran over him." I pause. "And the driver didn't bother to stop or call for help?"

Eric nods. "Pretty much. I know it makes little sense now, but after the coroner examines the body and provides more details, and after I trace Saxon's movements in the days before he died, and when we locate the vehicle that hit him, I'll be able to piece it together, and it'll make more sense."

The back door closes with a thud downstairs, distracting Sophie from her bowl of food and making her yelp.

"Adam," I say to Eric.

"We haven't notified Saxon's next of kin, yet. We're still trying to locate them," Eric explains quietly. "His death isn't public knowledge."

"I understand," I whisper, nodding. "I won't say anything."

"Meg, I don't know what your drink of choice is lately, but the barista told me you'd want a white chocolate and peppermint latte with extra whipped cream and a sprinkle of white chocolate shavings," Adam says without looking up, as he closes the apartment door behind him. "Hey, Eric," he says when he looks up. "I didn't know you were here, or I would've picked up a coffee for you."

"It's OK," I say. "Eric has a coffee." I hand Eric my mug and, mouth watering, liberate my latte from the tray. "Thank you, Mayor Martel," I say, raising the to-go cup in a toasting gesture.

"You saw the text?" Adam asks, sheepishly.

I think he's blushing. Adam doesn't blush easily.

"Congratulations, Adam." Eric extends his hand. "The best candidate won."

Adam and Eric's over-pumped handshake morphs into one of those half-hug-half-handshakes that men do where they slap each other on the shoulder.

While they shake hands, I send a quick text to Hannah to let her know her dad is officially the new mayor of Harmony Lake. I doubt she's awake yet, but she'll see it when she gets up.

"Megan mentioned you lost your keys last night?" Eric asks Adam.

I take my coffee to the leather club chair, cross my legs with my feet tucked under my butt, and settle in, ready to hear what happened at Sheamus's card game last night.

"I'm sure they're on the floor somewhere at Sheamus's house," Adam begins.

According to Adam, after Eric and I left the pub, Saxon Renaud and Rick Ransan showed up. We already knew that, but Eric doesn't interrupt Adam to mention it, and I don't either.

Adam says when Saxon arrived, the atmosphere at the pub changed. He said it went from relaxed and happy to tense and fractious. He says Saxon recommended that people congratulate him on being the next mayor of Harmony Lake, and even suggested they should buy him a drink to celebrate. Apparently, some residents booed at Saxon's comments, and others left the pub altogether. Adam thinks this annoyed or offended Saxon—or both. He reacted by telling everyone that this time next year, Harmony Lake would be a different town, a better town, and everyone would thank him. He said everyone who didn't vote for him would be sorry.

"We decided it was time to go to Sheamus's house to play cards," Adam explains. "Sheamus had to finish up a few things at the pub before he could leave, but he gave Pete his house key and the rest of us headed over there."

Pete is Pete Feeney. Pete was born and raised in Harmony Lake. The Feeney family is a town fixture. Pete's mum was the interim mayor until this morning when Adam was acclaimed as the new mayor, and his dad was the fire chief of the Harmony Lake Fire Department for many years.

"Other than you, Sheamus, and Pete, who else went to Sheamus's house?" Eric probes.

"The usual," Adam replies, shrugging. Then he counts people on his fingers. "Sheamus, me, Pete, Ryan, and because you weren't there"—he nods toward Eric—"Sheamus invited Rick Ransan so we'd have five players. You know how Sheamus is, he only likes to play if we have at least five players."

Ryan is Ryan Wright. He's part of my non-traditional modern family. His dad, Archie, is Connie's partner. Connie is like a mother to me, and Ryan jokes that he and I are stepsiblings.

"He invited Rick?" Eric sounds shocked. "Rick has never played cards with us before."

"He still hasn't played cards with us," Adam explains, shaking his head. "He didn't show up. Rick had an emergency and had to back out. He sent Saxon Renaud in his place."

Did I hear him correctly?

"Saxon Renaud?" I ask, certain I misheard Adam.

Adam nods. "Saxon Renaud," he confirms. "You

should've seen everyone's face when Sheamus opened the door, and we all saw Saxon and his stupid umbrella standing on the doorstep. He had the nerve to tell us he was doing us a favour because if he hadn't offered to take Rick's place, we would only have four players."

"Wow." I shake my head in disbelief, then sip my latte.

"I'm glad I missed it," Eric remarks.

"Dude, if you'd showed up, Saxon wouldn't have been there, and the game wouldn't have ended with fisticuffs and a search for a missing person."

"Tell me everything," Eric instructs.

Yes, Adam, tell us everything! Who got into a fight? Who went missing? I have so many questions.

I check the time on my phone. The store opens in just over an hour, but Connie is opening for me today, so I can be late if necessary. I don't want to miss anything Adam says about last night.

Adam speaks but is interrupted by a notification sound from Eric's phone. Eric glances at his phone, then places it screen-down on the breakfast bar.

"We're listening," I say encouragingly. I sip my latte and shift position in the oversize chair, so my knees are against my chest.

"Things were fine at first," Adam tells us. "Before we played the first hand, we agreed not to discuss politics, real estate, big-box stores, or anything else that could be controversial. We talked about the weather and hockey. It wasn't as much fun as usual, but it was tolerable." He shrugs.

"Fast forward to the fight," Eric urges.

Hearing nothing else, I'm already convinced Saxon was involved in the fight. I swear that man looked for trouble.

"Ryan was drinking Diet Coke, and Saxon was drinking rum and Coke. Sheamus's drinking glasses are all identical, so both drinks look the same. Saxon was sitting beside Ryan at the dining room table," Adam says as he provides background details relevant to the altercation. "Ryan picked up his glass and took a sip, then this funny look came over his face. He sniffed the glass and took another sip, then spat it out. He had picked up Saxon's glass by accident. The glass with rum and coke."

I gasp, my eyes wide with shock and concern. "Was Ryan OK?" I demand.

Adam shakes his head. "Not really. He pushed his chair away from the table and stood up. He accused Saxon of switching the drinks on purpose."

Ryan is a recovering alcoholic. His sobriety is important to him, and he works his program to avoid a relapse into active addiction. This could be a serious setback for him.

"Then what happened?" I ask, almost scared to find out the answer.

"Sheamus and I told Ryan we were proud of him for spitting it out when he realized it was alcohol. We told him it was a difficult thing to do, but he did it. We took him into the living room, away from the alcohol, and asked him if he wanted to call his sponsor," Adam replies.

"Good job." I take a deep breath, relieved. "Thank goodness you two were there for him."

"But we heard Pete and Saxon arguing in the dining room, so we went back in there," Adam continues. "Pete was accusing Saxon of switching the drinks on purpose. Sheamus always puts a wedge of lime in Ryan's diet coke, to avoid this situation."

"It's true," Eric agrees, nodding and looking at me. "Sheamus makes a point of reminding Ryan the wedge of lime is there to distinguish his drink from the alcoholic drinks."

"Did Sheamus forget the lime this time?" I ask.

"No," Adam shakes his head. "Pete held up the drink with the lime and Sheamus and I sniffed it. It was the rum and Coke. Pete suspects that when no one was looking, Saxon took the lime from the Diet Coke and put it in the rum and Coke to trick Ryan into drinking alcohol. We couldn't think of another explanation for how the lime got there. Ryan had already finished half of his diet coke. If the rum had been there before, he would've noticed earlier."

"That's awful." My eyes are welling up with tears.

I can't believe anyone would do such a thing, even someone as mean and bitter as Saxon Renaud. What joy could he get from tormenting Ryan and putting his sobriety at risk?

Could Ryan have been angry enough to kill Saxon?

"Who threw the first punch?" Eric asks, refocusing Adam and me on the purpose of the story.

"No one," Adam informs us. "But Ryan grabbed Saxon by the shirt collar and shoved him into the living room. Saxon tried to shove back, but Ryan shoved him again, harder. Our coats were laying over the chair in the living room. Ryan pushed Saxon into the chair so hard, our coats fell to the floor, and the chair slid across the room. When Saxon tried to get up and push back, his feet just pushed the coats around. My coat ended up under the sofa. In hindsight, my keys probably fell out of my pocket. Pete and Sheamus picked up the coats but must not have noticed my keys."

"How did the altercation stop? Who went missing?" Eric's notebook is open on the breakfast bar, and he's taking notes.

"After Ryan shoved Saxon the second time, I positioned myself between them," Adam replies. "Ryan couldn't get to Saxon without going through me. While Sheamus and Pete picked up the coats and put the furniture back, I turned around and suggested to Saxon it was time for him to leave. With none of us watching Ryan, he grabbed his coat and took off. It was more than a minute before we realized he had left, but as soon as we did, we grabbed our coats and went after him. We were worried he might be tempted to go somewhere and drink. When I got to my car, I discovered my keys weren't in my pocket. I checked all my pockets and the ground around my feet. By the time I realized I was stranded, everyone else was long gone."

"Where did Ryan go?" I ask.

I assume someone found him safe and sound, and sober, otherwise my phone would have blown up with calls and texts from the modern family group chat.

Adam shrugs. "I don't know where he went, but as soon as I woke up, I found my phone—thank you for charging it, Meg—and there was a text from Archie to everyone at the card game. It said we could stop searching because Ryan was safe."

"Thank goodness," I remark, exhaling a long breath I'd been holding onto.

"What did you do when you realized you didn't have your keys?" Eric asks.

"Panicked," Adam replies. "I checked my coat pockets, my pants pockets, and I retraced my steps from Sheamus's house to my car, in case I'd dropped the keys on the way. I didn't find them. It was snowing, and I thought maybe they had sunk into the snow. I used the flashlight on my phone to search through the snow but didn't find them. I finally stopped looking when my phone died, and I lost the flashlight. I walked around for a while to stay warm, then walked back to Sheamus's house, hoping he'd come home, and I could go inside and look for my keys. His car wasn't there, and I was freezing. I went to the pub in case Sheamus was there, but it was closed. Nothing else in town is open that late. I was stranded."

"Was your car at Sheamus's house when you went back?" Eric asks.

"Where else would it be?" Adam shrugs. "That's where I left it. But now that you mention it, everything was snow covered. I can't say for certain I saw my car when I went back." His gaze drifts off into the distance while he recalls the events of last night and whether he can be certain his car was there when he returned to Sheamus's house.

"So, that's when you came here," Eric concludes, distracting Adam from his thoughts.

"Right," Adam confirms. "Your place was close, and I was hoping you'd drive me to Meg's house because she has my spare keys. But you were at work, and her car was at home, so I crashed in your spare room."

"Where's your car now?" Eric asks.

"Parked across the street from Sheamus's house," Adam insists.

Eric shakes his head. "Your car isn't there, Adam. I sent a patrol car to check. The officer texted me a few minutes ago. There's no sign of your car."

"It has to be there," Adam maintains. "I texted Sheamus earlier to explain why I left my car there all night. I told him I was worried a snowplow might hit it, and he said he looked out the window and my car was fine. He said he'd look around for my keys."

To prove he's telling the truth, Adam unlocks his

phone and shows Eric the text conversation he had with Sheamus earlier this morning.

"Sheamus isn't home," Eric informs him. "His truck isn't there, and the snow on his driveway is still fresh. My officers suspect Sheamus hasn't been home since last night."

Where is Sheamus, and why did he pretend to be home when Adam texted him?

Where is Adam's car, and what time did Adam leave this apartment this morning?

The knot in my stomach is growing bigger by the minute.

CHAPTER 4

"ERIC, if my car isn't on the street outside Sheamus's house, it was stolen, and I need to file a report." Adam's voice is laced with either urgency, or fear, or both; I can't quite tell.

"Adam, we believe your car was involved in a serious incident overnight on Lake Access Road. I've been looking for you and your car all night, but it never occurred to me to check my apartment."

Before Adam can respond, his phone rings, startling him and me.

"It's Hannah," he says, looking at the screen.

"I texted her earlier to tell her you're the new mayor," I say.

"I'm answering it. Everyone act normal."

If there's something Adam and I do well together, it's act normal. When our marriage was unravelling, we separated emotionally before we separated physically.

For the sake of Hannah's senior year of high school, and to give ourselves time to work out the details of our separation, we lived under the same roof and maintained the pretense of a happily married couple for months before we told anyone we were splitting up.

Adam answers the call and puts our daughter on speakerphone. She congratulates him on being elected mayor and jokingly asks if she should call him Your Worship instead of Dad for the next four years.

The three of us laugh and play along, pretending there isn't a mess of a murder investigation unfolding around our family. We keep the tone of the conversation light and happy. We tell Hannah about the snowstorm and how pretty Harmony Lake is this morning.

Hannah wants to ask Adam a question about a paper she's working on for one of her law classes—she's studying pre-law—and Adam takes her off speaker and raises the phone to his ear to speak to her. I use the opportunity to talk to Eric alone and gesture for him to follow me downstairs to the store.

"Wow," I declare when we're alone.

Eric nods. "There's so much information to sort out."

"When you tell Adam that Saxon is dead, I think Jess, or me, or someone should be with him in case he freaks out. He's never been the last person to speak to someone before they died. It'll be a shock. It'll be an even bigger shock if it turns out his car was involved." Eric nods and envelops me in a hug and a kiss. I lean into him, inhaling his scent and listening to his heartbeat through his sweater. We both relax a little. "Adam's car should be easy to find," I theorize. "His fancy car comes with a fancy app that shows him where his car is and even shows him how it got there. You should be able to trace the route it drove last night."

Eric nods. "That's next." He sighs. "When I go upstairs, I'll ask him to show me the app." We cuddle on the sofa, in the cozy sitting area near the front of the store. "Do you know anything about Saxon's family?" Eric asks. "We need to notify his next of kin, but we don't know who to notify." He rubs Sophie when she jumps onto the sofa next to him.

"I would ask Rick," I suggest. "He's the only person who seemed to like Saxon. Other than that, he must have a lawyer. I mean, someone helped him close all those real estate deals."

"I have an officer looking into that," Eric says. "She's tracking down his lawyer as we speak."

Hearing him mention that he's delegated someone to find Saxon's lawyer reminds me that today is a big day for Eric too. Besides a new mayor, Harmony Lake gets a new permanent chief of police today.

"Congratulations," I say, nuzzling into his neck. "Today, you're the permanent chief of police. I know Adam's victory party is tonight, but how do you want to celebrate your achievement? Do you want me to plan something?"

"Thank you," he replies, squeezing me tightly. "I

don't feel very celebratory right now. Can we put it on the back burner for a while?"

"Totally," I agree, relieved.

I'm not feeling festive either, and I'm wondering if it's appropriate to have Adam's victory party tonight, considering his opponent died today, suddenly and suspiciously.

"Do you think given the circumstances we should postpone Adam's victory party?" I ask.

"Absolutely not," Eric replies without hesitation. "Everyone from the card game will be there. Along with other people who might have hated Saxon Renaud enough to want him dead. This party could lead to a break in the case. Also, all the friends and volunteers who helped with Adam's campaign deserve recognition for their contributions, regardless of what happened on Lake Access Road last night."

Eric returns to his apartment to continue talking to Adam, and I pull out my phone to text Connie.

Me: Good morning! I hear Ryan had a rough night. If you need to stay home today, I totally understand.

Connie: Ryan is fine. Archie will tend to him. Besides, I've already put my face on! I'll be there soon.

I should have known it would take more than a snowstorm and her stepson's near-relapse to keep Connie away from Knitorious.

Connie was the original owner of Knitorious. She passed it on to me before she semi-retired with Archie. Before that, I worked for her part-time for five years.

Now, we've switched roles; I own the store, and Connie works here part-time. Connie *is* Knitorious, without her the store wouldn't exist.

We met after Adam, Hannah, and I moved to Harmony Lake eighteen years ago. I was a young, recently married, new mother, living in a town where I didn't know anyone. If that wasn't enough to deal with, my mum died just before we moved here. Between missing my mum and an ambitious husband who was working all hours to build a career, I was overwhelmed.

I coped by knitting through my grief during Hannah's naps and after we put her to bed at night. One day, realizing I'd grief-knitted through my entire yarn stash, I pushed the stroller into Knitorious and met Connie. Our connection was instant. Connie took Hannah and me under her wing, filling the mother and grandmother-shaped holes in our hearts. We became friends, then quickly became family. She calls me her daughter-friend, and I call her my mother-friend.

"Good morning, my dear!" Connie sings as she breezes into the store from the back room.

At seventy-one years young, Connie is the most sophisticated, beautiful woman I know.

"Good morning," I say as Connie hugs me.

Her sleek silver bob tickles my cheek, and she smells like lilac, comfort and unconditional love.

"Your car isn't in the parking lot," she observes. "Did you and Sophie walk to work in the snow?"

"No," I reply. "We walked to work yesterday and spent the night upstairs."

"Very practical," Connie commends. "I'm glad you decided not to drive in this."

Says the woman who drove through the snow to get here.

"How's Ryan?" I ask.

Connie sighs and, knitting in hand, joins Sophie on the sofa. "He's all right. It was touch and go for a while, but he's using all his tools to stay on track."

"Thank goodness. Do you think it would be OK if I text him to tell him I'm rooting for him? I don't want to upset him or pressure him."

"Oh, I'm sure he'd love that, my dear! How did you hear about his unfortunate incident?"

Connie has a charming tendency to refer to everything she finds disagreeable as either "unpleasant" or "unfortunate."

"Adam mentioned it," I reply, pursing my lips into a tight smile and fighting the urge to tell her everything that has happened since last night.

"Have you heard anything about the unpleasantness on Lake Access Road?" Connie asks nonchalantly.

"There was some kind of car accident." I shrug. "Eric went there in the middle of the night."

She stops knitting, puts her needles on her lap, and looks at me over the top of her reading glasses. "Did he tell you what happened or who was involved?"

"We haven't really seen each other." It's not a lie.

"Adam slept in the spare room last night, and Eric and I bumped into each other when I walked Sophie this morning."

I avoid answering Connie's question directly because I can't lie to her. I'm not a good liar. Lying gives me anxiety, and I'll do anything to avoid feeling anxious.

"Why did Adam sleep here last night?" she asks.

"He lost his keys and couldn't get into his car or condo. Eric was at Lake Access Road, and my car wasn't here. The easiest solution was for Adam to crash in the spare room."

"Did he find his keys?" Connie asks.

I can tell she's suspicious. She knows there's more to the story. Even though I'm not lying to her, Connie knows I'm not being completely honest.

Saved by the bell, my phone dings, and I rush to the counter to fetch it.

Eric: Found Adam's car. On our way there now.

Me: Where is it?

Eric: Your house.

My house? Why? How did it get there?

"Is everything all right, my dear?" Connie asks, bringing me back to the here and now.

I nod, typing one more quick text to Eric.

Me: Drive safely. Let me know what happens.

Connie cranes her neck and looks toward the back of the store where the distant, muffled thumping of large, booted man-feet are clumping on the stairs. We both hear the familiar thud of the back door closing, then she looks at me expectantly.

"That was Eric and Adam," I explain. "Eric is taking Adam to find his keys." Connie continues to look at me, her facial expression unchanged. Her blue eyes wide with waiting. "Adam thinks he may have dropped them at Sheamus's house in the rush to leave last night to find Ryan."

Satisfied with my explanation, Connie opens her mouth in a silent "Ah," nods with a smile, and resumes knitting. "I hope he finds them," she remarks. "I've heard replacement keys for those luxury cars are very expensive. In fact, I'm told all the costs related to luxury cars are unnecessarily high."

Relieved at the change in topic, I nod encouragingly while Connie educates me about the inflated costs of everything related to luxury vehicles until it's time to unlock the front door and turn the sign from CLOSED to OPEN.

Within minutes of opening the store, my phone blows up with texts. People are asking if I'm all right, and curious to know why there are police cruisers and crime-scene tape around Adam's car in my driveway.

CHAPTER 5

ERIC: It's here!

Me: So I'm told.

People are even texting me photos of the scene in my driveway. I assume a crowd has gathered on the street in front of chez Martel, as my house is affectionately known locally.

I send a quick text to my confused and concerned best friend, April, explaining that everyone is OK and promising to phone her soon. Apparently, the brief text explanation isn't good enough, and she replies with a photo of her faux, fur-cuffed, rated-for-minus-forty-degrees winter boots standing in the snow outside Artsy Tartsy. This means her booted feet are marching toward Knitorious right now and will walk through the door any second.

Artsy Tartsy is the bakery April and her wife, Tamara, own. Tamara is a talented pastry chef, and her creations are locally famous. Artsy Tartsy is down the street from Knitorious.

I look at Connie and smile. She looks back at me, matching my smile.

"I'll wait until April gets here," she says, "so you won't have to repeat yourself."

I nod. How does she know April is coming? Did April text her, or is Connie freakishly intuitive? I decide not to ask.

Thanks to the fresh snow from last night's storm, the skiers and snowboarders will spend the day on the slopes and are unlikely to venture down from the mountain resorts to shop. Business will be slow today, which means I won't have any customers to use as an excuse when Connie and April ask me questions I want to answer but know I shouldn't. Like, was anyone hurt on Lake Access Road? And why is there front-end damage to Adam's car? And how did his car get to my house if Adam was here with me?

April walks through the door, carrying one of my favourite things: a white confectionery box with the Artsy Tartsy logo on the lid.

"You are a real-life snow angel!" I declare, relieving her of the box while she pulls down her white, faux, fur-lined hood and takes off her white puffy winter coat. "I'm starving!"

Whatever is in this box is fresh-from-the-oven warm and smells glorious. It's making my mouth water.

"I'll plug in the kettle and get plates," Connie

announces as she crosses the threshold from the store to the back room.

"It's not a treat," April clarifies as we hug, "It's a bribe. Something big is going on, and you know the details. Pastries for information. That's the deal, Megnificent." She winks as we pull apart.

April likes to call me random nicknames that are puns of my actual name. This morning I'm Megnificent.

April and I have been best friends since we met at a mummy-and-me group with our daughters eighteen years ago. Our daughters are the same age and are best friends. They even attend university together in Toronto. Besides their daughter, Rachel, April and Tamara also have a son, Zach who's sixteen.

Connie pops her head out of the back room. "Don't start without me."

We give her a thumbs-up.

April greets Sophie with rubs and tells her there's a treat in the confectionery box for her, then opens the box and pulls out a small white bag. At the sight of the bag, Sophie's ears perk up to full attention and her entire back end, not just her tail, wags with enthusiasm.

Besides yummy treats for humans, Tamara also makes pet treats under the brand name, The Barkery: Gourmet Treats For Well-Heeled Pets.

April puts her hand in the bag and pulls out what looks like a Sophie-sized bagel. "Peanut butter dog doughnut with carob icing," she explains to Sophie and me.

Because she's a good girl, Sophie contains her obvious excitement, sits, and waits patiently for April to put the treat on the floor in front of her. She eats it so fast, I wonder if she bothered to chew the thing.

"Start at the beginning, my dear," Connie urges, as she places the tea tray on the coffee table.

In between bites of my pomegranate-seed and cream cheese-topped puff pastry, I explain how Eric woke me in the middle of the night to tell me he had to go into work, then, after he left, a semi-frozen Adam knocked on the back door, looking for a ride to my house to get his spare set of keys because he lost his original set at Sheamus's house.

"Is that when Adam told you about Ryan?" Connie asks.

I shake my head. "No, I didn't ask for any details, and Adam didn't offer. We were both too exhausted for conversation. I found some pyjamas for him, and we went to sleep in our respective rooms."

"What happened to Ryan?" April asks, worried. "Was he involved in that accident everyone is talking about? The one on Lake Access Road?"

The Harmony Lake gossip network's dedication to spreading news is matched only by their speed. If I didn't know better, I'd swear they use telepathy to communicate because it feels like news travels throughout our community at the speed of thought. Even news about incidents that happen on remote

47

roads in the middle of the night during a snowstorm. They have eyes and ears everywhere, all the time.

"Haven't you heard?" Connie asks April.

Wide-eyed, April shakes her head, and Connie tells her about Ryan's "unpleasant experience" at the card game when, by accident, he sipped an alcoholic drink.

Upon hearing that Saxon was among the poker-night participants, April looks at me and asks, "Do we think it was an accident, or do we think it was Saxon being Saxon?"

I shrug. "Adam believes it was intentional. He says everyone else who was there believes it was intentional too." I tell her and Connie what Adam told Eric and me about the lime wedge mysteriously moving from one drink to another.

A low, animalistic growl emanates from the back of April's throat, and she rolls her eyes. "That man is infuriating!" Though she doesn't refer to him by name, I know she means Saxon Renaud. He evokes this reaction from people. "I swear causing trouble for other people is how he entertains himself. He collects enemies the way some people collect stamps."

I'm about to correct April's present tense statement by replacing the verbs with their past tenses, but stop myself by biting my lips. His death isn't public knowledge yet, and I promised Eric I wouldn't say anything. It's difficult, though, because I tell April and Connie everything. I remind myself it's only temporary until the police notify Saxon's next of kin.

"What were you about to say, my dear?" Connie asks, raising her eyebrows and nodding at my forcefully closed mouth.

"Just that it would be a strange coincidence, if the only time Ryan accidentally confuses an alcoholic drink with his non-alcoholic drink is the one time Saxon is there and seated next to him." It's a quasi-lie. I would've said this *after* I corrected April's remarks and made them past tense.

"How did Adam's car end up at your house if Adam wasn't driving it?" April asks.

I shake my head and shrug. "That's the million-dollar question," I reply. "Adam thinks he lost his keys in the rush to leave Sheamus's house and look for Ryan. He said when he walked away from Sheamus's house, his car was parked across the street. If it's not there now, it was stolen."

"Someone else must have found his keys," Connie surmises.

April nods. "Adam's car has a decent security system. It would be difficult to steal without the keys."

I nod in agreement.

We finish our tea and pastries while we discuss how uncommon auto theft is in Harmony Lake. To the best of Connie's recollection, the last time a car was stolen was the mid 90s. A coach's car was taken for a joy ride by the players from a rival hockey team in Harmony Hills. The rival team plastered the coach's car in Harmony Hills Hockey Association bumper stickers before abandoning it on the side of the highway.

"Are you suggesting a rival lawyer stole Adam's car and took it for a joyride?" I ask jokingly when Connie finishes her story. "Or a rival mayor?"

"If they covered it in bumper stickers, Adam will go berserk!" April laughs with that contagious laugh she has, making Connie and me laugh with her.

We're interrupted when Connie's cell phone rings. April and I suppress our giggles while Connie steps away from the cozy sitting area to answer the call.

I can't hear most of what she says because Connie gravitates away from us and toward the back room. She straightens and fusses with random skeins of yarn on the shelves as she moves through the store and talks quietly on her phone. The few words I hear are imbued with a tone of worry. And when she glances at us, her facial expression matches the concern in her voice. Her eyes are wide, and her mouth, which usually smiles, is pressed into a thin, tense line.

"What's going on?" April whispers.

"I don't know, but it's not good," I reply.

"Do you think it's Ryan?" she asks.

"I hope not."

Connie hangs up and, looking stunned, pulls out one of the Parsons chairs from the harvest table and sits down. April, Sophie, and I join her.

"Connie, what's wrong?" April asks, sitting in the chair beside her. "Did something happen?"

"Whatever it is, we're here for you," I remind Connie as I sit in the chair on the other side of her.

"That was Archie," Connie tells us, referring to her boyfriend. "He said a police officer came and took Ryan to the station for questioning."

Ryan is Archie's son.

"Questioning about what?" I ask, wondering if the officer said Ryan was being questioned about Saxon Renaud's death.

"Archie doesn't know." Connie's concern is morphing into fear. I can hear it in her voice and see it on her face. "What if Saxon is pressing charges against Ryan because of their shoving match last night?" Connie looks at April, then at me. "Ryan has a record. This could be really bad for him."

Several years ago, when Ryan was a young man with a drinking problem, he moved to Ottawa to work for his uncle's construction company. While he was there, he made some bad decisions. He caught some of his co-workers stealing supplies from the construction site, and instead of turning them in, he agreed to look the other way for a cut of the proceeds from the sale of the stolen goods. Unbeknownst to Ryan, one of the co-workers involved in the scheme was an informant who was working with the police to bring down the theft ring. When the takedown happened, Ryan was arrested and charged, even though he didn't steal or resell anything. Benefitting from the theft was enough to get him convicted. He spent a few months in jail, followed by a few years on probation. The experience was a wake-up call for him, and he got sober and made better decisions.

Ryan has been an upstanding member of our community since. He moved back to Harmony Lake and started working with his dad. They own the handyman company, The Wright Men For The Job. Ryan is a one-man operation nowadays because Archie is semi-retired and only works occasionally. I trust Ryan, and so do most of the other town residents. He's in and out of our homes and businesses regularly, fixing things, installing things, and keeping our town running smoothly. I would trust Ryan with my life. I would trust him with Hannah's life. I don't believe for a moment that Ryan could kill Saxon Renaud, no matter what Saxon did to provoke him.

"I don't think Saxon filed a complaint about Ryan to the police." I can't stand to see the tears welling up in Connie's eyes. I need to reassure her there's no way Saxon filed a complaint against Ryan.

"But you don't know that for sure," Connie responds. "How could you?"

"Trust me," I say, putting my hand on top of hers.

"You know what Saxon is like," Connie says. "Maybe when he found out he lost the election, he went looking for someone to take out his frustration on and set his sights on Ryan. Saxon Renaud could be at the police station right now, spinning a web of lies about what happened between him and Ryan last night."

"Saxon Renaud is not at the police station," I insist confidently, shaking my head.

"How do you know?"

"Because Saxon Renaud is dead." Adam is standing in the doorway between the store and the back room.

CHAPTER 6

"ADAM?!" I say, not sure if I'm more surprised by his sudden appearance or his use of the back door.

Adam never uses the back door at Knitorious, and this is the fifth time he's used it in less than twelve hours.

He steps into the store and joins us at the harvest table. "Saxon died last night in the incident on Lake Access Road."

Connie doesn't seem reassured by this explanation, and I understand why. She's already concerned that Ryan is being questioned about shoving Saxon, and now she realizes it's possible he's being questioned in relation to Saxon's death. A much more serious crime, with much more serious consequences.

"Is Saxon's death public knowledge?" I ask quietly, looking at Adam.

Adam nods. "Eric said it's fine. They found a brother to notify."

"Oh," I say.

The four of us sit together in silence while Connie and April process what they just heard. I break the silence when I notice Jess standing in the back room. She must've come in with Adam. I'm glad she's here with him.

"Hi, Jess." I greet her with a hug, and she joins us at the harvest table.

"Hi, everyone," she mumbles. "What a day, huh?"

Connie asks Adam to go to the police station as Ryan's lawyer and stay with him while they interview Ryan. Adam explains that he can't do that because he's also a person of interest in the case and offers to refer Ryan to another lawyer.

Connie decides she should be with Archie, so they can anxiously wait for Ryan together. We all offer to drive her home. In fact we try to insist that someone should drive her home and stay with them, but she won't accept any of our offers and insists she will drive herself. She promises to call if she or Archie need anything.

After giving everyone the opportunity to hug her and reassure her that Ryan did nothing wrong and will probably be home before lunchtime, Connie goes to the back door and puts on her coat. I follow her and ask one more time if she'll let me take her home.

"No, my dear, I'll be fine. I promise." She brushes a

stray curl away from my face then puts on her gloves. "I need you to be my eyes and ears," she whispers. "Find out everything you can about how Saxon died, so we can prove Ryan and Adam had nothing to do with this unpleasantness."

I nod. "I'll do my best."

We kiss cheeks, and I close the door behind her after she leaves.

Adam takes out his phone and shows us some photos of the front-end damage on his car. They parked the car at the bottom of my driveway.

"You'd think hitting a grown person would cause more damage to the car," I observe, looking at the photos.

"That's what I said," Adam agrees. "But Eric thinks Saxon was already lying on the road when my car ran over him."

Why would Saxon be lying in several inches of snow, on the road, in the middle of the night? Did the killer render Saxon unconscious, then run him over? Was Saxon drugged? Is it possible Saxon was already dead? But if he was already dead, why bother running over him at all?

Maybe whoever ran over him wanted to cover up the fact that Saxon was already dead and his actual cause of death. Or maybe they wanted to make it look like Adam killed Saxon. I wonder if Eric has heard from the coroner yet. I resist the urge to text him with all my questions because he's probably questioning Ryan, and I don't want to interrupt them.

"So, it was your car that hit Saxon?" I ask. "The police know for sure?"

"Not one hundred percent," Adam replies, "but according to the app, my car was on Lake Access Road last night. It took a rather indirect route to get there, but it was there, and my car's movements coincide with the 9-1-1 call from the anonymous witness who said they saw my car leaving the scene. We're waiting for forensics to confirm it, but it's safe to assume it was my car."

Jess, April, and I exhale almost in unison.

"Are you a suspect?" Jess asks Adam.

Adam nods.

"How?" April asks, then she points to the ceiling. "You were asleep upstairs. How could you drive from Lake Access Road to Megan's house, dump your car, lose your keys, and walk to Eric's apartment in that short time?"

"Also," I add, "didn't you say you stopped at the pub to see if Sheamus was there? Before you came here?" If he stopped in at the pub, someone would have seen him and can confirm he was there and not in his car near Lake Access Road.

"I went there, but the pub was closed," Adam clarifies.

"They're open until 2 a.m.," Jess counters.

Adam shrugs. "I guess they closed early because of the weather."

He looks exhausted and defeated. I ask him if I can have another look at the photos on his phone.

"They parked your car at the very bottom of my driveway," I point out. "The back end overhangs the driveway." I look at Adam. "Don't you think that's strange?"

"I think this whole situation is strange, Meg," he replies. "Eric checked the security footage, and the cameras didn't pick up my car at all. He thinks whoever left my car there knew about the security system and parked like this to avoid the cameras."

While you'd think this information would narrow down the number of potential suspects, it doesn't. Harmony Lake is a tiny town, and everyone knows about the state-of-the-art security system at my house. Adam had it installed before he moved out because someone broke in, laid in wait for me, and tried to kill me.

Eric can check the camera footage because he has access to the app that came with the security system. He can lock and unlock the house, arm and disarm the security system, and view the camera footage.

"Who cleared the snow from the driveway?" I ask, although I'm sure I already know the answer.

"Who do you think?" Adam answers my question with a question.

"Phillip," April and I answer in stereo.

Phillip Wilde is my next-door neighbour at home and at work. His florist shop, Wilde Flowers, shares a wall and a parking lot with Knitorious. Phillip is a thoughtful, diligent neighbour who likes to ensure the curb appeal of the neighbourhood meets a certain minimum standard. If I don't clear my snow quickly enough, Phillip will clear it for me—and the other driveways in the immediate vicinity of his house—when he clears his own driveway with his snowblower.

He's wonderfully thorough about it too. Looking at these photos, there isn't one flake of snow left on my driveway. Or on Adam's car.

"Did he clean the snow off your car too?" I ask.

"He sure did," Adam confirms with a hint of exasperation in his voice. "He said there was no point in doing the driveway if I was going to come along and just brush the snow from my car onto the freshly cleared driveway."

"Of course, he did," I commiserate, realizing Phillip might have also unwittingly erased critical evidence like footprints in the snow, hair, or other DNA that might have fallen off the culprit when they abandoned the car. "He meant well, Adam. Phillip couldn't have known he was disturbing a crime scene."

"I know," Adam acknowledges somberly. "I thanked him for doing it."

"Did you get your spare keys while you were there?" April asks.

"Yes, and the ones he lost were in the ignition of his car," Jess replies. "The police have them now to check them for evidence, but at least we know where they are.

But I think it's a good idea to change his locks, anyway. What if they made copies?"

"Jess is right, Adam," April advises. "Maybe you should call Ryan and get him to change the locks at your office and condo."

An uncomfortable silence follows the mention of Ryan's name. We're all reminded that a crime has taken place, and two members of our modern family are persons of interest.

Jess looks at Adam with a concerned expression on her thin, fair face. Her seafoam green eyes are heavy with worry, and her mouth is frowning. She rubs Adam's arm.

"Why don't we get you home? You haven't eaten yet today, and you look like you could use a nap before tonight," Jess suggests to Adam.

Adam rolls his eyes. "I forgot about tonight." He looks back and forth from me to Jess. "We should postpone the victory party," he says.

Jess and I look at each other. She shrugs.

"I talked to Eric about postponing it," I tell everyone. "He wants it to continue as planned. He's hoping a room full of people who didn't like Saxon Renaud might yield some clues or information about what happened last night."

"Makes sense." Adam nods and gets up from his chair. He buttons up his navy peacoat and looks at Jess. "What do you think?"

Jess also stands up. She nods. "Whatever it takes to clear your name and put this behind us."

The four of us exchange hugs, and April and I tell Jess and Adam to call us if they need anything.

"This puts a damper on his first day as mayor, doesn't it?" April asks, after Adam and Jess have left.

"It sure does," I agree. "Even in death, Saxon Renaud can ruin everyone's day."

I feel bad as soon as I hear the words pass my lips. As much as I didn't like Saxon, he's not here to defend himself, and I shouldn't speak ill of the dead.

"Ryan and Adam had nothing to do with this," April proclaims.

"I know," I agree, nodding. "But unless the coroner concludes that Saxon's death was caused by either an accident or natural causes, someone killed Saxon Renaud. Someone local."

I know the murderer isn't Adam or Ryan, but to prove it and clear their names, I need to find the killer.

CHAPTER 7

"HI, MARLA."

"Hi, Megan."

I place the mouse tail I'm knitting on the coffee table in front of me and watch my part-time employee take off her coat while she hurries through the store to the back room.

We've only had two customers in the two hours since the store opened, and neither of them bought anything. I think one of them came in to escape from the cold for a few minutes, and the other made a beeline for the front window where Sophie was having her morning nap. She said she saw Sophie in the window and couldn't resist coming in to pet her. Neither person was familiar to me. I'm sure they were tourists.

After April left to get back to the bakery, I texted Marla and told her she was welcome to take the day off because last night's snowstorm brought today's business to a halt. Marla insisted she'd be here, and true to her word, here she is, right on time.

Like Connie, Marla was born and raised in Harmony Lake. She's the same age as Connie, and they've known each other all their lives.

"Did you hear what happened?" Marla asks, still trying to catch her breath as she smooths her salt-and-pepper pixie cut into place.

"Can you be more specific?" I ask. "It's been a busy day for news. Are you referring to the election results? The accident on Lake Acce…"

"Saxon Renaud is dead!" The words explode out of Marla's mouth like there's a prize for the first person to say them. "And so far, Ryan, Adam, Sheamus, and Pete are being questioned by the police."

I nod. "Yes, I heard about that. Sad. We don't know for sure they're being questioned about Saxon's death, though," I remind her.

"Why else would the police want to talk to them?"

She makes a good point. Time to change the subject.

"Saxon went to your church, didn't he?" I ask. "Did you know him well?"

Marla nods and joins me in the cozy sitting area with her knitting.

"He was a very polite, proper gentleman," Marla says, lowering her reading glasses from the top of her head to her eyes.

"Really?" I ask, skeptical at the suggestion Saxon Renaud had any redeeming qualities. "I hear he has a brother somewhere. Did Saxon ever talk to you about his family?"

Marla screws up her face and shrugs. "Saxon had a way of revealing nothing about himself, yet talking to you in a way that made you feel you knew each other well. He learned a lot about everyone else while revealing nothing about himself."

"So, he was a private person," I surmise.

Marla puts down her needles and considers my comment. "Not private. Secretive." Satisfied with her response, she picks up her needles and resumes knitting.

"What's the difference?" I ask, confused about the distinction.

"Well," Marla pauses, once again lowering her knitting to her lap, "privacy is passive, and secrecy is active."

"Go on," I urge.

I'm intrigued. Nothing about Saxon Renaud has ever intrigued me before, but this has my interest piqued.

"Private people don't hide information, but they don't broadcast it either. It's there, they just don't bring attention to it. Secretive people keep information hidden intentionally, out of fear. They're afraid if they reveal their information, something bad will happen. Saxon was secretive."

"That's deep, Marla. How do you have so much insight into Saxon? Did he tell you his secrets?"

She shakes her head and chuckles. "No. But after seven decades of people watching, you notice a few things."

"Did you notice anything else about Saxon?" I ask. "Anything that might help to piece together his last moments? Can you think of any reason he'd be on Lake Access Road?"

Marla shrugs and shakes her head. "I wish I could help, Megan, but I didn't know Saxon very well. We were acquaintances."

I smile, thank Marla for trying, and make a mental note to mention our conversation to Eric. Maybe Saxon had other friends in his church community who know more about him than Marla.

Marla and I knit in comfortable silence until we're interrupted by the jingle of the bell over the door.

"Cold enough for you?" The postal carrier asks as she drops a stack of mail on the counter.

The three of us make small talk about the weather until the postal carrier overheats underneath her winter gear and needs to escape to the cold air outside.

Sifting through the stack of mail, I find two items addressed to Wilde Flowers.

"Marla, will you be all right on your own while I pop next door and drop off Phillip's mail?"

"Of course," Marla insists, "take your time."

I nip into the kitchenette and grab the white confectionery bag that contains the last remaining peanut butter dog doughnut.

"Why, Megan Martel, where on earth is your coat?" Phillip asks melodramatically with one hand on his hip and the other waggling a finger at me scoldingly.

"I'm feeling impetuous," I tease, closing the door behind me. "With reckless abandon, I risked walking the few metres between our doors coatless." I mock gasp and bring my hand to my mouth.

"Scandalous," he replies sarcastically, clutching pretend pearls. "What will the neighbours think?"

We giggle, and I drop the envelopes on the counter of the florist shop.

"Some of your mail was delivered to Knitorious." I hold up the white confectionery bag and shake the contents. "And I have an extra dog treat from The Barkery. May Kevin have it?"

"Kevin, would you like a treat?" Phillip asks.

Kevin is Phillip's chihuahua. They go everywhere together. Kevin is perched regally atop his royal blue velvet pillow with gold piping and tassels. I let Kevin sniff my hand. After I pass his smell test, he positions his head so I can scratch between his ears.

I place the doggie doughnut on the velvet pillow. Kevin sniffs it cautiously, then takes small, chihuahua-sized bites.

"Thank you for clearing my driveway this morning," I say to Phillip, who's opening the mail I left on his counter.

"Anytime." He flicks his wrist dismissively and puts down the mail. "What's the deal with Adam's car?" he asks.

"It was stolen," I explain. "Sometime last night, someone either found or stole his keys and took his car. Adam didn't realize it was missing until this morning, and I spent the night at Eric's, so we didn't know it was in my driveway until this morning."

"I saw some front-end damage when I brushed the snow off his car," Phillip explains. "Any idea what happened to it?"

"Not exactly," I reply honestly. "The forensics people have the car. They should have some answers soon."

"It was involved in the accident on Lake Access Road, wasn't it? Everyone's talking about it. Saxon Renaud died."

I nod. "So I've heard."

"I thought it was odd that Adam's car was there when you weren't home," Phillip observes. "And odder still, it was parked at the very foot of your driveway. Adam never parks like that. It makes sense now that you say someone stole the car."

"How did you know I wasn't home when you noticed Adam's car?" I ask.

It's not like I check in with Phillip when I spend the night away from home, and my car is always in the garage this time of year, making it more difficult to tell whether I'm home.

"Sophie," he explains. "When I clear your snow, or

pull a few weeds from your garden, or water your plants, or whatever, Sophie watches me from the living room window. No Sophie, no Megan." Phillip shrugs.

"Ahhh," I say, "very observant of you."

As much as I want to ask more questions about how often Phillip tends to the garden and snow maintenance at my house, I stop myself, because who am I kidding? If it weren't for Phillip Wilde, my house would have no curb appeal. We both know he does at least half the work.

"I should get back," I say. "Marla is on her own, and it's time for Sophie's midday walk."

"Before you go," Phillip rushes around from behind the counter. "I think this rightfully belongs to you."

He reaches into his pants pocket and produces a shiny, copper penny.

"A penny?" I ask.

"A penny saved is a penny earned, as my mother used to say." Phillip presses the penny into my palm and closes my fingers around it.

"Thank you?" I'm confused. "But why is it rightfully mine?"

"I found it on your property," he explains. "It fell off Adam's back bumper when I was brushing the snow off his car. It's amazing I noticed it in all that snow. I would've missed it if it wasn't so shiny. It must be a lucky penny."

"It must be," I agree, looking down at the shiny penny in my hand.

"You know what they say." Phillip waggles his index finger at me. "See a penny, pick it up, and all day long you'll have good luck." He smiles.

"Thank you," I say, holding up the penny between my thumb and forefinger as I walk to the door.

Once upon a time, finding a penny was an everyday occurrence, but Canada hasn't had pennies in circulation since 2012. This one-cent coin is a relic from the past. These days, the only places to find pennies in Harmony Lake are old piggy banks, and the coin slots of Saxon Renaud's penny loafers. How did this penny end up on the rear bumper of Adam's car? If this penny is a clue in Saxon's murder, maybe it really is a lucky penny. Lucky for me, unlucky for Saxon's killer.

"MARLA, I'm taking Sophie for a walk, then I have to run an errand."

"No problem, Megan. Take as long as you want. If it's OK with you, I'm going to move some yarn around to display the reds, pinks, and purples for Valentine's day next month."

"Brilliant idea!" I tell her as I collect my bag from underneath the counter.

I put the penny Phillip gave me in the zippered coin slot of my wallet.

I bundle up myself and Sophie, put my Airpods in my ears under my ear warmer, and put my playlist on shuffle. With Adele's sultry vocal stylings crooning *Hello* in my ear, I warn Sophie to brace herself for the chilly walk home.

According to the text updates I've received from most of the town, the scene in my driveway has cleared up. With the crime-scene tape gone, and Adam's car towed away by the police, I can get my car out of the garage. My plan is to leave Sophie at home for the afternoon, drive to the police station to drop off the penny to Eric, then drive back to Knitorious and relieve Marla.

If this penny is from Saxon's penny loafer, how did it find its way onto Adam's back bumper? In the photos I've seen, there was no damage to the rear of his car, so it's unlikely Adam's car backed up over Saxon's body. And if the penny was there since the car left Lake Access Road, how did it get all the way to my house without blowing off the bumper? Maybe this penny isn't evidence after all, maybe it's a coincidence. I sigh. Whether the penny is relevant to Saxon's murder isn't for me to decide, it's for the police to determine.

While I'm deep in thought, my phone rings, startling me back to the here and now.

I reach under my ear warmer and tap my right Airpod to answer the call. "Hello?"

"Hey, babe! How's your day?"

The familiar echo tells me that Eric is in his car.

"Less eventful than yours," I reply. "Are you in the car? I thought you were interviewing witnesses."

"Another officer is helping me with the interviews.

I'm on my way home to have the shower I didn't get to have earlier. If you haven't walked Sophie yet, maybe you can wait for me and we can walk her together?"

"You're too late, Chief! Sophie and I are walking as we speak."

"Are you at the park? I can meet you."

"Nope, we're on our way home to pick up my car," I respond. "If you meet me there, I'll make you lunch and maybe give you some evidence for dessert."

"What kind of evidence?"

"It's a surprise," I tease.

Most women probably surprise their partners with fancy meals or sentimental gifts. Not us, we give each other clues and evidence. The gifts that keep on giving.

"Give me a hint," Eric pleads. "What size evidence bag should I bring?"

"The smallest one you have."

CHAPTER 8

I MAKE a quick omelette for Eric and me with some leftover ham and chopped onion I find in the fridge.

Eric hasn't put down his phone since he walked through the door. His thumbs are forever typing and have been since he accepted the interim chief of police position three months ago. His phone has a bigger presence in our lives than it ever did before; it's like an unwanted third person in our relationship. Even when he's not at work, he's invisibly tethered to the station thanks to the magic of Wi-Fi and 5G cell phone networks. Days off don't exist for him anymore.

Before he was chief, Eric's phone was only this active when he was working a case, but now it never stops. It rings, dings, vibrates, beeps, and buzzes twenty-four hours a day, seven days a week. At first, I told myself it was a transitional phase, and the need to be constantly reachable would slow down once he settled into his new role. Now, I'm not sure. I'm having flashbacks to being married to Adam, and look how that turned out.

"Thank you," he says, without looking up from his phone when I put his plate in front of him.

Finally, he turns the blasted thing upside down and pushes it to the other end of the table.

"Can I ask you something?" I push some omelette around my plate with my fork.

"Of course," Eric replies, "you can ask me anything." He bites into his toast.

"When you found Saxon, did both of his penny loafers have pennies in them?"

"You found it?" Eric garbles, still chewing. His eyebrows almost disappear into his hairline, and he swallows with a loud gulp. "Where did you find it?"

I shrug one shoulder. "I didn't find it. It found me. Phillip gave it to me. He didn't seem to realize it might be evidence."

"He didn't think it was evidence?" Eric sounds dubious. "What did he think it was? Where did he find it?"

"He thought it was good luck," I reply, and I recite the little rhyme Phillip told me when he gave the penny to me earlier. "Look at it from Phillip's perspective," I suggest. "When Phillip cleared the snow earlier, he didn't know about the accident on Lake Access Road or about Saxon's death. It didn't occur to him that Adam's car was a crime scene or that he might come across evidence."

"Phillip thought finding a shoe with a penny in it was good luck?" Eric clarifies, suspiciously.

I think we're talking about different things.

"No, he thinks the penny he found on the rear bumper of Adam's car was good luck. He thinks it's a lucky penny," I explain. Then I realize what I'm missing. "Was Saxon missing an entire shoe? Not just the penny?" I ask.

Eric puts down his fork. His phone has been buzzing the entire time we've been talking, and he glances over at it. I can tell he wants to pick it up. He restrains himself.

"The shoe is a holdback," Eric tells me.

A holdback is a piece of evidence from the scene of a crime the police don't disclose to the public. Something only the culprit or someone with inside knowledge of the crime would know about. The holdback is used to confirm a suspect's confession or expose a false confession. According to Eric, false confessions happen more than you'd think.

"I won't tell anyone," I assure him.

"I know." He takes my hand. "The umbrella is a holdback too. We can't locate it, either."

"His umbrella is missing?" I swallow to suppress a smile. There's poetic justice in Saxon Renaud being separated from his beloved umbrella. "Do you think he poked the wrong person with it, and they killed him?"

I'm half-joking, half-serious. "Or he drew another battle line in the snow, and it made someone angry?"

"Maybe," Eric replies. "Based on the coroner's preliminary findings, Saxon was already dead when Adam's car ran over him. He was likely murdered somewhere else, then transported to Lake Access Road. The cause of death is strangulation. The coroner isn't sure if the killer yoked him from behind, or did it face-to-face, but Saxon's neck was compressed with a straight, blunt object."

A straight, blunt object like an umbrella, maybe?

"And now you can't find his umbrella. You suspect the cause of death is strangulation, and the manner of death is the umbrella," I deduce.

Eric nods.

In cop speak, the cause of death is how the victim died, and the manner of death is how the cause of death was delivered.

So, the killer—or killers—put Saxon's dead body in Adam's car, drove to Lake Access Road, removed Saxon's body from the car, positioned it in the road, and drove over it. Why? We're either looking for one very strong person, or multiple average-strength people. Lugging a dead body around isn't easy.

We finish eating, and while Eric clears the dishes from the table, I retrieve the penny from my wallet and meet him in the family room.

"I haven't ruled out anyone yet," Eric says as he seals the evidence bag with the penny in it. "Everyone at the card game last night is a suspect. And if Adam lost his keys *outside* Sheamus's house, the pool of potential suspects gets even bigger."

I cozy up next to him on the sofa and pull the blanket over our legs. He yawns and sinks deeper into the sofa. Because yawns are contagious, I yawn too. His eyes are tired and bleary. Can he even see me clearly?

"Adam said his car took an indirect route to Lake Access Road," I say. "Could the murder scene be somewhere along that route? The killer either brought Adam's car to Saxon's body or brought Saxon's body to Adam's car. The former would be easier and less conspicuous than the latter."

"Officers are searching the route inch by inch," Eric explains. "So far, there's no indication of a murder scene. They haven't found a shoe or an umbrella, either. I think the indirect route might have been a tactic the killer used to avoid being recognized while driving Adam's car."

"That confirms my suspicions that whoever killed Saxon is a local," I conclude.

"Why? What else makes you think the killer is local?" Eric asks, pulling away to look me in the eye.

"Well, they knew about Lake Access Road," I begin. "Only people who live in Harmony Lake or visit frequently would know about it and how to get there. Also, we were having a snowstorm, and you wouldn't be here in a blizzard if you didn't live here. Harmony Lake is too remote to enter and exit in terrible weather.

And they left Adam's car at my house. They associated this address with him and wanted his car to get back to him. It all screams local to me."

"The last part is the part that bothers me," Eric reveals. "It doesn't make sense to leave Adam's car at your house." He looks at me. "Why not abandon it at Adam's office? Or the parking lot at the pub? Or in front of Sheamus's house, where they found it? All of those places would have been lower risk than your house because none of them have security cameras. They chose the only house in town with security cameras. And they knew about your cameras because they parked the car to avoid them. There's a reason the killer left the car here, and if I can figure it out, it might lead us to the killer."

"The only thing I can think of," I say, trying to help, "is that all the places you listed are either too high traffic or too remote."

"Everything in this town is downtown or remote," Eric points out. "There's no in between."

"Adam's office and condo are both at the eastern most point of town. If the killer didn't have another car handy, it would be a long walk in a snowstorm to get anywhere," I reason. "The pub parking lot is busy and well-lit, even during a snowstorm. It snows here six months of the year. The residents of this town are used to snow. They won't let a blizzard stop them from a night at the pub. If the killer didn't know the pub closed early because of the storm, they would avoid the parking lot for fear of being seen dropping off Adam's car. Same with Sheamus's house. He lives right behind Water Street, and his street gets a lot of foot traffic when people stumble home from the pub."

"Those are good points," Eric cedes, then yawns again, "but it doesn't explain why they chose this specific house." He gestures around himself.

"Either their car was near here, or my house is walking distance to wherever they went next," I speculate. "And I live on a quiet street, far enough away from Water Street that it was unlikely anyone would recognize them walking up the street in a blizzard."

"We don't even know which direction they went after they left the car." He sounds dejected.

"The falling snow covered up any footprints or tire tracks they left, and Phillip's dedication to snow removal blew away any evidence the killer might have left near the car."

"Except the lucky penny," I remind him. "And maybe the forensics team will find something inside Adam's car that will help identify whoever did this."

"Let's hope," Eric mutters.

Could one of my neighbours be a murderer? The thought makes me visibly shudder. Eric squeezes me tighter, and I pull the blanket up to my shoulders.

Eric's phone is in his other hand again, and he's scrolling through messages.

"Why did Sheamus lie about being home when Adam texted him this morning?" I ask.

Eric sighs. "I don't know. I can't verify Sheamus's alibi." He stops typing and puts his phone on the armrest of the sofa. He blinks rapidly and rubs his eyes with his free hand. "He says he was driving around looking for Ryan, and when he got the text saying Ryan was found and was safe, he parked at the pub and walked home. He claims he turned off his phone and went to bed. Which would explain why Adam didn't see Sheamus's truck in the driveway when he went back to his house."

"Why would Sheamus park at the pub and walk home?" I ask. "His house is only a short drive from the pub."

"He blamed the weather," Eric explains. "He said visibility was terrible, and he didn't want to drive."

"Sheamus drives a huge four-wheel-drive pickup truck with a snowplow attachment in the winter. But he didn't want to drive for five minutes in the snow? OK," I say, with sarcasm oozing from each word.

"I know, babe, but I can't prove Sheamus is lying. His truck was in the parking lot where he said it would be, and it was covered in several hours' worth of snow accumulation."

I look up at him, and his eyes are tired and bloodshot.

"Will you do something for me?" I ask.

"I'd do anything for you," he replies, once again looking at his phone. "What do you want me to do?"

"Take a nap."

"A nap?" he asks, returning his phone to the armrest.

I nod.

"You want me to sleep?" He looks at me. "Now?"

I nod again. "With your phone turned off."

"It's day one of a murder investigation. I can't take a nap," Eric reasons. "And I can't just turn off my phone."

I take a deep breath and prepare to make my case. "Honey, it's a day and a half past your bedtime," I tell him. "You've slept less than two hours out of the last thirty, and you still have Adam's victory party tonight because *you* insisted that it continue as planned, so you could observe the suspects in the same room at the same time."

"Can I nap with my phone on?" he counters, attempting to negotiate.

I shake my head. "It never stops, and you won't sleep. The world won't end if you unplug for a few hours."

"What if you have an emergency and need to reach me?" He's grasping for reasons to keep his phone on.

"Nap here. If I need you, I'll call the landline," I propose, shutting down his argument. "I'll wake you in plenty of time to shower and get dressed for tonight," I assure him, making it more difficult to find a reason not to nap. I make one last plea and try to appeal to his sense of duty. "You'll be a more effective investigator if you recharge your battery." I rest my case.

"I have to take the lucky penny to forensics." He shrugs, smirking triumphantly.

I didn't expect this argument.

"I'll drop off the penny on my way to the store. Just tell me who to give it to." Ha! Argue with that, Sloane!

"Fine," he surrenders with a sigh.

I tuck in Eric and Sophie for a nap, plug his phone into a charger in another room, and turn it off before the lucky penny and I get in the car and head to the Harmony Lake Police Station.

CHAPTER 9

TODAY REQUIRES extra caffeine if I'm going to stay awake long enough to attend Adam's victory party tonight. At least, this is what I tell myself to justify having two coffees today. I was going to justify it by getting one for Marla and telling myself I may as well get one for myself while I'm here, but I texted Marla, and she said it's too late in the day for her to have coffee.

While I stand in line at Latte Da, waiting for the barista to finish making my white chocolate and peppermint latte with extra whipped cream and a sprinkle of white chocolate shavings, I text Connie to make sure she, Archie, and Ryan are OK. She insists everyone is fine, and they're still planning to attend the victory celebration tonight. It will reassure me to see them in person and gauge for myself that Ryan is OK.

Coffee in hand, I lower my sunglasses from the top of my head to my face and step onto the sidewalk. A sunny day after a fresh snowfall is always brighter than usual because the sunlight reflecting off the snow makes everything appear brighter. A sunny, winter day can be brighter, and harder on the eyes, than a sunny summer day.

Sheamus O'Brien is loitering on the sidewalk outside Hairway to Heaven. Is he peering in the window? I get the impression he's trying to look discreet about it, but his awkward attempt to appear nonchalant makes his vibe more creepy-stalker than casual passerby. I guess it's hard to be inconspicuous with a head of bright red hair and pale Irish complexion. When tourists at the pub comment on Sheamus's stereotypical Irish pigmentation and ginger hair, he jokingly tells them it's because of the lack of sunlight inside pubs.

Hairway to Heaven is the hair salon next door to Latte Da, and across the street from the pub. The owner, Kelly, is my hairdresser and good friend.

Curious to see how this plays out, I hang back for a few minutes and watch what Sheamus does next. Leaning against the wall between the two stores, I sip my latte and watch Sheamus spy on whatever is happening inside Hairway to Heaven.

He's wearing that scarf again; the chunky hand-knit one he wore last night. The yarn is even more beautiful in the daylight, and I'm dying to ask him about it.

"Hi, Megan," Sheamus says when he notices me. "Cold enough for ya?"

"Hi, Sheamus." I smile. "Whatcha doin'?"

He shrugs. "Nothing much." He fidgets when I push myself off the wall and crane my neck to look at the window he was just peeping through, then look back at him. "I was thinking of getting a haircut," he explains, "but it looks like they're busy. They probably won't be able to fit me in." He shrugs again and self-consciously shifts his weight from one foot to the other.

I nod. Why is he uneasy? He's not usually uneasy; he's usually laid back and relaxed.

Sheamus doesn't look like he's due for a haircut. The longest hair on his ginger head appears to be only an inch long. I cup my free hand against my temple and squint, looking in the window. Two stylists sit at the reception desk, chatting and giggling.

"Doesn't look busy to me," I observe.

Sheamus shoves his ungloved hands in his jeans pocket and rocks back and forth on his heels. "Kelly's busy though. I only like Kelly to do my hair."

I look in the window again and scan the salon for Kelly. Sure enough, there she is with her back to the window, leaning over a sink, washing a client's hair.

"Me too," I admit. "Kelly is the only hairdresser who's touched my hair in a dozen years." I smile.

"She's the best." Seamus grins widely and blushes.

"May I touch your scarf?" I ask, proud of myself for checking first, instead of just reaching out and petting it, like I'm tempted to do.

"Absolutely," he replies, pulling the rest of his scarf

out from inside his zippered coat. "A special friend made it for me," he explains. "She said she chose the yarn because the colours remind her of Ireland. She paired it with white yarn. It reminds me of the Irish flag."

"Yes, it looks a bit like the Irish flag," I agree, enjoying the squishiness of the stitches. "Alpaca?" I ask, already certain it is.

The soft, spongy texture and the fuzzy haze surrounding the fabric is a dead giveaway that this yarn is mostly, if not entirely, alpaca.

Sheamus nods. "Yes. Her aunt has an alpaca farm and spins and dyes the fibre herself. The whitish yarn is natural, undyed, and the yarn with reddish and green flecks is called *Ashes to Ashes, Rust to Rust.*"

"It's beautiful," I say, smoothing the scarf against Sheamus's coat and taking a step back. "You know a lot about your scarf. Most non-knitters aren't as well-informed about their hand-knit gifts."

"Well," he blushes, "it's my favourite scarf." He tucks the ends back inside his coat.

"Sheamus," I start hesitantly, "what happened last night?"

We stroll toward Knitorious, and I sip my latte while Sheamus recounts his version of events. The details of his story are almost identical to Adam's description of what happened.

"At the height of the storm, visibility was awful, Megan. I parked my truck and walked home."

"It must have been bad," I sympathize. "But when Adam texted you this morning, you told him his car was still outside your house and you said it was untouched. Why did you tell him that? His car disappeared hours before he texted you."

Sheamus sighs. "I was still asleep when Adam texted me. His text woke me up. I was groggy and looked out the window to ease his mind because I could tell he was worried a snowplow had hit his car. There were two snow-covered cars parked on my street. The snow was smooth and untouched." He shrugs. "I assumed one of them must be Adam's Jag, so I texted him back and told him his car was fine."

That makes sense, except for the part where Adam's text woke up Sheamus. I'm sure Eric told me that, in his statement, Sheamus said he turned off his phone before he went to bed. If his phone was off, a text message couldn't have woken him.

Is Sheamus lying to me, or did he lie in his statement to the police? Or is the status of his cell phone a minor, insignificant detail that he's confused about?

* * *

"Hello?" I already know who it is because my phone has call display.

"It's dead here!" April declares. "It wasn't worth opening the bakery today. T and I should have gone tobogganing instead."

"You and T go tobogganing?" I ask. "I had no idea."

"Sometimes," April replies. I can picture her shrugging as she says it, even though we're talking on the phone. "You should come with us next time. It's fun."

"Yes, please!" I used to love tobogganing. I haven't done it since my daughter was little. "I still have Hannah's old sled in the rafters of the garage."

"The reason I'm calling," April says, as if she's ever needed a reason to call me, "is to ask if we can bring a lot of baked goods to the party tonight. T baked them fresh for all the customers we didn't have today. Do you think it would be OK?"

"It has nothing to do with me," I remind her. "It's Adam's event. He and Jess planned it with Sheamus."

A loud sigh comes through my AirPods. "Sometimes, for whatever reason, I still think of you and Adam as a single unit," April admits quietly. "I'm sorry, Megapixel."

"No worries," I assure her. "Twenty-year habits are hard to break." Slightly uncomfortable pause. "But check with Jess about the baked goods, I think she chose the menu for tonight," I add, changing the subject. "And check with Sheamus, too, since he's catering." I look around the store, even though I know I'm the only person here because Marla left to take her break. "Speaking of Sheamus…"

"Have you seen him? Did you ask him about last night?" April gasps. "You *did*!" How does she know when I haven't answered her question yet? I swear this woman can read my mind. "Tell me everything," she demands.

"Sheamus is a friend, and I want to believe he's telling the truth," I conclude at the end of my story.

"But you aren't sure if you believe him?" April asks. "I'm not sure I believe him either, Megnolia. I've seen Sheamus drive his truck in all kinds of bad weather. Heck, I've seen him use his snowplow attachment to clear snow when it's too snowy for the real snowplows to come out. And if he couldn't tell for sure if one of the snow-covered cars outside his house was Adam's, he should've said so instead of lying and saying he could see Adam's car. His story doesn't feel right."

"That's what I thought," I admit, relieved I'm not the only one who thinks Sheamus might be lying or leaving out an important detail or two.

CHAPTER 10

WHEN I GET HOME after work, I'm relieved to hear water *whooshing* through the pipes because it means Eric is in the shower. When I called the landline earlier to wake him, he was so drowsy I thought he might roll over and go back to sleep as soon as he hung up the phone.

According to Jess, tonight's event will have appetizers, finger food, and—thanks to the snowstorm keeping skiers and snowboarders in the mountains and out of Artsy Tartsy—a lot more pastries than were on the original menu

"I won't be late tonight, Soph," I explain to the corgi while I fix myself a small plate of cheese and crackers to sustain me until the party.

I don't want to eat a full dinner because I know I won't be able to resist the siren song of Tamara's delicious desserts, and I plan to indulge my sweet tooth to the fullest extent possible. After all, it is a celebration.

"Are you hungry, Sophie? Do you want dinner?" I wash a handful of grapes and add them to the plate of cheese and crackers, then dry my hands on a towel.

"Don't fall for her hungry dog act." Eric winks from the kitchen doorway where he's rubbing Sophie. "I fed and walked Sophie before my shower."

"Thank you," I say, extending my plate toward him. "Snack?"

He takes two pieces of cheese and a few grapes. "I warmed up the last piece of lasagna while Sophie was eating," he explains.

For me, tonight's function is a party, but for Eric, it's a work event. While I nibble, he explains that there will be a few non-uniformed officers at the party, watching and listening for anything that might pertain to Saxon Renaud's death and the incident on Lake Access Road. Eric says he hopes to glean some insight from watching the card game participants, in particular, and how they interact with one another.

"Do you need me to do anything?" I ask.

"Just enjoy yourself," Eric replies and puts his hands on my hips. "I'm sorry I have to work this event. I wish we could go together as a proper couple."

"It's fine," I assure him. "If it leads to a break in the case, it will be worth it." I hug him. "How was your nap?"

He kisses my forehead. "About my nap," he says. "Now that I've had some rest, I realize how overtired I was. I feel much better, and the world didn't fall apart without me for a few hours. Thank you. You were right."

"I usually am," I tease. "You just forget sometimes." I stand on my tippy toes and kiss him.

I mentally debate whether now is the right time to tell him about my conversation with Sheamus, but Eric checks his watch and announces that we should get going. He wants to be early, so he can talk to his colleagues before the guests start to arrive.

"I'll take my car and meet you there," I suggest. "I need to change and freshen up. Also, I told April and T that I'll meet them outside, and we'll go in together."

THERE'S no point trying to park at the pub because I already know the small parking lot will be full. Instead, I park behind Knitorious, beside Phillip's white floral-wrapped delivery van. April is already here, sitting in her warm car, waiting for me.

"Where's T?" I ask when April gets out of her car alone.

"I dropped her off at the pub," she explains as we hug hello. "I helped her carry the baked goods inside, and she stayed to organize and plate them. I drove here to park the car and meet you."

We walk from the store to the pub, and I'm grateful the sidewalks were plowed and are clear of snow, allowing me to wear my stiletto heels. I hate wearing boots to a function and going through the hassle of changing into my shoes when I get there.

Approaching the pub, I see Jess standing outside talking on her phone. Her gesticulations and facial expressions are familiar to me. I recognize a fellow mum arguing with a teenager when I see one. I've made those same faces and thrown around those same hand gestures when bickering with Hannah. Jess has three kids; her youngest is seventeen years old and recently started driving. Raising one teenager was stressful enough, I can't imagine raising three, especially when they're as close in age as Jess's kids are.

I give her a sympathetic smile, and she holds up her index finger telling me to wait as she puts the call on hold.

April gets a text from T who needs help plating pastries in the kitchen. I tell April to go inside and help her wife, and we'll see each other later.

Jess takes a deep cleansing breath. "Teenagers!" She rolls her eyes. "This one insists that I promised him two weeks ago that he could have two friends sleep over at our house tonight. There's no way I promised that. I would never approve a sleepover and allow three teenagers in my house when I'm not there to monitor it."

"Oh my," I sympathize. "Is there anything I can do?"

"Would you rather deal with an irrational teenager or with Adam's anxiety? I can't decide which one is less fun," she says. Her voice has a teasing tone, but her face is tense and serious.

"Adam is anxious?" I ask, knitting my brows together. "About what?"

Adam is one of the most poised people I've ever met. Even when he's stressed, most people would never know because his steady demeanour is usually unflappable.

"Nerves, I think." Jess shrugs. "He's freaking out about his speech."

"Really?" I reply, at a loss for words. "Huh."

The Adam I know loves an audience. I've watched him give speeches, keynote addresses, toasts, and emcee large events without ever breaking a sweat. Charming a room is his happy place.

Jess nods and holds up her phone. "Let me finish dealing with this teenage drama, and I'll join you inside when I'm done." She smiles.

"Good luck," I say opening the outer door to the pub.

I suspect the true source of Adam's stress isn't his speech, but the stress of Saxon's murder, on top of being elected mayor, and having his car stolen; it would be a lot to handle for anyone.

Inside the pub, it's business as usual downstairs with tourists and locals laughing and having a good time. The jovial atmosphere is accompanied by a DJ mixing music and an alcohol-induced, cheerful buzz in the air. Tonight's party is on the second floor in one of the function rooms, so I weave my way through the crowd toward the stairs. At the bottom of the stairs, an employee moves the velvet rope aside, I thank him, and begin my ascent.

At the top, I pause and look and take in the scene. They have converted one of the smaller offices into a coat-check room for the night, so I head over there to check my coat. As I take off my coat and hand it to the attendant, Adam approaches me from the side.

"There you are!" He looks flustered. "When Eric showed up without you, I panicked. I thought you weren't coming. Where were you?"

Jess wasn't kidding. Adam is definitely anxious.

I've only seen Adam anxious four times in the entire twenty-two years we've known each other: when he proposed to me, when I was in labour with Hannah, when he was waiting to find out if he made partner at the firm, and when we were separating and he had to tell me we were being blackmailed because he was having an affair with a married colleague.

"I'm here now," I assure him. "What's wrong?"

"My speech. It's all wrong. It's a mess. Everything's a mess. Can you go over my speech with me?" Adam isn't a fast talker. His usual tone is calm and authoritative, but right now his voice is urgent and uncertain. "This is the first speech I've written without your help. What if my jokes are inappropriate?"

He has a point; Adam's sense of humour can be a

little raunchy for an all-ages audience. But I'm sure Jess would've helped him tone it down.

I thank the coat-check attendant when they hand me my ticket, then take Adam by the arm, and lead him to a quiet corner where we can speak privately. The rest of the town's residents need not see their newly elected mayor having a meltdown.

"Didn't Jess listen to your speech already? I thought you practiced with her."

"Yes," he admits. "She listened, and she made a few suggestions, but it's not the same. Meg, I need your help." He shakes his head and adds, "This is a mistake! Why did I do this? I shouldn't be mayor."

"Adam, you'll do great. You always give great speeches. You're a natural public speaker. You've done this hundreds of times, and it's always gone off without a hitch. Tonight will be no different."

I did not expect this evening's festivities would begin with me giving my ex-husband a pre-speech pep talk, but here we are.

I point toward the large function room where his guests are waiting to congratulate him and celebrate his victory. "Everyone in that room voted for you because they believe in you. They voted for you because they *want* you to be mayor. They are our friends and neighbours, and they knew what they were getting when they voted for you. If you can speak to a room full of hundreds of lawyers, you can speak to them."

"That's the problem Meg," he explains, throwing

his hands up in frustration. "I'm used to speaking to lawyers and law societies, not friends and neighbours who are depending on me to keep our town happy and safe. Outside of Harmony Lake, I'm Adam the lawyer, and I know how to do that, but inside Harmony Lake, I was always Megan's husband or Hannah's dad. Now I'm just Adam Martel, and people don't know me. They know *you* and like *you*, not me. Don't you get it? Your nice personality offsets my egotistical personality. Without you to soften me and make me more likeable, everyone will see me for the arrogant fraud that I am." Adam catches his breath, loosens his tie, and undoes the top button of his shirt. Beads of sweat dot his brow.

Shocked by Adam's sudden capacity for self-insight, and starting to feel anxious myself after watching his anxiety-fuelled rant, I decide to try to calm down both of us.

"Heavy shoulders, long arms." I take a deep breath.

Adam nods and takes a couple of deep breaths.

"Calm down. We'll figure this out," I say comfortingly. "You're usually the calm, rational Martel, and I'm usually the emotional Martel."

"Well, we're switching roles tonight, Meg! Tonight, I get to be the emotional Martel, and you get to be the calm one!"

I reach out and turn the doorknob to Sheamus's office. It's unlocked. I open the door and gesture for Adam to follow me inside.

"Go ahead. Let it out. I'll stay with you until you feel better." I hand him a tissue from my clutch purse.

Adam paces around the crowded office, dabbing his sweaty brow, until he calms down. After he composes himself, he recites his speech to me, and it sounds great. I make a few small suggestions to tone down a couple of his jokes, and I remind him that less humour might be better considering his political opponent was murdered today. Adam wrote the speech before Saxon's death and admits that, because of today's chaos, he didn't think to change it to reflect a more sombre mood.

While Adam types into his phone, changing his speech, I sit in a chair across from Sheamus's desk and look around the cluttered room.

Sheamus's office is more like a storage locker than a functional office. The lighting is dim, and there are no windows to provide natural light. There are spare bar stools stacked in one corner with boxes of unopened straws, napkins, and toothpicks stacked precariously on top of the barstools like a real-life game of Jenga: Irish Pub Edition. Against another wall, folding chairs and tables lean against each other, along with the A-frame sign that Sheamus puts outside the pub in the warmer weather with the day's specials written in chalk.

There are piles of folded table linens, white bar towels, and old menus on top of the filing cabinets. Leaning against the wall in the corner farthest from where I'm sitting is... a whangee-handled, black umbrella? Are my eyes playing tricks on me? I blink and do a double take, in case the dim light is messing with my vision. Could that be Saxon's missing umbrella? Without taking my eyes off the umbrella, I open my clutch purse, take out my phone, and snap a quick photo.

The flash distracts Adam from his speech, and he looks at me quizzically.

"Oops," I say. "I didn't mean to do that." I hate lying, but the umbrella is a holdback, and I don't want to make up a bigger lie to explain why I'm taking a photo.

"What do you think?" Adam asks, handing me his phone with his speech open.

I skim it, make a few small edits, and hand it back to him.

While he reads the changes and commits them to memory, I do up the top button of his shirt, then tighten and straighten his tie.

"Do you feel better?" I ask.

Adam nods and gives me a small smile. "Thank you, Meg. I'm fine now. I don't know what I would do without you."

I smooth his lapels and step away, looking him up and down to make sure he's stage ready, when Jess pokes her head in the door.

"There you are! I looked everywhere for you. What are you doing in here?"

"We went over Adam's speech, made a few minor changes to reflect today's events, and removed a couple of jokes that may or may not have been inappropriate for the audience," I reply. "I'm off to join the party. I told April I'd meet her, and Eric will wonder where I am." I smile, pick up my purse from the chair, and leave.

I close the office door behind me and pull out my cell phone. I text the photo of the umbrella to Eric.

Me: Found this in Sheamus's office.

CHAPTER 11

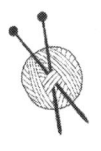

INSIDE THE FUNCTION ROOM, I am but one drop in a sea of familiar faces. I pause, take a breath, and survey the room, looking for Connie, Archie, or Ryan, but don't find them in my initial scan of the crowd.

"You look beautiful," Eric says, then kisses me hello. "Wow! That dress is flattering and kind of distracting."

I'm wearing my navy-blue wrap dress. It has long sleeves and a lapel collar. My favourite features are the pockets! The wide-belted waist flatters my curves. I have an hourglass figure, and I learned a long time ago that I feel more comfortable in clothes that flatter my shape than in clothes that try to hide my shape. It's easier to work with what I have than to try to make myself into something I'm not. I don't have a long, willowy body like April, but I'm pretty happy with the body I was born with. I'm happiest when I wear clothes that work with me instead of against me.

"Thank you," I reply, squeezing his hand. "Did you get my text?"

Eric nods. "I've already asked Sheamus if we can take the umbrella. He said yes. I sent an officer to secure it."

A server comes by with a tray of sparkling drinks. "Champagne?" she asks.

"I'm tempted, but I'm driving," I reply, the disappointment obvious in my voice.

"Ginger ale?" the server asks, pointing to one of the champagne flutes on her tray.

"Thank you." I smile and take the ginger ale.

Eric furrows his brow. "You're not staying at my place tonight?" he asks when the server moves on to the next cluster of guests.

"I have to go home. Sophie's there."

"Can I stay over?" he asks.

"Always," I reply. "But I'll probably leave before you, so I'll drive myself home and meet you there."

"I can drive you home and come back," he suggests.

Why is he in bodyguard mode?

"Why are you being so protective? Did something happen you haven't told me about?"

"Megan, someone, who is likely a murderer, left a stolen car in your driveway last night and avoided your security cameras. I'd feel better if I took you home myself."

Eric has a talent for saying things in a way that makes them sound scarier than I think they are.

He's here to do a job, and I don't want to distract him with an argument, so we agree to discuss it later. He goes on his way, eavesdropping and watching everything around him.

"Have you seen Ryan yet?" I ask April when we find each other and after we ooh and aah over how amazing we both look.

She shakes her head. "I don't think they're here yet." April slouches so her mouth is closer to my ear. "Kelly's here," she hisses at me in a loud whisper. "She said she wasn't coming, but she's here."

Our friend, Kelly, hasn't been out and about much since her husband passed away just over a year ago; it was his murder that brought Eric to Harmony Lake. Since her husband's death, Kelly has kept to herself. We've tried to encourage her to come out, socialize, and have fun, but she just wasn't ready yet.

I follow April's gaze to Kelly, who is smiling and chatting with a group of people that includes Sheamus.

"It's such a relief to see her happy," I say blinking tears out of my eyes. "I was beginning to think we'd never see her laugh again."

"Well, if anyone can make her smile again, Sheamus is the guy to do it. He's the most outgoing and extroverted person we know," April observes.

"It's true," I say, nodding.

Watching the small group of people interact, I notice Sheamus is wearing that scarf again. Isn't he warm? He's wearing a thick alpaca scarf inside a crowded upstairs room of a pub. I guess he wasn't kidding when he said it was his favourite scarf.

Kelly spots us looking at her. She smiles and waves, then comes over. We exchange hugs and hellos.

"It's so great to see you here, Kelly," I tell her. "We've missed you!"

"If we knew you were coming, we could've come together," April says.

"Thanks, ladies," Kelly smiles and nods. "It feels good to see everyone again. I'm glad I came. It was a last-minute decision. A couple of my stylists were coming, and I wanted to congratulate Adam in person. Thank goodness he beat Saxon and saved us from the big-box stores."

Kelly, April, and I chat until someone approaches Kelly from behind and taps her on the shoulder. She turns around to say hello to them, then turns back to us.

"Ladies, I'm going to mingle and catch up with people I haven't seen in forever." Kelly points at me. "Don't forget our appointment next week."

"Never," I respond. "My hair and I need to spend some time with you. See you on Monday."

Kelly wanders over to another group of people, which again includes Sheamus because he somehow is everywhere all the time. April and I watch Kelly smile and laugh. We comment that seeing Kelly enjoy herself again makes us feel warm inside.

"Do you sense a spark between them?" April asks.

"Between Kelly and Sheamus?" I ask.

April nods slowly. "The heat between them is so hot I can feel it from here."

"You think?" I watch Sheamus and Kelly. April's right, There's chemistry. "Kelly has barely left her house for over a year," I remind her. "I don't think she's started dating yet."

"I don't know if they're dating, but I know chemistry when I feel it, Megapop," April says.

The clinking of glasses grows louder than the collective murmur of the crowd, and everyone turns toward the stage where Adam is ready to give his speech.

I make my way to the buffet table and fix a plate of pastries to eat while I listen. I notice Eric standing near the buffet table, deep in conversation with Pete Feeney. I wonder what they're talking about, and whether Eric is learning anything that could help solve Saxon's murder.

April and I find a spot close to the stage, and I eat pastries while Adam speaks.

When his speech is over, the room cheers and gives Adam a round of applause. As the crowd disperses and everyone divides themselves into cliques, I overhear several comments about how good his speech was and how relieved and happy people are that Adam is the new mayor of Harmony Lake.

To his credit, Adam said some lovely words about Saxon which couldn't have been easy. He also announced that the flags at the Harmony Lake town hall will be at half-mast for the next three days in Saxon's honour. He must've added the part about the flags after I edited his speech because I don't recall it being there before.

Eric and Pete are still talking, and I'm contemplating casually drifting toward them until I'm within eavesdropping range, when a light touch on my shoulder makes me flinch.

"Ryan!" I say when I spin around and realize it's him. I throw my arms around him and give him a hug. "It's so good to see you."

"It's good to be seen," he replies jokingly.

I let go of him and hug his partner, Lin. Then I hug both Connie and Archie. When I stand back and look at them as a group, it's obvious they're uptight and tense. But other than that, everybody seems fine, and most important, Ryan is sober.

We talk for a while, limiting our conversation to small talk. We don't venture beyond anything more interesting than the weather, or what each of us is wearing, because we're aware of the many eyes and ears around us.

"Is it OK if I come by the store tomorrow morning to change the locks?" Ryan asks.

"Why do you want to change the locks?" I answer his question with a question.

"Adam asked me to take care of it because he had a spare key on the key chain that went missing with his car," Ryan explains.

"Come by whenever, someone will be there all day."
I forgot Adam had a spare key to Knitorious.

April and Tamara and I work the room for a while, stopping to talk to friends and neighbours. I make sure to gently steer us in the general direction of the buffet table, so I can have a few more cheesecake bites before I leave.

We finally reach the buffet table, and someone stops Tamara to compliment her mini Black Forest cupcakes. While a fellow-pastry lover tries to coax the recipe out of Tamara, I quietly say goodbye to April, interrupt Tamara to give her a quick hug goodbye, and start the process of saying goodbye to friends and neighbours on my way to the coat check.

"I'm tired," I say when I approach Eric. "I think I'll go home now."

"I'll drive you." It's a statement, not a question or a suggestion.

"I'll be fine," I insist. "I'll text you as soon as I get home."

"At least let me walk you to your car," Eric negotiates.

"If you leave, you might miss something important," I rationalize. "You need to stay here and find clues to solve Saxon's murder. This investigation is making everybody crazy. I've never seen the people I love so stressed and worried." I tell him about Adam's breakdown, and how tense Connie, Archie, and Ryan are.

"Good evening, you gorgeous couple," Philip says, giving me a double-cheek kiss and exchanging an air kiss with Eric.

Philip takes my hand and looks me up and down. "Sweetie, you are throwing off serious Jane Russell vibes in that dress, and I *love* it!"

"Thank you," I say demurely, slightly embarrassed at the attention.

"Megan, am I to understand you're leaving now?" Philip asks, then looks at Eric. "Why don't I see Megan home safely, and you can stay here and do what you do best. I'm leaving now, anyway. I have an early delivery at the shop." He looks at me. "Baby's breath and roses for a bridal bouquet."

"Were you eavesdropping on our conversation, Phillip?" I ask.

"Only half of it," he replies. "Eric's half. You speak too quietly."

Well, at least he's honest.

"It would be great if we could walk to our cars together," I say. "I parked next to you."

"Perfect! I'll follow you home in my van and make sure you arrive at chez Martel safe and sound."

We both look at Eric. "Are you comfortable with this arrangement?" I ask.

He nods. "Thank you, Phillip."

Phillip flicks his wrist casually. "It's the least I can do since I might've blown away all your evidence with my snowblower." He extends his hand, palm up, and looks at me. "Give me your coat-check ticket, sweetie. I'll get our coats while you say goodbye to lover boy."

I give Phillip my coat-check ticket, and he turns and leaves.

"I'll likely be asleep when you get home," I tell Eric, and stretch to my tallest height to kiss him. "Good night, I love you. I'll see you tomorrow."

"I love you too. Please text me when you get home. Remember to lock the doors and arm the security system."

On my way out, I stop and say goodbye to friends and neighbours as I pass them.

"Your speech was great. I told you it would go off without a hitch," I tell Adam when I encounter him and Jess.

"Thanks, Meg. And thanks for coming tonight," he replies.

"Thank you for doing Adam-management while I dealt with my teen troubles," Jess says, hugging me.

"No problem," I reply. "I think I got the easier of the two tasks."

We wish each other good night and remind each other to drive safely. I head out of the function room and into the large open area. I don't see Phillip anywhere.

"Meg! Wait a sec," Adam hisses, jogging to catch up with me.

I turn around. "What's wrong?"

"Nothing," Adam replies, coming to a stop in front

of me. "Thank you, again. If you hadn't shown up, I don't think I would've been able to go in there and give the speech." He smiles.

"No problem," I say. "You'd do the same for me." I turn to walk away.

"You look beautiful, by the way," Adam calls after me. "That's one of my favourite dresses. You bought it in Montreal when we were there for my parents' forty-fifth wedding anniversary, remember?"

I remember, but I'm surprised Adam does. In our two decades of marriage, he never once said anything about what I wore to various events, let alone mentioned where I bought it or whether he liked it. Is the stress of this investigation making him snap? Is he having some kind of breakdown? Or is this a midlife crisis? Whatever it is, it's weird. The quicker we rid ourselves of this murder investigation and get back to normal, the better.

"Thank you." I smile. "Enjoy the rest of your party."

With no sign of Phillip upstairs, I decide to head downstairs and see if he's waiting for me by the door. Sure enough, I spot him by the door talking to Rick Ransan.

"Sorry I kept you waiting, Phillip," I say, then I look over at Rick and smile. "Hi, Rick."

"H-hi, Megan. You look nice," Rick responds.

"Thank you," I reply.

Before I can tell Rick I'm sorry that his friend Saxon died, Phillip is behind me, saying goodbye to Rick and slipping my coat sleeves over my arms. The next thing I know, I'm dressed for the outdoors. I blurt a quick goodbye to Rick as Phillip pulls me by the hand through the inner doors of the pub, then the outer doors, not letting go until we're standing on the sidewalk where I finish buttoning my coat.

"I had to get out of there," Phillip explains, taking a deep breath and lowering the zipper of his coat to expose his neck. "It's too hot and stuffy in that crowded bar when I'm wearing this goose down-filled coat." He extends his elbow, offering me his arm.

"I understand," I sympathize, hooking my arm through his. "Are you and Rick Ransan close friends?" I ask as we meander down Water Street.

"No," Phillip replies. "I'm closer to Trudy than Rick, but because Rick and Trudy are close, I guess that kind of makes Rick and me friends."

Trudy Nakata is an elderly resident of Harmony Lake. She's active in our community and a member of the book club. She and Rick Ransan are neighbours; Rick dotes on Trudy and helps her live independently in her home.

"I didn't know you and Trudy are close," I say.

"Oh, yes, Trudy and my mum were good friends back in the day," Phillip explains. "And Trudy looks after Kevin when I'm not home. Tonight, she took Kevin outside to do his business and gave him his bedtime snack." He looks around to make sure no one is listening, then tilts his head toward me and adds quietly,

"Aaaaand, Trudy is Rick's alibi for when Saxon was killed."

"Really?" I ask, shocked. "I didn't know that." In a quieter voice, I add, "Tell me more."

It didn't occur to me that Saxon Renaud's only friend could also be his murderer. But I guess it makes sense that he would be a person of interest. Rick was one of the last people seen with Saxon. He backed out of the poker game at the last minute, and who knows where Rick went after he dropped off Saxon at Sheamus's house.

"Well, according to Trudy, when Saxon was murdered, Rick was rescuing Cat Benatar," Phillip explains. "She said she spent hours looking for Cat Benatar when she heard his meows coming from the ceiling. The cat found its way up there but couldn't find its way out. She phoned Rick in a panic, and he rushed over to rescue the cat. Rick had to drill holes and everything. Trudy says it was an awful mess but was worth it because Cat Benatar got out unharmed."

Cat Benetar is Trudy's cat, and he's a climber.

"How did Cat Benatar get up there?" I ask.

"Loose ceiling tile in the laundry room," Phillip replies. "Trudy says Rick fixed all the holes he made and the loose ceiling tile, so Cat Benatar couldn't climb up there again. She says Rick was there all night."

Rick sounds like a good person. He cares for his elderly neighbour, saves her cat, and stays up all night repairing the damage he made saving the cat to ensure it won't get stuck again. What could Rick Ransan and Saxon Renaud have in common?

"Why would a nice person like Rick hang around with someone like Saxon Renaud?" I wonder out loud.

"I don't know," Phillip replies with a shrug. "I know Rick worked for Saxon, but why they were friends beyond that is a mystery to me."

It's a mystery to me too. For now.

CHAPTER 12

Saturday, January 16th

I take one of the hand-knit display scarves and wrap it around my neck, then hug myself with my hand-knit cardigan, and shiver. It's freezing in the store because Ryan has the door open while he changes the lock. Even Sophie is chilly; she's curled up in a tight little ball on her dog bed, still wearing her purple and white argyle sweater.

"Thanks for coming in early to meet me, Megan," Ryan says as he works on the front door.

"No problem," I reply. "I'm an early riser, so I was up, anyway." I smile. "So, how are you feeling Ryan? I mean, how are you doing after Friday night?"

"You mean when I accidentally drank Saxon's rum and Coke?" He answers my question with a question. "It's OK, Megan, you can mention it. It's not a trigger for me."

"OK," I respond. "If you're sure... What happened after you drank the rum and Coke and confronted Saxon? Where did you go?"

Ryan tells me from his perspective how the evening played out. His story is remarkably similar to both Adam and Sheamus's versions of events. At least everyone agrees on the events that led up to Saxon's murder.

Ryan tells me that when he left Sheamus's house, he got in his car and drove with no particular destination in mind.

"I wanted to put as much distance as possible between me and that rum and Coke. Finally, I decided to drive either to Harmony Hills or the city and find a twelve-step meeting." Ryan finishes with the front door, closes it, locks it, and joins me in the cozy sitting area where he continues his story. "Driving was horrible. There was no visibility, and the roads were covered in snow. I realized it would take hours to get anywhere, and I wouldn't find a meeting anyway, not in this weather."

"So, what did you do?" I ask.

"I pulled into the parking lot at the Hav-a-nap motel," Ryan replies.

The Hav-a-nap motel is on the west side of town, near the ramp to the highway, and, coincidentally, near Lake Access Road. Could Ryan be the witness who reported seeing Adam's car leaving Lake Access Road?

"Is that where Pete Feeney found you?" I asked.

"Pete didn't find me." Ryan shakes his head. "No one found me. I called my sponsor from my cell phone. After a while, he talked me off the ledge. Then I called my dad, and he stayed on the phone with me while I drove home."

By process of elimination, I assumed Pete Feeney found Ryan. I knew it wasn't Adam because he had no car and showed up on Eric's doorstep. Sheamus said he went home when he got a text saying that Ryan was safe. Rick was at Trudy's house tracking Cat Benetar through the ceiling to rescue him. I figured it couldn't be Saxon because he was murdered, and who are we kidding, it's doubtful Saxon would have been concerned enough about Ryan's well-being to help look for him, anyway. That left Pete Feeney. If Pete didn't find Ryan, where was he when Ryan parked at the Hav-a-nap motel?

"When you parked at the motel, were you parked where you could see Lake Access Road, by chance? Did you see Adam's car near there?"

Ryan shakes his head. "My car was facing the opposite direction," Ryan explains. "And the snowfall was too heavy. Snow started accumulating on my windshield as soon as I put the car in park. I couldn't see anything, and I'm sure no one would have been able to see me, either."

This proves my point. Unless they were super close

to it, how would a witness have been able to see Adam's car clearly enough to identify it?

I smile. "We were all relieved that you were OK," I tell him.

"Thanks, Megan." Ryan gets up, picks up his toolbox, and gestures for me to follow him to the back of the store.

I sit on the stairs that lead to the apartment while Ryan gets to work changing the lock on the back door.

Ryan stops working and looks up at me. "I didn't kill Saxon Renaud," he says, making what feels like deliberate eye contact with me. "I didn't like him, and I'm not sad he's dead, especially after what he did to me on Friday night. But I didn't kill him. I wouldn't kill anybody."

"I know," I reply. "No one thinks you did it. And we'll prove it by finding out who did."

"You should have a lot of suspects to choose from," Ryan observes as he resumes working on the lock. "Few people liked Saxon, and he owed many people money."

"What?" I ask, correcting my posture and sitting at full attention. This is the first I've heard about Saxon owing money to anyone. "Who does Saxon owe money to? Who told you about his debt?"

Money is a common motive for murder; maybe an angry creditor killed Saxon.

"Jay Singh told me," Ryan explains.

Jay Singh is Ryan's friend, and a local money lender,

though he prefers to call himself an alternate lender. In exchange for a higher rate of interest than one would pay at a bank or other traditional lending institution, Jay will discreetly lend money with no questions asked. His job often makes him privy to intimate details of his clients' lives. Details his clients would prefer to keep private. Once, when I was a person of interest in a murder investigation, Jay helped me by sharing a tidbit of information with me to help clear my name.

It surprised me when Jay told me he counts several residents of Harmony Lake among his clientele. It's the paradox of this tight-knit community; while it seems like everyone knows everything about their friends and neighbours, our town is still full of secrets.

"Did Saxon owe money to Jay?" I ask.

"That's what Jay told me," Ryan replies. "He said Saxon owed money to other lenders too. Jay said Saxon was overextended." Ryan puts air quotes around *overextended*. "Jay didn't come out and say it, but I got the feeling Saxon was behind on his repayments. Jay hates that."

"I'm sure he does," I agree, nodding.

To look at Saxon, you wouldn't think he had financial difficulties. He drove a newer mid-range car, he wore designer, albeit older clothes, he carried that expensive umbrella everywhere he went, and he conducted himself with an air of self-importance. Not to mention all the property he owned around Harmony lake. Combined, his property holdings must be worth a lot of money.

If Ryan is correct, and Saxon was over-leveraged, he hid it behind a carefully cultivated image of affluence.

Saxon wouldn't be the first person who looks wealthy but isn't. It's possible to be asset-rich and income-poor. Owning lots of property doesn't mean lots of cash flow. It's feasible that the income from Saxon's real estate investments wasn't enough to cover his expenses. Also, some of his properties were older and likely required expensive maintenance.

The sound of someone knocking at the front door, followed by Sophie's excited yelps, distracts me from my thoughts, and I check the time. Only a few minutes until it's time to open the store. I bet Marla is knocking, wondering why her key doesn't work. I remind Ryan that I need a few extra keys, excuse myself, and rush to the front door.

"My key doesn't work," Marla says, holding up the offending key as evidence.

"Sorry about that," I respond. "Ryan just changed the lock. We lost a spare key to the store yesterday."

"Oh my," Marla says, her eyes wide.

I leave the front door unlocked and turn the sign from CLOSED to OPEN.

A few minutes later, Ryan finishes working at the back door and gives me the keys on his way out. After he leaves, Connie arrives and the three of us take turns serving customers and ringing up sales.

Knitorious is busy today, which isn't a surprise because we're in the middle of the winter tourist season, and the ski resorts in the Harmony Hills mountains are booked solid. The skiers and snowboarders like to wander into town on Saturdays to soak up the ambience, eat at our fabulous restaurants, and shop at our local stores.

Between customers, Connie, Marla, and I talk about last night's party. We chat about who was there and who wasn't, review the food, and inevitably find ourselves talking about who killed Saxon Renault.

According to Marla, the rumour mill favours either Adam or Ryan as the prime suspects in Saxon's murder. Adam's alleged motive was to eliminate his political rival, and Ryan's supposed motive was revenge after Saxon tricked him into drinking alcohol.

Connie tells us she heard mumblings last night that Sheamus might be the murderer. Sheamus is vehemently opposed to any big-box stores or restaurants in Harmony Lake. The rumour mill speculates that Sheamus would have more to lose than many small businesses because big-box restaurants and sports bars would likely be among the first new inhabitants of our small town under a Saxon Renaud-led town council.

"It's true, big-box restaurants and sports bars would be tough competition for the Irish Embassy Pub," I agree. "But using that logic, every business owner in Harmony Lake is a suspect." I bring my hand to my chest. "*I* would be a suspect." I laugh, and Connie and Marla laugh with me.

"Well, there are other rumours about other potential suspects," Connie teases.

"Who?" I ask.

"Rick Ransan is a favourite choice among the charity knitters," she replies.

"Connie's right," Marla confirms. "Some of the charity knitters talked about it last night."

The Charity Knitting Guild is a local organization whose outward mission is to use knitting to raise money and awareness for good causes.

We also have a book club. The book club is a local group of book lovers whose outward mission is to read and discuss best-selling fiction.

I say outward mission because the whole town knows the inward mission of both groups—the true reason they exist—is to preserve Harmony Lake's small-town charm by eliminating anything that threatens it.

The membership of both groups comprises many of Harmony Lake's older, wiser, female residents. The groups have a matriarchal hierarchy with the elder, more experienced members training the younger members to eventually take over.

Harmony Lake might have a democratically elected mayor and town council, but everyone in town knows the knitters and the readers wield the real power.

In fact, Adam ran for mayor because the knitters

and the readers joined forces to recruit him. They spear-headed his campaign and used their influence to keep the big-boxers out of power. Never have two groups of sweet, nurturing women been so loved and so feared at the same time.

Connie and Marla are the only two crossover members; they belong to both groups. I don't belong to either group, but the charity knitters meet at Knitorious every Wednesday afternoon to knit and plan their upcoming projects, so I interact with them regularly.

"The book club thinks Rick might be the killer too," Connie adds, "but they don't dare talk about it in front of Trudy."

"Of course." I nod.

Trudy is a member of the book club, and Rick Ransan's neighbour. They look after each other. She wouldn't like to hear the other readers accuse him of murder.

"Why would Rick want to kill his friend, Saxon?" I ask. "I mean, neither of them seemed to have any other friends."

"Rick was Saxon's employee, he did odd jobs and helped maintain Saxon's properties," Marla reminds me. "But people say Saxon was mean to Rick. They say they've heard Saxon call Rick nasty names and make fun of his stutter. Maybe Rick was sick and tired of Saxon's abuse. Maybe Rick finally snapped and ran over Saxon with Adam's car."

The accuracy rate of the Harmony Lake rumour mill

is shockingly high, and knowing Saxon, it's believable that he might have bullied and verbally abused Rick. That being said, I can't imagine Rick would murder Saxon to make it stop. This is the same man who gave up a night's sleep to save a cat from a ceiling, for goodness' sake. People who save cats don't commit murder, right?

CHAPTER 13

COMING IN FROM THE COLD, dry outside air, I sniffle. What's that splendid smell? When I inhale again, my nostrils twitch, then flare to maximum capacity to let in as much of the glorious aroma as possible.

"It smells like coffee in here, Soph," I mutter as I detach her leash after our midday walk. "My coffee. White chocolate and peppermint latte," I elaborate, taking off her sweater.

"With extra whipped cream and a sprinkle of white chocolate shavings."

Who said that? Is Eric here? I look up, shocked to see Eric sitting at the table in the kitchenette, his face focussed on his phone screen as his thumbs type so fast they appear to hover over the keyboard. He'll get repetitive stress syndrome if he's not careful.

"Hey, handsome! What are you doing here?" I ask,

joining him at the table and cracking the lid on my coffee.

"I was nearby, so I stopped by to say hi and bring you a coffee." He smiles, laying his phone face down on the table.

"Thank you," I say, taking a small sip. "You must have used the front door," I speculate.

We keep the back door locked, even when the store is open.

He tilts his head and looks at me inquisitively. "I did. I came from Latte Da, so I came in the front door and said hi to Marla and Connie," Eric confirms. "How did you know that?" He rubs Sophie's head when she puts her front paws on his knees.

I set my coffee on the table and raise my index finger. "Stay here. I have something for you."

"Is it an early anniversary gift?" he calls after me as I walk out of the back room.

A surprising thing I've learned about Eric as our relationship grows is that he's a hopeless romantic. He's prone to romantic gestures so sweet, they verge on corny. As someone who is more practical than senti-mental, I wasn't sure at first how to respond to his increasingly frequent romantic words and gestures, but now I think it's one of his most endearing qualities. On the outside, Eric is a hunky, muscle-bound man who carries a gun, but on the inside, he's a soft, sentimental, gentle soul who tears up at the end of romantic come-dies. I admire his ability to deal with horrible situations and criminals every day at work, without letting it harden him and make him emotionally unavailable. If sentimentality and romanticism are his coping mechanisms, I'll embrace it.

"Not an anniversary gift," I say when I return a moment later and place a key on the table in front of him. "Ryan changed the locks this morning," I explain. "Your key wouldn't have worked if you tried to come in the back door." I explain to Eric that a spare key to Knitorious was on Adam's stolen key chain.

"Speaking of keys," Eric responds. "The forensics people didn't find any fingerprints or DNA on Adam's keys. Whoever stole them wiped them clean before abandoning them with the car."

My sigh conveys the defeat I feel. "I was hoping the killer left evidence in the car," I explain. "Evidence that would lead straight to them, so this fiasco would end." I wrap my hands around my coffee cup and take comfort in the warmth.

"Don't give up hope," Eric says, enveloping my hands and coffee cup with his big, warm hands. "I'm on my way to meet with forensics and get the report for the rest of the car. Maybe they found something we can use."

"Don't they usually email forensics reports to you?" I ask, sipping my latte.

Eric nods. "They want to show me something. They said it's visual." He shrugs. "But they did email me a report about the umbrella you found in Sheamus's office last night."

"And?" I ask.

"It's not one of Saxon's umbrellas," Eric replies, flipping his phone over and quickly checking his notifications, before turning it face down again.

"One of? Saxon had multiple umbrellas?" I ask.

"We found multiple umbrellas when we searched his house," Eric explains. "It seems he kept back-up umbrellas. They're all identical. Same manufacturer too. Anyway, the one in Sheamus's office isn't the same, and they recovered no fingerprints or DNA from it to prove Saxon ever touched it. Sheamus said a customer left it at the pub about four months ago and never came back for it. He said his office is the informal lost-and-found for the pub. We questioned the server who found it four months ago, and she corroborated Sheamus's story."

Now I feel bad that Sheamus had to go through being questioned again, and have one of his employees questioned, because I hastily mis-identified an umbrella in his dimly lit office.

I lean in and speak quietly, so anyone hanging around the door to the back room won't hear me. "If Saxon had multiple umbrellas, could the umbrella you're looking for, the holdback," I mouth the word holdback, "be amongst the umbrellas you found at his house?" I ask.

Eric shakes his head. "It's a good thought, but forensics checked," he replies. "The umbrellas we found at his house were brand new. They were sealed in plastic from the manufacturer and had tags on them."

"Did he have multiple pairs of penny loafers too?" I ask rhetorically, my voice thick with sarcasm.

"He did. They were still in boxes with store tags on them," Eric says.

"I was talking with Ryan this morning, and he mentioned that he parked near Lake Access Road around the time Saxon was killed. He said there was no visibility. How did the witness who identified Adam's car actually *see* Adam's car?" I ask.

"I don't know, babe. I'd love to question that witness, but I don't know who it is."

"The 9-1-1 dispatcher couldn't trace the call?" I ask.

Eric shakes his head.

"Is there a tape of the call?" I plead, hopeful. "Maybe if I listen to it, I'll recognize the caller's voice."

He shakes his head again. "The witness didn't call 9-1-1, they called the tip line at the station."

"I didn't know the tip line is still a thing," I retort.

Several years ago, most police departments in our area set up toll-free tip lines. These tip lines encouraged anyone who had any information about any crime to come forward anonymously. The tip line doesn't have call display to reveal the phone number the tipster is calling from, and calls are neither traced nor recorded. The caller's anonymity is guaranteed.

"It's a thing," Eric confirms, "and the witness used it on Friday night, er, Saturday morning."

REAGAN DAVIS

"Unless they were at the scene, there's no way they saw Adam's car," I insist.

"Agreed." Eric nods, then whispers, "I think the witness who called the tip line is likely the killer."

My mind is blown. I sip my latte and take a moment to let what he said sink in.

Finally, barely above a whisper, I ask, "Why would the killer report themself to the police? If they drove away and returned Adam's car to where they found it, in front of Sheamus's house, Saxon's body probably wouldn't have been discovered until spring thaw. Saxon would have been presumed missing, and the killer would have gotten away with murder. For now."

"I have a couple of theories," Eric leans closer and lowers his voice. "Either the killer has a conscience and couldn't live with abandoning Saxon's dead, damaged body to freeze and go unfound until spring, or they saw Adam walking alone after he'd lost his keys and realized he had no alibi, so made the call to frame him." He sits up and in his normal speaking voice, adds, "But it's impossible to get inside the head of someone unhinged enough to commit murder."

Eric picks up his phone to check the time and gets distracted by the notifications that have accumulated since he put it down a few minutes ago. "I have to get going," he says, standing up. "Dinner later? I'll make a reservation at Pastabilities." He pulls me in for a hug and bends down to kiss me.

"Pastabilities sounds amazing," I say, thinking about

their shrimp and mushroom risotto. "I'm not sure we'll get a table with a same day reservation, though. Not on a Saturday night during tourist season."

Eric winks. "I'll turn on the charm."

"In that case, we'll get a table for sure," I tease. "Remember to make the reservation for three."

Eric looks down at me. "Three?" he asks, confused.

"You, me, and your phone," I reply.

"Ha Ha... hilarious!" He kisses me again. "I'll text you with the time." He winks, then disappears through the back door.

CHAPTER 14

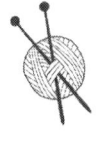

"Hi, Mayor Feeney." Is that the correct way to address a former mayor? I make a mental note to look it up later. "It's nice to see you. Are you starting a new project?" I ask.

"Hello, Megan," Mayor Feeney smiles sweetly. "I was just telling Connie and Marla how excited I am to have the time to indulge my hobbies now that I'm retired. I'd like to knit my youngest grandson this lovely sweater." She holds up an aged and tattered paper pattern that's flimsy from being folded and unfolded many times.

Mayor Feeney is a tiny, wrinkled octogenarian, who smells like lavender and cedar, and has a saccharine-like sweetness to her voice. Her short blue-grey hair is treated with a blue rinse every two weeks and a perm every four months. She is a walking, talking stereotype of the ideal grandmother. Except this grandmother is a force to be reckoned with. Alice Feeney has been a fixture in Harmony Lake's local political scene for the better part of fifty years. Prior to her twenty years as deputy mayor, she was a member of the town council, a school board trustee, and before that, Alice Feeney was Harmony Lake's first ever female police constable. She did all these things while also being married and raising four children. Her husband was the fire chief of the Harmony Lake Fire Department for many years. She's a pioneer who blazed a trail for the generations of strong Harmony Lake women who followed in her footsteps.

"It's lovely," I say in response to the paper pattern. "Have you decided which yarn you'd like to use?"

"Connie was just getting some samples for me to choose from." Mayor Feeney squints and points toward the back half of the store. "I think I like that baby blue yarn over there." She walks toward it before she finishes her sentence.

With Connie in tow, Mayor Feeney makes her way over to the baby blue yarn in the worsted weight section, and I notice her son, Pete, sitting in the cozy sitting area, scrolling his phone while he waits for his mum.

Pete is one of those people whose hair greyed prematurely. As a result, though he's only in his early fifties, his hair has already gone through the various stages of grey, and is already pure white. The whiteness of his hair matches the whiteness of his teeth. The contrast of his white hair and teeth against his blue eyes is captivating when you meet him for the first time. Somehow, Pete's white hair doesn't age him at all. In fact, his healthy physique and smooth skin make him appear younger than his actual age.

"Hi, Pete," I say, making my way to join him in the cozy sitting area. "Are you shopping for yarn too?"

I'm teasing. Pete doesn't knit, at least not that I know of. Pete's probably too busy to knit. Between his full-time job as a firefighter and his part-time job as a real estate agent, I can't imagine he has much time for hobbies.

"Oh, hi, Megan," he says, smiling and looking up from his phone. "No," he chuckles, "I'm on chauffeur duty today. My mum's mind might be sharp as a tack, but her reflexes aren't what they used to be, no matter what she tells you. We try to save her the trouble of driving, when she lets us. Especially in poor weather. Which means we get to be at her beck and call at least six months of the year."

"She's lucky to have you," I comment, and sit down next to him on the sofa. Pete slips his phone into the pocket of his black pea coat. "Listen, Pete, thank you for the other night."

"The other night?" Pete asks with an expression stuck somewhere between shock and confusion.

"Yes, thank you for looking out for Ryan at Shea-mus's card game the other night. We appreciate you searching for him despite the weather and hazardous road conditions."

"Oh, that," Pete says, nodding. "There's no need to thank me, Megan. I really didn't do anything. In fact, I had to abandon the search and rush to my parents' house to remove a squirrel that got stuck in their chimney."

"Oh?" I asked. "In the middle of the night? That's what I call good service. If a squirrel gets itself stuck in my chimney in the middle of the night, I know who I'll call." I smile and we both laugh.

"I had no choice," Pete explains. "The thing was chattering, and scratching, and making all sorts of noises. My parents couldn't sleep, and my mother was afraid it might be injured or possibly die."

"Was the squirrel OK?" I ask.

"Yes, I'm pleased to report the squirrel came through the entire incident without a scratch. I put it in a box with an old blanket and some peanuts until I could release it yesterday morning."

"I'm glad it worked out for everyone involved." I pause while I figure out how to broach the subject of Saxon's murder without sounding nosy or confrontational. "So," I say, smiling. "How about all those rumours about Saxon Renaud's murder?" Pete nods in acknowledgement. "Which one of the many rumours do you subscribe to?" I ask.

Pete sits back and brings his right ankle to his left

knee, holding it there with his right hand. "Have you heard the one about the money lender?" he asks.

"Yes, I have," I reply.

Pete tilts his head toward me and in a lower voice says, "Well, I know his lawyer—we've done a few real estate transactions together—and he says the money lender, Jay Singh, started legal proceedings to force the sale of some of Saxon's properties. The money lender isn't happy, and it wouldn't surprise me if he took out Saxon to set an example to his other clients." He raises his eyebrows and nods.

Does Pete mean he knows Saxon's lawyer, or Jay's lawyer? It makes little sense to me to kill someone who owes you money. It's more difficult, and expensive, to collect money from a dead person than a living one. Estates can take years to settle; it would be more efficient to deal with the debtor instead of their estate.

I help Connie and Mayor Feeney by finding the size of knitting needles the pattern calls for to get gauge. Then, when Mayor Feeney and Connie have gathered all the yarn and notions that she'll need to complete her project, I ring up the sale.

"If you don't mind waiting until tonight to start your sweater, Mayor Feeney, we can wind the yarn for you in the store, and I can drop it off at your house on my way home tonight," I offer.

"That's sweet, Megan, but I don't want to be any trouble."

"It's no trouble, Alice," Connie interjects, using

Mayor Feeney's first name. "Megan lives around the corner from you. She has to drive past your house to get home."

I nod. "We're practically neighbours," I confirm.

"That's right," Mayor Feeney responds. "I forgot you and I live in the same neighbourhood." She smiles. "In that case, thank you. I'd love it if you would wind the yarn for me."

"I'll drop it off around 6 p.m.," I tell her as I place the needles she purchased in a bag. "If you don't get gauge with these needles, Mayor Feeney, be sure to bring them back, and we'll exchange them for a different size." I put her receipt in the bag and hand it to her across the counter.

"Thank you, Megan. I'm sure these will be fine. I always get gauge. It's a natural gift."

If I had a nickel for every time a knitter told me that, I'd be the wealthiest woman in town.

Mayor Feeney and Pete turn to leave, and Pete turns back, looking at me and snapping his fingers.

"Megan, before I forget," he says, pointing at me, "can you tell Eric that I printed those listings for him? I forgot them at home, but I'll drop them off over the next day or two."

"I'll tell him." I'm sure the tone of my voice conveys my confusion. "What listings did Eric ask you to print?"

"He wants to see what's available in Harmony Lake, you know, to get a feel for the market," Pete explains. "I was telling him how I expect to be busy in the next few weeks because of the spring market, and he mentioned he'd like to buy a house now that his position as chief is permanent. So, I told him I'd print some listings. I forgot to bring them with me. I left them at home on top of my printer." He rolls his eyes and smiles.

Pete turns to leave and flips up the collar of his black pea coat in an almost identical way that Adam does. Pete opens the store door for his mum, takes her shopping bag from her, and gestures for her to leave first. Such a doting son.

"What's this about Eric moving, my dear?" Connie asks, concerned.

Dumbfounded, I shake my head. "I have no idea. It must be a misunderstanding. If Eric was planning to move, he would've mentioned it to me."

I'm sure he would've mentioned it to me. I know he's eager for us to move in together, but he wouldn't go house hunting without discussing it with me first. He knows I'm not ready for us to live together yet. He says he understands, and except for an occasional hint disguised as a joke, he's supportive and patient. Has his patience run out?

CHAPTER 15

Connie and Marla take turns going on break, and the time passes quickly. But by mid-afternoon, traffic has slowed down, and we have time to putter around the store, straightening and organizing. I take this opportunity to organize the back room and make space for new stock we're expecting next week.

"Megan?"

"In here, Marla," I call from the storage closet.

"There's someone here to see you," she says.

"Who?" I ask, gathering my curls into a messy ponytail with the hair elastic I always keep on my wrist.

"Rick Ransan," Marla replies. "He asked for Eric first. I told him Eric isn't here, and he asked to see you."

My curiosity is piqued.

"You can send him back here, Marla. Thank you." I smile.

My initial instinct is to talk to Rick in the store, but

he asked for Eric first, making me think he might want to talk about Saxon or Saxon's murder, so I decide it's best if we speak in the back where it's more private.

"Are you sure that's a good idea, Megan?" Marla sounds worried.

"I'll be fine, Marla. You and Connie know we're back here, and I won't close the door all the way. I'll make sure I have an escape route available."

"If we see the door to the back room close all the way, we'll call for help," she tells me.

I nod.

Satisfied with our plan, Marla smiles and nods, then turns and rushes back to the store to get Rick. I step out of the back room, brush off my clothes, and make my ponytail a little less messy. I sit at the table in the kitchenette, choosing the chair closest to the door.

"Over here, Rick," I say when his head pokes through the doorway.

"There you are! H-h-hi, Megan. I've never been in a knitting store before." Rick looks at the kitchenette and back room with fascination.

I study his facial expression as he beholds the room in awe, and for a microsecond, I glimpse the curious little boy he once was.

Rick is a large, hefty man. Everything about him is thick. He has a thick neck, thick torso, and thick fingers. His light brown hair is thick and curly, with curls looser than mine. His beard is short, but thick, and he dresses like Ryan, which makes sense, I guess, since they're both handymen. I don't see Rick often, but when I do, he's wearing broken-in jeans, work boots, and a flannel shirt.

"How are you, Rick?" I ask, gesturing for him to take the chair opposite me.

"I am fine, Megan. How are you?" he asks, smiling.

"Very well, thank you," I reply. "I didn't get a chance last night to tell you I'm sorry for your loss. I understand that you and Saxon were friends, and I'm sorry you lost a friend."

"Thanks, Megan," he responds. "To be honest, w-w-we weren't as close as people seem to think. He was my employer. He didn't h-have any friends, and I don't have any friends, so we just kind of hung out friendless and alone together."

"Friendless and alone together" might be the saddest description of a relationship I've ever heard.

"Oh." I'm not sure how to respond to his disclosure. "Well, you've lost someone significant in your life, and for that, you have my condolences." I give him a small smile. "What will you do now that your employer is… gone?" I ask.

"Don't worry about me, M-Megan. I'll be all right. I own a few rental properties around the lake and two condos."

I didn't know Rick was a property investor. It must not be common knowledge, or I'm sure I would've heard about it from the rumour mill. I'm glad he has something to fall back on and won't struggle while he looks for another job. He continues to tell me about his rental properties and mentions that the cottages he owns "around the lake" are on the same side of the lake as Lake Access Road. Coincidence? Eric always says investigators don't like coincidences in murder investigations.

"Good for you!" I say.

"I paid close attention when I worked for Saxon. Watching him and some of the mistakes he made was more valuable than the wages he paid me." Rick chuckles. "I learned what to do and what not to do."

I offer Rick a cup of tea, but he declines.

"Saxon's death is why I'm here," Rick discloses. "I phoned Chief Sloane, but he hasn't gotten back to me, yet. I didn't know what else to do, so I came here to see if he's home, but he's not."

I shake my head. "Eric is at work today. I don't know when he'll be home. Is there anything I can help you with?"

"I hope so," Rick replies. "I'm worried about Clawdia."

I search my memory bank for anyone named Clawdia but come up blank.

"Who is Clawdia?" I ask.

"Saxon's cat," Rick replies.

"Saxon had a cat?" I blurt louder than I intend.

I can't imagine Saxon Renaud having any love or affection for another living being.

Rick nods. "He s-sure did. I'm worried about her. Is

she still in his house? Did the police take her some-where? If she's there, is she alone, scared, and hungry?"

Oh, my. Now, I'm worried about Clawdia too. I do some quick mental math and realize that Saxon has been dead for thirty-six hours; a long time to go without fresh water, food, or a clean litter box.

"Did you mention Clawdia to the police when they questioned you?" I ask.

Rick shakes his head. "I was nervous and didn't think about her until after," he replies. "I have a key to Saxon's house, and I went there, but there's police tape on the door, so I didn't go in."

I hate to admit it, but I might not have been as truthful in Rick's situation. If I was worried about the health and welfare of an animal, I might've just moved the tape, let myself in, then re-sealed the tape on my way out.

"You want to ask Eric if you can enter Saxon's house to check on Clawdia?" I ask.

He nods. "I want to get Clawdia. And maybe her food and litter box, too, if Chief Sloane will let me. I can take her back to my house. I don't mind taking care of her. She's a shy cat. She hides from strangers, and she probably hid when the police searched the house. She would have been terrified. Or worse, maybe she got scared and escaped while they were searching. It's freezing outside, Megan, and goodness knows where she is…"

Rick's voice is panicky, and his words increase in

speed as he speaks. His concern is palpable, and I notice that over the course of our conversation, his stutter has almost disappeared. I raise my hand in a stop motion, and Rick stops talking and takes a breath.

"Let me see if I can get hold of Eric," I suggest, unlocking my phone screen.

I know even if he's in a meeting, Eric will reply to my text, but I don't tell Rick that.

"Megan, if he says I'm allowed to pick up Clawdia, would you come with me? It feels weird going to Saxon's house alone, now that he's… you know… and I don't have anyone else to ask.

I nod. "Of course, I will," I respond.

Me: Did you know Saxon had a cat? Rick wants to enter Saxon's house to get Clawdia and take her back to his house.

Eric: Are you with Rick right now? Is he at the store?

Me: Yes and yes. He was looking for you.

Eric: We know about the cat. I assigned an officer to feed the cat and scoop the litter. Saxon's brother has until Monday to get the cat, otherwise someone from the Animal Centre will pick it up.

My inner animal advocate doesn't like this. If Saxon's brother doesn't pick up Clawdia, she'll be alone for almost ninety-six hours. What if she's scared and doesn't understand why her human isn't coming back?

I read Eric's last text to Rick, and we're of the same mind; we'd both prefer for Clawdia to stay with him.

Rick tells me he doubts that Saxon's brother will want Clawdia.

"Saxon had hardly any contact with his family. He wasn't close to them. I doubt they'll come all the way to Harmony Lake just to get his cat. But if I'm wrong, and his brother wants the cat, I'll give her to him. In the meantime, I think Clawdia would be happier staying with me. Other than Saxon, I'm the only person she knows."

"Let's see what we can do," I say to Rick while looking at my phone and typing a text to Eric.

Me: Can Rick pick up Clawdia? He has a key. If Saxon's brother wants the cat, he can just as easily get her from Rick's house as he can from Saxon's house.

"Three dots," I say to Rick. "He's typing a reply."

The three dots disappear, and I startle when my phone rings.

"It's Eric," I tell Rick as I answer the call.

"Hello?" I stand up, stepping away from the table and walking toward the stairs for privacy.

"Hey, babe. Is Rick still there?"

"Yes," I reply, nodding even though Eric can't see me. "I'm sorry to interrupt you at work, but Clawdia isn't used to being alone, and we're worried about her."

"Can you go somewhere quiet with Rick and put me on speaker?"

I return to the table and put Eric on speaker.

"We can hear you," I say.

"Hi, Chief Sloane," Rick says, waving as if Eric can see him.

"Hi, Rick, I'm sorry I haven't called you back. I've been in meetings all day. Does the cat have any health issues? Does it require medication or anything?"

"Not that I'm aware of," Rick replies. "And I think Saxon would have mentioned it. He talked about Clawdia a lot."

Eric sighs. "Rick, I'll have an officer meet you at Saxon's house in one hour. You can take the cat, her food, and her litter box. You cannot remove anything else from the house. The officer will take photos of everything you take."

"Thanks, Chief Sloane, we'll be there," Rick replies.

"We?" Eric asks. "Megan, are you going with him?"

"Yes," I reply.

"Can you take me off speaker now, please?"

I take the call off speaker, and once again wander toward the stairs.

"If I tell you I'm uncomfortable with this, are you going to go anyway?" Eric asks.

"I think so," I reply honestly.

Another deep sigh from his end of the phone.

"An officer will be with you. I'll tell them to make sure you aren't alone with Rick." It's another one of those statements that is neither a suggestion nor a question.

I thought the police confirmed Rick's alibi. If they eliminated him as a suspect in Saxon's murder, why is

Eric uncomfortable with me being alone with him? I want to ask but know that Rick is only about ten feet away, so I save my question for later.

"I understand," I say.

"I'm a phone call away if you need anything. I love you."

"I love you too," I say.

"Dinner is at 7 p.m."

"I can't wait," I reply.

We end our call, and I tell Rick I'll meet him at Saxon's house in an hour. He thanks me for helping him and Clawdia, then leaves through the back door, mumbling something about borrowing Cat Benatar's kitty carrier from Trudy.

CHAPTER 16

CONNIE AND MARLA insisting they'll be fine without me at Knitorious makes me feel better about leaving to meet Rick at Saxon's house.

Before I left, Connie and Marla tried to think of anyone they know of, other than Rick, who has been inside Saxon's house. They couldn't come up with anyone. They're curious and excited about my visit, and I'm under strict orders to report back to them. They tried to convince me to take photos, but I can't do that. It feels too much like violating someone's personal space, even if that someone is dead.

If the way Saxon presented himself indicates what his home is like, I expect a tidy, organized space with carefully chosen, tasteful, and collectible antique furniture and knickknacks.

I roll to a stop, pulling up behind Rick's car, outside Saxon's house on Mountain Road. Mountain

Road is one of the oldest streets in Harmony Lake. It's on the east side of town and is one of only two roads that leads to the resorts in the Harmony Hills mountains.

The lots are large with mature, shady trees and large Victorian-era homes setback far from the street. Old-timey reproduction, Victorian-era streetlights add to the charm of the neighbourhood.

Saxon owns several houses on this street. Most of them were renovated and repurposed from their original single-family-residential status, to either professional office spaces or multi-residential rental properties. I've never been inside Saxon's home, but I believe he lives in a renovated duplex.

Rick and I exit our cars at the same time. We look around, then at each other, and shrug. There isn't any sign of a police car nearby.

"I guess the police officer who's accompanying us isn't here yet," I observe.

"I guess not," Rick agrees.

I check the time on my phone, and we're a few minutes early. We stand by our cars while we wait for the officer to arrive. Today is less frigid and windy than the last few days. I use this opportunity to ask Rick a few more questions about Saxon. Maybe he can give me some insight into Saxon's life, a clue about who killed him or why.

"Rick, earlier when you told me about your job with Saxon, you said you learned a lot from watching him.

You said you learned what not to do. What did you mean by that?"

"It's like my mum always said," Rick replies. "You'll catch more flies with honey than with vinegar. Saxon was all vinegar and no honey."

"You mean he wasn't very nice to people?" I clarify.

"Exactly," Rick says. "Saxon was nasty. Sometimes, it seemed like he was mean and difficult on purpose." Rick shrugs one shoulder. "He made his life more difficult than it had to be. If he was nicer to people, life would have been easier for him."

"Easier how?" I ask.

"Saxon was always fighting with someone. He was always threatening to sue someone, or someone was threatening to sue him. For example, he owed a lot of people money and was always late making repayments. He wouldn't apologize when his payments were late. He would try to come up with a reason that it wasn't his fault. Nothing was ever his fault, if you asked him. Saxon was always the victim of other people's choices."

This is the third time today someone has mentioned that Saxon had a debt problem. First Ryan told me that Saxon owed money to Jay Singh, then Pete, and now Rick.

"Why did Saxon have so much debt?" I ask.

"Saxon's properties are mortgaged to the hilt," Rick explains. "He bought them on spec. He never planned to keep them. Saxon's plan was to buy as much real estate as he could, then sell it for a profit to investors and developers who want to build in Harmony Lake. He underestimated how difficult it would be to get around the big-box policy. He protested the policy for years, but the town council and most of the residents are opposed to big-box companies coming here. Saxon got stuck with these properties. His payments were so high, the rental income barely covered the expenses. As the value of a property would go up, he would increase the mortgage against it and use the borrowed money to keep himself afloat."

"You can only do that for so long," I conclude. "Eventually, you've borrowed as much as any lender will allow, and your monthly payments are so large you can't maintain them. Never mind the costs of maintaining the properties on top of the regular expenses."

"Exactly!" Rick says. "Saxon's only hope to dig himself out of debt was to win the mayoral election and reverse the big-box policy. Then he could sell his properties to the investors and come out of it with money in his pocket."

If this is true, this election was Saxon's last hope, his Hail Mary pass. Saxon's entire financial future depended on him winning the mayoral by-election.

"What was his backup plan?" I ask. "What was Saxon planning to do if he lost the election?"

Rick shakes his head. "I don't know, Megan. He never mentioned a backup plan. I think in his mind he had no other option."

"What do you think of the big-box policy?" I ask,

assuming Rick would be of the same opinion as Saxon. "If the policy were reversed, would you sell your properties to developers and walk away with a profit?"

"I voted for Adam," Rick divulges. "I like Harmony Lake the way it is, small and uncommercialized. Judging by the landslide results, most of the town's residents feel the same way."

I'm shocked at Rick's disclosure. He spent so much time with Saxon, I just assumed they were of the same opinion about the big-box policy. That'll teach me to go around making assumptions. Could Rick feel so strongly about it he killed Saxon to make sure if he won the election the policy wouldn't be reversed?

"Who do you think killed him?" I ask.

"I don't know for sure," Rick replies. "But Saxon and Pete Feeney had quite a few meetings together in the weeks leading up to the election. Secret meetings."

"If they were secret, how do you know about them?" I ask. "Do you know what they talked about?"

"Saxon would tell me he was meeting with Pete, but he wouldn't tell me what they were meeting about. They would meet on FaceTime."

I wonder what they were meeting about? Pete is a firefighter and a real estate agent. It's unlikely they met multiple times to discuss fire safety. Was Saxon so confident about winning the election that he was already arranging for Pete to sell his properties? Odd that Pete didn't mention this earlier when we talked about Saxon's death. I wonder if he disclosed these meetings to Eric? I add it to the mental list I'm keeping called, things-to-mention-to-Eric. The list is getting long.

"I hear you saved Cat Benatar's life on Thursday night," I say changing the subject. "It was nice of you to give up a whole night to save Trudy's cat."

"It was as much for me as it was for Trudy," Rick explains, chuckling. "It was the third time this winter Cat Benatar found his way into the ceiling and got stuck there. I closed off every hole I could find so I wouldn't have to save him again." We laugh.

"You're a really nice person, Rick," I tell him. "I don't think many people realize how nice you are because you're quiet, and you spent so much time with Saxon. People might've assumed because you were friends with him, that you and he were alike, but you're not."

"It isn't easy for me to make friends, Megan," Rick confides. "I have bad social anxiety. It's difficult for me to hang out in groups. And when I was growing up, I was teased and bullied because of my stutter. A mean group of popular boys tormented me about it for years. So now, when I'm around smart guys like Adam, athletic guys like Eric, or funny, confident guys like Sheamus and Ryan, I feel like that bullied kid again. I get uncomfortable, and my stutter gets worse, which makes me more anxious, and it becomes a vicious cycle. It's easier to avoid those situations."

"I'm sorry that happened to you," I say. "But the people you mentioned aren't like that. Adam, Eric,

Sheamus, and Ryan would never tease you or bully you because you stutter. Trust me, I wouldn't be friends with people like that. Also, I notice when you and I talk one-on-one your stutter disappears."

"It's not as prevalent when I'm speaking with one person, especially someone like you, who's easy to talk to. I know Saxon was one reason I don't have many friends," Rick admits. "I think on some level it worked for me. As long as I hung around with Saxon, I didn't have to worry about being socially awkward because everyone avoided me."

"Is it true that Saxon was a jerk to you?" I ask. "I heard he said some unkind things to you sometimes."

Rick nods. "It's true," he admits. "Saxon had a short temper and, sometimes, I was the closest person he could take out his frustrations on."

Maybe Marla is right; maybe Rick got fed up with how Saxon treated him and killed him in a fit of rage or revenge. But how could Rick be the murderer when he was at Trudy's house, saving Cat Benetar from the ceiling?

"Well, without Saxon around," I respond, "it'll be more difficult to hide that you're a nice, funny person who's pleasant to be around, and people might want to be your friend," I warn him.

"I hope so," Rick admits. "I think I'm ready to extend my friend group beyond Trudy, Cat Benetar, and Clawdia." He laughs.

We're interrupted when the patrol car shows up.

Rick collects the kitty carrier from his car, and we follow the officer to the front door where he removes the crime-scene tape blocking the keyhole. Rick uses his key to unlock the door, and the three of us step inside.

The inside of Saxon's house is not what I was expecting. Instead of the tidy, organized space I imagined, I'm standing in a space not comfortable enough to call a home. The furnishings are sparse and barely functional. There's a small, dented, metal folding table with two folding chairs that I assume was Saxon's kitchen table. A TV so old it has a picture tube sits on top of a stack of two sideways milk crates that house a record collection. Across from the TV is an old floral sofa with three sunk-in seat cushions that look like they have almost no padding left. The velour upholstery is worn so thin, it's see-through in some spots.

The lighting in the house hasn't been updated, so there are few overhead lights. Instead there are lamps on the floor throughout, and the heavy velvet draperies are pulled closed, preventing any natural light from coming in.

The walls near the windows are water-stained, and the wood floors are about thirty years overdue for refinishing. A litter box sits in one corner of the kitchen, and a bowl of kibble and a bowl of water are in the opposite corner. Scattered cat toys dot the floor.

Rick walks through the space, making kissing sounds and calling Clawdia's name. He alternates the kissing sounds with *ssspssssp* sounds.

"I think I know where she's hiding," Rick whispers to me.

The police officer and I follow him down the hall, then up the stairs. We enter what I assume was Saxon's bedroom. He didn't even have a proper bed; he slept on a mattress on the floor. Maybe this wasn't Saxon's bedroom. It doesn't look very lived in. But when Rick opens the closet door, I see a whangee handle umbrella leaning against the wall and several identical shoeboxes lining the shelf above the clothing rack. I know this was Saxon's bedroom. Rick shoves the shoeboxes aside, exposing a small, very timid, wide-eyed kitty.

"There you are Miss Clawdia," Rick coos to the small cat.

He reaches up and pulls Clawdia from the shelf, bundling her in his arms and rubbing her head with his bearded chin. When she nuzzles into his neck, it's obvious she knows him and is happy and relieved to see him. Rick and Clawdia are old friends.

I pick up the kitty carrier and open the door, holding it toward Rick so he can slide Clawdia inside. Loud, guttural meows fill the room. She does not like the kitty carrier and registers her dislike verbally.

The police officer follows Rick and I downstairs. In the kitchen, I collect the bag of kitty kibble and Clawdia's food dishes. I dump the water out of the water dish, and I gather a few of the cat toys that are scattered on the floor. The police officer collects her litter box and the unopened box of fresh litter. The three of us take

Clawdia and her accessories to Rick's car, then return to the front door so Rick can lock it, and the officer can re-seal the keyhole.

"Thank you for coming with me today, Megan. I appreciate it," Rick says as he closes the trunk with the litter box inside.

"No problem," I reply. "I'm glad I could help. Clawdia is lucky to have you looking out for her. I don't think anyone else in town knows she exists."

"I'm happy to take her," Rick says. "She's a sweet cat. Hopefully she's not a climber and doesn't find her way into the ceiling like Cat Benatar," he jokes.

After Rick drives away, I knock on the passenger side window of the patrol car. The young officer lowers the window, and I thank him for his time and help. On my way to Knitorious, I prepare myself to answer tons of questions from Connie and Marla about the inside of Saxon Renaud's home.

CHAPTER 17

ON MY TIPPY TOES, I scan the Pastabilities dining room for Eric. I don't see him, but because of how the tables and booths are arranged, it's difficult to see who occupies them. I know he's here somewhere; he sent me a text a few minutes ago to let me know he was seated. Also, he's never late when we meet. Ever.

Even when Pastabilities is fully booked, it's neither loud nor crowded. They configured the restaurant for intimacy with tables and booths spaced farther apart than most restaurants. The sense of seclusion is further enforced with strategically placed coat racks and floor plants that double as privacy screens.

The maître d' spots me waiting, smiles, and comes over. He teasingly chides me for being late, though I'm less than ten minutes late, and gestures for me to follow him. We pass several coat racks and floor plants before I spot Eric, laser focussed on his phone, in a quiet semi-circular booth in the corner. We're seated at one of the best tables in the restaurant, a bit big for a party of two but definitely a premium location.

"I'm sorry I'm late," I apologize as I slide into the semi-circular booth next to him. "I stopped at Mayor Feeney's house to drop off some yarn she purchased. We started talking, and you know how it is," I explain.

"No worries," he says with a smile. "I've waited way longer for way less." His wink makes my tummy flutter like a charm of hummingbirds just took flight inside me.

I sense Eric is about to lean over and kiss me, but we're interrupted when the maître d', still standing next to our table, speaks.

The maître d' congratulates Eric on his appointment as police chief and tells him it's an honour to have the chief of police dine in their humble establishment. After much smiling and thank yous by all three of us, the maître d' takes our drink order, leaves us with menus, and disappears.

Finally alone, Eric leans over to kiss me hello, then holds up his cell phone between us, opens my bag, and drops the phone inside.

"No phone until after dinner," he declares. "You first, then work."

"Wow," I say in response to his gesture. "Are you sure? What if there's a break in the case and they need to reach you?"

"It can wait an hour," he insists, then adds, "besides,

if something big happens, word will get to us through the rumour mill before the official channels, anyway."

We laugh because it's true.

"Thank you," I say. "I was starting to forget what it's like to spend time together without your phone providing a constant digital soundtrack."

"I know, and I'm sorry." He covers my hand in his and strokes my knuckles with his thumb. "You've been so patient the last few months while I figure out how to do this police chief job. Starting tonight, I'm implementing a daily detox of at least an hour with no phone and no computer."

The server arrives with our drinks and attempts to take our order, but we haven't opened our menus yet. She gives us a few more minutes and leaves. Before we open our menus, I already know what I'm having. Shrimp and mushroom risotto with spinach salad. It's my favourite dish at Pastabilities. Eric decides on the chicken Asiago, chicken breast stuffed with Asiago cheese, spinach, and caramelized onions. To start, we order the antipasto plate.

"How was your visit to Saxon's house?" Eric asks after the server leaves with our orders.

"It was… educational," I reply.

"I'm listening," Eric says.

I tell Eric about my visit to Saxon's house, starting with pulling up behind Rick's car before the officer arrived. I tell him how shocked I was at the inside of the house and the conditions in which Saxon lived. Then I tell him Rick's disclosure to me about his relationship with Saxon and what he observed during the time they spent together.

"My instincts tell me Rick didn't murder Saxon," I say. "But I have to admit, he had a lot of motive. As if wanting revenge against Saxon for the mean abusive things he said to Rick wasn't enough, it turns out Rick didn't even vote for Saxon because he didn't want the big-box policy to be reversed."

"There's a hole in Rick's alibi," Eric reveals. "That's why I was uncomfortable with you going to Saxon's house with him today. Rick is an unlikely suspect, but he's a suspect. There's at least an hour-long gap in his alibi. Trudy fell asleep and can't vouch for Rick's whereabouts. She can't even confirm how long she slept."

"But Rick was at her house before Trudy fell asleep and then still there when she woke up?" I ask.

Eric nods. "That's right, but there's a large enough gap of time unaccounted for that I can't rule him out as a suspect."

"Speaking of holes," I make a play on words, "Rick created several holes when he was chasing Cat Benetar through the ceiling. Also, Trudy's laundry room has ceiling tiles. It was because of a loose ceiling tile that Cat Benetar could get into the ceiling."

"And?" Eric urges.

"And it would've been easy for Rick to shove something in those holes before he sealed them."

"Ah," Eric says. "You mean like an umbrella or

penny loafer."

I nod. "It's worth a look, isn't it?"

"We asked. Trudy doesn't want us poking around in her ceiling. I'd have to get a warrant, and I'm trying to avoid it if possible. I don't want to upset her or get blamed if Cat Benetar gets lost in the ceiling again."

"When I asked Rick if he had any theories about who killed Saxon, he named Pete Feeney." I watch Eric's face for a reaction, but he gives nothing away.

"Did he say *why* he thinks Pete would kill Saxon?" Eric asks.

"Rick said Saxon and Pete had several secret meetings together over the last few weeks. Rick said they met over FaceTime. He said Saxon wouldn't tell him what they talked about."

"Interesting." Eric looks down and to the left, something he does when he's thinking. "Pete didn't mention these meetings in his statement."

"He didn't mention them to me either," I say.

"You spoke with Pete?" Eric asks, wide eyed. "My goodness, you have had a busy day."

I nod. "He was in the store earlier with his mum. She was shopping for yarn, and he was her driver, so I sat with him while he waited, and we talked."

I tell Eric about my conversation with Pete, and how Pete suspects that a money lender might be behind Saxon's murder.

"We're beginning to get a picture of Saxon's financial situation," Eric discloses. He shakes his head. "It wasn't good. Saxon had a lot of debt. He was in over his head, behind in payments to everybody, and his income was less than his expenses."

"It wasn't a very well-kept secret," I tell him. "Today alone, three different people have told me that Saxon was in debt and was behind on his repayments."

"Did you learn anything else from your conversation with Pete?" Eric asks, taking a sip of his drink.

"I did," I reply. "He asked me to pass on a message to you." Eric raises his eyebrows with interest. "He wants me to tell you he printed the listings you asked about, but he forgot them on top of his printer. He said he'll drop them off in the next day or so." I look at Eric and wait for a response. Nothing. His facial expression gives nothing away. "Are you moving, Eric?" I finally ask.

"Only if you're evicting me," he replies playfully.

"Why does Pete think you want to buy a house?"

"I think Pete misunderstood the conversation we had at Adam's victory party last night," Eric explains. "I was standing by the buffet table, and Pete was telling me how busy he is every year between January and April with buyers and sellers hoping to move in the spring. I told him I miss having my own home. I mentioned that I'd like to own a house again, someday. That's all I said. Being the salesman he is, Pete jumped on it and decided he should sell me a house."

"So, you aren't house hunting?" I clarify.

"No, I wouldn't do something like that without

talking to you first," Eric replies, using his finger to sweep a stray curl from my face. "But one day, I want to own a home again," he admits. "The apartment above the store was supposed to be temporary, until I figured out if I liked living and working in this town enough to stay here, and until I could convince the cute yarn store owner I had a crush on to go on a date with me." He smiles, and I'm sure I'm blushing. "It's been over a year now. I love my life here, and I'm still sitting on the money from my divorce settlement. I set aside that money to buy my next home."

"So, you're not fed up with waiting for me to be ready for us to live together? You haven't given up and moved on without me?"

"Never," Eric insists. "Pete misunderstood our conversation. I didn't realize he was so keen to make a sale. I'll have a word with him and make sure he understands I'm not in the market for a house."

When I saw Eric and Pete by the buffet table at Adam's party, I assumed they were talking about Saxon's murder, but I guess Pete was trying to sell Eric a house.

"I know you're ready for us to live together," I say, rubbing Eric's knee, "and I really appreciate you not pressuring me, while you patiently wait for me to catch up." I take a deep breath and admit, "I want us to live together, too, but I don't want to move. I know it sounds selfish, but I raised my daughter in this house, and I have good memories there. I live on a great street, my neighbours are fantastic, I love my gardens and the southern exposure, and I'm just not ready to sell it and leave."

"You think I want you to sell your house?" he asks. "You don't have to sell your house. If you want us to live in your house, I'm happy with that."

"Seriously?" I'm shocked. I'm not sure I'd live in a house Eric shared with his ex-wife. "When I imagine us living together, I imagine us in a home we choose together. A fresh start in a house where neither of us has a past. It never occurred to me that you'd want to live at chez Martel."

"Babe, I don't care where we live," Eric explains. "I agree with everything you said about your house. It's a great house in a great neighbourhood, and it's Hannah's home. I understand why you'd want to keep it. I also understand if you don't want me to live there with you, but for the record, I'd move in with you in a heartbeat."

"Can I think about it?" I ask. "I'm not procrastinating, I just want to make sure we make the right decision at the right time. If we do this, I want it to work."

"I'm not going anywhere," Eric assures me, then sighs deeply. "I can't tell you how relieved I am that location is what's holding you back. I was scared you were hesitating because you have doubts about us."

"No doubts," I reassure him, leaning in and nuzzling his neck. "Thank you for not rushing me." Eric kisses the top of my head.

"Maybe there's a compromise," he suggests. "We could renovate your home and make it our home. Whenever we watch those home-reno shows, you say there are things you'd like to change about your house. We could do that. We could time it for when Hannah is at school, so she's not inconvenienced while she's home. And we can stay at my apartment when the renovations are in progress, so we aren't living in a construction zone."

This is a brilliant idea.

"You might be onto something," I say, then bite my lip thinking about the possibilities.

Proud of himself, Eric grins widely. "We can take it one project at a time," he suggests. "We can renovate as fast or slow as we want so neither of us feels rushed."

He uses the phrase, "neither of us" liberally. We both know he means me. I'm pretty sure if I booked a church and chose a wedding dress, Eric wouldn't feel rushed.

The server brings our appetizer, and we decide not to talk about Saxon's murder or real estate for the duration of our meal. Instead, we talk about gloriously mundane things like the TV shows we watch together, the weather, and what's going on with his family back east.

"Do you miss your phone yet?" I ask over our shared tiramisu.

"Not at all," Eric replies. "But after dinner, I want to show you a photo I took today when I met with forensics."

"A photo of something they found in Adam's car?" I put down my fork and nudge the plate with the remaining tiramisu toward Eric.

I wipe my mouth with my napkin and leave the napkin on the table like a flag of surrender. An official signal that I can't eat another bite. Everything was so delicious that I stuffed myself until I couldn't possibly swallow another crumb.

Eric nods with a mouth full of cake. Why doesn't he ever get full?

"They didn't find much in Adam's car," he says, managing my expectations. "No fingerprints at all. The steering wheel, seatbelt, gearshift, and door handles were wiped clean. At the very least, forensics expected to find Adam's fingerprints, but they didn't. They found trace DNA belonging to Adam, and they're running DNA on a few long strawberry blonde strands of hair recovered from the front passenger side of the vehicle. I assume they'll come back as belonging to Jess. And a few long brown curly strands I assume will come back as Hannah's."

"This is enough to eliminate Adam as a suspect, right?" I coax. "First, he has an alibi. He was in your apartment with me when Saxon died. Second, it wouldn't make sense for Adam to wipe his own finger-prints from his own vehicle when it would be expected for them to be there. Obviously, somebody who isn't Adam killed Saxon Renaud."

"I don't believe Adam is the killer," Eric says, using

his gentle voice.

I recognize this tone of voice; he's about to say something I don't want to hear, something like Adam is still a suspect.

"But…" I argue prematurely.

"I can't eliminate him as a suspect," he says, interrupting me. "You can't be sure he was in my apartment all night. I have to assume he showed up to give himself an alibi, snuck out while you were sleeping so he could clean and dispose of the car, then snuck in again before you woke up."

I can't argue with that. I can't confirm what did or didn't happen or who was or wasn't in the apartment while I slept, but if Adam left and came back while I was asleep, Sophie would have alerted me to it. I mention this to Eric, but he says Sophie's lack of bark is neither admissible evidence nor reliable testimony, and not sufficient to verify Adam's whereabouts the night someone killed Saxon.

"We suspect the killer is the same height as Adam or very close. The driver's seat and mirrors weren't moved. Or, if the killer adjusted them, they re-adjusted them to the original settings before they abandoned the car in your driveway. Either that, or they couldn't figure out the seat and mirror controls and gave up."

"Pretty much anyone who attended the card game could be a suspect if height is a requirement," I counter. "Even you could be a suspect using that criteria. You, Adam, Pete, and Rick are within about an inch of each other's height. Sheamus and Ryan are both a little shorter, maybe five foot nine and five foot ten. Does this eliminate Sheamus and Ryan because they're a few inches shorter than whoever may have driven the car?"

"No, they're both close enough in height that they would be able to drive the car without changing the settings," Eric explains. "The evidence found in the trunk rules out Saxon as a driver and confirms what we've suspected all along—he was killed elsewhere, then transported to Lake Access Road."

"You thought Saxon might've driven the car?" I don't understand how Saxon could be a suspect in his own murder.

"I couldn't rule out the possibility that whoever killed Saxon forced him to drive to Lake Access Road, then killed him and ran over him. But thanks to the evidence we found in the trunk I've eliminated that possibility."

"What did you find in the trunk?" I ask.

He shrugs. "A few strands of Saxon's hair, some fibres from his clothes, and a few other unidentified fibres. Those are the photos I want to show you, the unidentified fibres."

I spy our server in the distance and raise my hand to get her attention. When she looks at me and smiles, I smile back and make a check mark with my thumb and forefinger to indicate we're ready for the bill. I want to get out of here and see the fibre evidence from Adam's trunk.

CHAPTER 18

WHILE ERIC LOVES up Sophie and reacquaints himself with his phone, I change into my pyjamas, wash my face, and brush my teeth. No longer able to deny that I've become one of those people who, more often than not, falls asleep with their knitting in their lap watching TV after dinner, I've embraced it and get ready for bed before I get settled on the sofa.

"The forensics team found some unidentified fibres in the trunk of Adam's car and around the driver's seat. They found similar fibres on Saxon's coat and in his hair." Eric opens his messenger bag and hands me a plastic evidence bag with a few kinky, frizzy strands of fibre. "They determined that the fibres from Saxon's coat and head, the driver's seat, and Adam's trunk originate from the same source…"

"Animal fibre," I interrupt. I hold the bag closer to

my face to look at the fibres as closely as possible. "This is haze. From yarn." I look at him.

Haze is the halo of fuzz that surrounds certain animal fibres like cashmere and alpaca.

"I knew you'd recognize it." He sounds equal parts impressed and astonished.

"Mohair? Cashmere?" I ask, once again inspecting the fibre through the plastic barrier of the evidence bag.

"Alpaca," Eric replies.

I furrow my brow. Why is this familiar? I'm having one of those déjà vu moments. Even though I'm not touching the fibre directly, I feel like I've touched it before. I remember feeling the squishy, soft stitches between my fingers.

"What is it?" Eric asks. "Do you recognize this fibre? Do you know where it came from?"

I shake my head. "I'm not sure. I touch alpaca every day at the store. Maybe it reminds me of something we have in stock." I squint at the strands of fibre. "It might help if I know what colour it is."

Was the murderer wearing something made with alpaca yarn from my store? The thought makes me momentarily queasy.

Eric unlocks his phone and opens the camera roll. "I have photos of microscopic images of the fibres," he explains. "There are multiple colours. Some were white, like this one. The forensics report said the white ones are undyed." He hands me his phone and shows me a fuzzy picture of what he says is an undyed alpaca fibre, then he takes it back and swipes to another photo. "Some are dyed one of two solid colours, and some are dyed with both colours. I told the forensics guy that the term for that is variegated, and he was pretty impressed with my yarn knowledge."

As soon as Eric says the word variegated, I flashback to Sheamus walking from table to table at the pub on Thursday evening after the election. He was wearing that hand-knit, bulky scarf. The next day, when I saw him outside Hairway To Heaven, he was wearing the scarf again, and he let me touch it while he told me about the variegated colours. Later that night, at Adam's party, Sheamus wore the scarf again, and I remember thinking it was too hot for such a thick scarf.

"Anyway, the other two colours are…"

"Red and green." I finish his sentence. "Or should I say, *Ashes to Ashes, Rust to Rust,*" I add, recalling the name Sheamus used for the variegated yarn.

"Babe, do you remember who bought this yarn?"

I shake my head. "No, I didn't sell it to anyone."

In shock, I feel behind me to make sure the sofa is there before I sit down.

Sheamus O'Brien killed Saxon Renaud? Sheamus can't be a murderer, he's my friend. Heck, he's everyone's friend. He's the friendliest, happy-go-luckiest person in town. No way.

"Can you find the purchasers on the store computer?" Eric asks.

I shake my head again. "No, we don't sell it at Knitorious. I'm told this yarn was hand spun and hand dyed by someone who owns an alpaca farm," I explain.

Eric sits down next to me. "Told by who?" he asks.

"Sheamus," I reply. "The fibres are from his scarf."

"Are you sure?" He looks as shocked as I feel.

I nod. "As sure as I can be."

Eric curses out loud. "His alibi is unverified."

"What does that mean?" I ask.

"He was alone when Saxon was murdered. There's no evidence to prove or disprove his whereabouts." Eric shrugs. "He may as well have no alibi at all."

"That reminds me." I pivot so my body faces Eric. "Did you say Sheamus turned *off* his phone before he went to sleep on Thursday night?"

"That's right," Eric replies, nodding. "That's why we couldn't get a location on his cell phone." He narrows his eyes. "Why? Did you hear something different?"

"Sheamus told me he was asleep when Adam texted him to check on his car on Friday morning. He said Adam's text woke him up, and he was confused when he said he saw Adam's car in front of his house."

"How can a powered-off cell phone wake you up?" Eric asks rhetorically.

"Exactly," I reply.

"The officer who went to Sheamus's house on Friday morning to look for Adam's car said it looked like Sheamus hadn't been home all night. The snow was undisturbed, and he didn't respond when my officer knocked on the door. He said he was in the shower, but again, I can't verify it."

"I don't believe Sheamus is a murderer," I say. "It doesn't feel right. The evidence against him is circumstantial, right?"

"Right," Eric says. "I'm not sure we have enough to charge him, but there's enough for me to question him again and ask him to surrender his scarf for examination."

I pivot more toward Eric, and bring my feet up onto the sofa, crossing them in front of me.

"Here's the thing about alpaca." I begin my fibre lecture. "The haze is always shedding, and it sticks to everything. It's like a bad rash or craft glitter—just when you think you got rid of it, and you haven't seen it in months, it suddenly reappears, stuck to you, and you realize you can never get rid of it."

"OK," Eric says. "How is this relevant to Saxon's murder?"

"Saxon was at Sheamus's house. It would be reasonable for Saxon to have alpaca haze on him." I wave my hand in front of me. "Scratch that. It would be reasonable for everyone at the card game to have alpaca haze on them. And they likely transferred it to their cars. And depending where Sheamus's scarf was located when Saxon and Ryan had their shoving match, lots of haze could have been disturbed and become airborne, landing on whoever and whatever was nearby."

"If the scarf was with the pile of coats, the coats could have picked up some of the fibre," Eric speculates.

"Precisely," I say, poking his arm.

"So, the haze on Saxon might not be from the killer, he could've picked it up before he was killed," Eric surmises.

"And," I think out loud, "it means the killer wasn't necessarily at the card game. Saxon could have transferred haze to his murderer when he was strangled or when the killer moved his body. Then the killer could have transferred some of the haze to the driver's seat of Adam's car. The stuff can move from person to person like a cold virus."

"So, I could use this alpaca fibre as evidence against the killer, and the killer could use the same fibre as evidence of their innocence," Eric concludes, unlocking his phone. His thumbs move back and forth across the keyboard at record speed.

"What next?" I ask.

"I need to make sure Sheamus's scarf is, in fact, the source of these fibres, and I need to ask everyone who was at the card game to provide the clothes and coats they wore for examination." He types on his phone again.

Anyone at the card game could have found Adam's keys and used his car to run down Saxon. Even someone who wasn't at the card game could have done it. If Adam dropped his keys on his way to his car, someone else could have found them. Maybe someone saw him searching in the snow for them, waited for Adam to give up searching and leave, then found them. Instead of eliminating suspects, the list of potential suspects is growing.

CHAPTER 19

APRIL: *We're supposed to get two more inches of the white stuff tonight! Want to go sledding with T and me tomorrow?*

Me: Yes! When and where?

April: Whenever you finish brunch, at Harmony Lake Elementary School

Me: See you there!

CHAPTER 20

SUNDAY, January 17th

I slept in this morning, if you can call it that. Sleeping in for me means until sunrise, but it was still nice to have the extra sleep. The last few days were hectic and overwhelming.

When I get off the elevator, a savory aroma invades my nostrils. The glorious smell gets stronger as I get closer to Adam's door.

"Good morning." Adam and I kiss cheeks.

"Good morning. What is that amazing smell?" I step inside and close the door behind me.

"Brunch," he states the obvious. "It's almost ready. I just need to clear the table so we have somewhere to eat."

Adam closes his laptop and gathers the papers and folders scattered across the top of the table.

"I'll do that," I offer. "You finish making breakfast,

and I'll clear and set the table." I swoop in and take over gathering and shuffling the papers while Adam rushes to the kitchen.

Adam brings out two plates of bacon and egg sandwiches and puts one in front of me. Breakfast looks as good as it smells.

"It looks yummy," I say, picking up my sandwich. I take a bite without waiting for him to sit down. "Mmmm," I moan, rolling my eyes in bliss. "Is this your mum's recipe?" I ask with my mouth full of food, forgetting my manners.

Adam nods and smiles proudly. "It is," he confirms. "It's her recipe for bacon and egg sandwiches with smoky barbeque relish. I know how much you and Hannah like it, so I asked her for the recipe."

Adam's mum is an amazing cook. She used to make this for breakfast when we would visit them in Montreal. For Hannah and me, breakfast was always one of the culinary highlights of the trip; a simple yet traditional breakfast with a twist—the twist being her secret smoky barbeque relish.

"You did an outstanding job following her recipe," I tell him. "Next time I talk to her, I'll tell her. She'll be very proud." Then I add, "I can't believe you convinced her to give you the recipe. I've been asking her for it for years, and she wouldn't give it up. She told me she'd leave it to me in her will."

"Well, she's so happy I'm finally learning to cook

that she'll do anything to encourage it, even if it means sharing a few of her secret recipes."

Adam unlocks his tablet and FaceTimes Hannah. While we eat, the three of us catch up and talk about our lives. Hannah has heard about Saxon's murder, and she has questions. I'm not surprised she's heard about it. She has a lot of friends in Harmony Lake, and our rumour mill would win the gold medal for speed if such an event existed. We answer her questions honestly and reassure her that her dad isn't a suspect, even though he and I know he is. The last thing we need is for Hannah to sit in her dorm room four-and-a-half hours away, worried about something she can't control, when Adam and I are perfectly capable of worrying enough for all three of us. We keep the tone and mood of the conversation relaxed and upbeat.

Hannah is jealous when I show her my sandwich with her grandma's smoky barbeque relish, and Adam promises to make it for her the next time she's home.

When we end our call with Hannah, I help Adam clear the table and load the dishwasher. I'm about to thank him for breakfast and get ready to leave when, out of the blue, he asks me if Eric and I are planning to buy a house together.

"Why would you ask that?" I ask, taken aback.

Adam shrugs. "Pete mentioned that Eric is looking to buy a house, so I assumed you were looking with him."

"No one is buying a house," I begin.

I stop myself from explaining the misunderstanding between Pete and Eric and remind myself that I don't owe Adam an explanation about anything; we're divorced. "I wouldn't make a big decision like that without discussing it with Hannah first." The last sentence sounds more defensive than I intended.

I'm sure he's asking as a concerned parent. It's a big decision, and it would affect our daughter.

"Just asking," he says with his hands in front of his shoulders in a surrender-like gesture. "But while we're talking about buying houses, can I run something past you?"

"Sure," I say, resuming my seat at the dining table. "What's up?"

"I hear through the grapevine that Saxon Renaud was having financial difficulties before he died," Adam says, picking up his laptop and pile of papers and carrying them to the table. "This could be an opportunity, Meg."

"An opportunity for whom?" I ask.

"For us, and for Harmony Lake as a whole," he replies. "Saxon's creditors will want their money sooner rather than later. If someone offered to take these properties off their hands and pay off the debt, I'm sure the creditors and the executors of the estate would be very grateful."

"Why would we do this?" I ask, biting my lip and wondering how taking over Saxon's troublesome properties could possibly benefit our family.

"Well, for starters, it would be a good investment," Adam replies. "And purchasing a few key properties could be a more effective way of protecting Harmony lake from big-box developers than our current strategy of winning elections every four years. I can't be the mayor of Harmony Lake forever, Meg, and at least we'd know the properties we own would never be sold to developers."

Though we're divorced, and live mostly separate lives, Adam and I still have a few financial connections. I do the bookkeeping for Adam's law practice, and his car is in my name. Adam still manages the insurance for my house, his condo, his law practice, Knitorious, and both vehicles, and we still share a few joint investments.

I stop biting my lip. "Are you suggesting that by strategically choosing which properties we purchase, the remaining properties would be less desirable to investors?"

Most of the properties in Harmony Lake are too small to be useful to developers or big-box corporations. They would need to purchase groups of connected properties to build anything worthwhile. I think Adam is suggesting we choose properties that would break up the most desirable clusters of lots. We could thwart any future development plans we don't like by refusing to sell our lots. This is the type of strategic plan I would expect from Adam's brilliant mind.

"Exactly!" Adam declares. "Earlier this morning, I

was looking at a map of Harmony Lake and marking off the properties I know Saxon owns. I also looked at our investments, and I think if we pool our resources, choose the locations carefully, and take advantage of Saxon's estate's desire to settle his affairs quickly, we could do something beneficial for us and for the town's future."

I take a deep breath. "There's a lot of risk in owning so much real estate," I say. "I mean, look how it worked out for Saxon. All our financial eggs in one basket. It would tie up all of our money in real estate. I'm not comfortable with that."

"I get it," Adam says with forced cheerfulness. The undertone of disappointment in his voice betrays the smile plastered on his face. "I thought I would suggest it. No harm in talking about it."

While my initial instinct is that this would be too risky for Adam and me alone, he makes valid points about the advantages of such a strategy.

"What if we form a syndicate," I suggest, thinking out loud. "It would reduce our risk and give other people who love this town the opportunity to take part in preserving it."

Adam tilts his head. "It could work," he responds. "Who are you thinking of?"

I shrug. "I don't know. Connie and Archie, maybe Eric."

"Can you run some numbers?" Adam asks. "Maybe

you could talk to Pete and get an idea of how much Saxon's various properties are worth."

I've always handled our investments. When we were married, Adam and I made big investment decisions together, but I did the research, executed the decisions, and monitored everything. I was happy to do it. My educational background is economics and accounting, so spreadsheets are my happy place, and since I was a stay-at-home mum for most of our marriage, managing our money kept me intellectually engaged. Also, Adam worked so much, he didn't have time for the minutiae of our household finances.

"Sure," I reply. "If you'll do something for me."

"What do you want me to do, Meg?"

"Invite Rick Ransan to your next guy thing," I reply. "You know, the next card game, or night at the pub watching hockey, or whatever."

"Why?" Adam sneers and raises one thick eyebrow.

"Because he just lost his only friend," I explain. "And he's a nice guy. He's kind of shy and doesn't make friends easily. I'm not asking you to invite him to *everything*. I'm just asking you to give him a chance."

"It's a deal. I'll see what I can do." Adam extends his hand and I shake it.

"Thank you," I say.

Adam's phone dings, and he reaches into his pocket to retrieve it.

"It's Eric," he says, reading the screen. "He's sending a cop over here to pick up the coat and clothing

I wore on Thursday night." Adam looks up at me. "What's that about?"

"It's not just you," I reassure him. "Everyone at the card game is receiving the same text. He wants to do a fibre analysis or something." Adam's facial muscles tense, and the creases in his forehead are suddenly deeper than usual. "It's not a big deal," I tell him. "No one thinks you killed Saxon Renaud."

Adam sighs. "I'm not worried about what people think, I'm worried about where the evidence is pointing."

So am I.

CHAPTER 21

APRIL WAS RIGHT, Harmony Lake received two more inches of fresh snow overnight.

At the elementary school, sledders are lining up at the top of the hill, waiting their turn to barrel down to the bottom.

"If you and Adam go ahead with this real estate scheme, T and I might like to take part too," April says over the swishing of our snow pants as we climb the hill to join the queue and wait our turn. "I'll talk to her about it later, and let you know for sure."

I tell her I'll keep her informed, then Tamara runs up behind us, toboggan in hand, and the three of us trudge up the hill together.

"Have you decided what to get Eric for your anniversary yet?" April asks as we inch forward in line.

"I'm working on it," I reply. "He said something at dinner last night that gave me an idea."

"No pressure," Tamara interjects. "But he put a lot of thought into your anniversary. It means a lot to him."

April shoots her wife a look that silently screams, *stop talking!*

"What do you mean? What's he planning?" I ask, my eyes darting back and forth between April and Tamara. I glare at each of them equally hard and for an equal amount of time, applying the same amount of pressure to both of them.

"We don't know what he's planning," April says slowly and clearly. Then she looks at Tamara. "*Do we, T?*" she asks through clenched teeth.

Tamara shakes her head exaggeratedly. "Nope. We know nothing. Pretend I never said anything." She purses her lips into a tight, thin line, raises her eyebrows, and pretends to zip her lips with her gloved thumb and forefinger.

"You know, and you won't tell meeeee?" I whine so loudly the two kindergarten-aged kids in line ahead of us turn and look up at me.

"If we say anything, Connie will kill us." April sounds serious and her eyes are wide.

"You mean she'll kill *you*," Tamara clarifies. "It was you who was told in confidence, not me."

"Someone tell me something!" I demand, interrupting their domestic dispute.

"No way," April responds, shaking her head. "Have you seen Connie angry? She's scary."

"One hint," Tamara holds up her gloved index

finger. "Do you remember what you wore on your first date with Eric?" she asks.

"I think so," I reply cautiously.

Actually, I remember *exactly* what I wore. I wore my Lanesplitter skirt from the fall 2010 edition of Knitty, a black T-shirt, my black leather moto jacket, and black knee-high boots with heels.

"You should wear it again this Thursday," Tamara suggests with a wink. "It'll be a nice touch."

The two little kids ahead of us are next. As they position themselves on their runner sled, I remind them to hold on tight, and they turn to look at me. Twins. I know these kids.

"Hey, you're Jacob and Justin Singh," I say. "Are your mum and dad here with you?"

Twin number one nods. Twin number two points at the bottom of the hill and says, "Our dad's over there." The boys wave to their dad, and he waves back, then gives them a thumbs-up.

The twins finish arranging themselves and their sled, and I give them a little nudge to get them started. As they careen down the hill, I glance down at their waiting father. When we make eye contact, I smile, and wave; he reciprocates, smiling and waving in return. Their dad is Jay Singh, the money lender to whom Saxon was allegedly behind in making repayments.

When the twins are a safe distance ahead of me, I sit on my knees on Hannah's old saucer sled and push off down the hill. I zoom down the hill, veering toward Jay Singh with questions swirling in my head.

"Well, well, well, if it isn't the first lady of Harmony Lake." Jay bows with mock formality.

"I'm not the first lady of Harmony Lake," I correct him. "Mayor Martel and I finalized our divorce months ago."

"Details," Jay says, sweeping away my comment. "Everyone in town knows you two are still tight, and your boyfriend is the chief of police. If those connections don't make you the first lady of Harmony Lake, I don't know what does."

I decide not to argue because I have more pressing things to discuss with him. After the obligatory pleasantries and small talk, I get to the point.

"I hear our town's latest murder victim owed you a lot of money."

Jay smiles and waves to his boys, who are once again waiting in line at the top of the hill. "It's true," he corroborates. "Saxon was into me for a lot of money. He was behind on his repayments, and I suspect he'd reached the point where he couldn't catch up. My lawyer started paperwork last week to force the sale of some of Saxon's properties."

"I bet Saxon didn't like that," I venture a guess.

"He sure didn't." Jay chuckles. "I have a phone full of angry voicemails from Saxon detailing how much he didn't like it."

"Did you share those voicemails with the police?" I ask.

"Of course I did, Megan. What kind of person do you think I am? I am an upstanding, legitimate businessperson."

"I know," I assure him. "You don't have to convince me. I think your business model is brilliant."

Jay fights an uphill battle regarding his reputation. Despite counting several of Harmony Lake's residents among his clientele, at least that's what he tells me, his reputation is akin to that of a mafia-style loan shark like the violent, intimidating money mongers portrayed in Hollywood mobster movies. But in actuality, Jay provides a legitimate service and is transparent about the terms and conditions of his loans. He provides full disclosure on his website.

"You're one of the few people around here who gets it," he says. "And before you ask, I was out of town with my family until Friday afternoon. Me, Jenna, and the kids drove into the city on Thursday to have dinner with her parents and ended up staying overnight because of the snowstorm. I already told Eric, and he verified my alibi."

"I didn't think you were a good suspect," I confide. "You're too smart to kill someone who owes you money."

"Right?!" He shrugs with his hands in front of him. "Why don't people get that? Why don't they see that it would be bad for business if I went around killing my clients?"

I shrug.

"I can tell you this." Jay looks around, then moves closer to me, putting some extra distance between us and the cluster of elementary school-aged children standing nearby. "I'm not the only lender Saxon owed money to. He was in over his head. Things would've come crashing down around him in the next few weeks if he hadn't died."

"So I hear," I say. "Who do you think killed him and why?"

"I don't know who," Jay replies. "But I have a theory about why. Have you talked to whoever was helping him fix the election?"

What? Did I hear him correctly? Saxon Renaud was plotting to fix the election?

"Who was helping him fix the election? And how do you know he was trying to fix the election?" I hiss in a whisper-yell.

If this is true, Saxon's election-fixing scam failed. He didn't win. He didn't even come close to winning.

"I don't know, and he told me." Jay's voice is low and calm.

"Keep talking," I urge.

"I don't know if he was lying or not, and I don't know any details," Jay qualifies what he's about to tell me with a disclaimer and I nod in acknowledgement. "It's possible he was so desperate, he said whatever he thought might buy him more time, but Saxon begged me not to contact my lawyer until after the election. He told me he was going to win. He said it was a sure thing. He told me someone owed him a favour, and his winning the election was a done deal. He said his properties would be sold, and he would pay me in full within thirty days of the election."

Mind blown, I'm speechless.

"You better close your mouth before you catch flies, Megadoodle," April calls from the bottom of the hill where she, Tamara, and Jay's twins march toward us, dragging their sleds behind them.

I close my mouth and look at Jay. He raises his index finger to his mouth and makes a silent *shhh* gesture as April, Tamara, and the twins get closer. I nod.

I glance behind Jay, and they're still a good thirty feet away. I whisper, "You told the police about this, right?"

Jay shakes his head. "I have no proof, and my lawyer advised me not to tell the police more than they ask."

Lucky for me, I'm not the police.

CHAPTER 22

Knitorious is closed on Mondays, so Monday is the day I run errands, clean the house, and get caught up on the not-so-fun maintenance tasks of my life.

I pull into the parking lot behind Knitorious and choose the spot closest to the back door. I check the time on the dashboard of the car. Fifteen minutes. I have fifteen minutes to get these groceries upstairs, put them away, and get to my appointment with Kelly at Hairway to Heaven. I should have left Eric's groceries at my house when I stopped at home to put away my own groceries and take Sophie for her midday walk. I could have gone back to get them later and skipped this game of beat-the-clock.

Before hitting up the grocery store, I went shopping for Eric's gift, which took longer than I expected. Then, I found myself grocery shopping for two houses because, while I was cruising the aisles at the Shop'n'Save, I remembered a bunch of stuff that Eric is out of at his apartment. I don't normally do Eric's grocery shopping for him, but I know how busy he is with Saxon's case. A lot of the stuff he was out of is stuff I use, so it behooved me to pick up his groceries too.

Before I knew it, the day was half over, and now, I'm dangerously close to being late for my hair appointment with Kelly.

"Megan!"

I spin when I hear my name. "Oh, hi, Pete." I Look down at the grocery bags in my hands and shrug. "I'd wave, but you know," I joke.

"Yes, you've got your hands full." He secures the letter size manila envelope he's carrying under his arm, nods toward the bags in my hands, and says, "Can I help you with those?"

"No thank you," I reply. "They're not heavy, just awkward."

"At least let me get the trunk for you," Pete offers, then he reaches up and closes the trunk of my SUV.

"Thank you," I say. "Are you looking for me?" I assume he is; otherwise, why would he be here? "Knitorious is closed on Mondays. Is there a problem with the yarn your mum purchased on Saturday?"

"Oh no, nothing like that. I was hoping to see you or Eric," Pete replies.

"Eric is at work," I tell him. "But here I am. What can I help you with?"

Pete pulls the manila envelope from under his arm and holds it up. "These are the listings I promised to drop off for Eric," he explains. "If you have a few minutes, I'd be happy to come inside and go over them with you."

I guess Eric hasn't talked to Pete and cleared up the misunderstanding about Eric buying a house. But to be fair, this case is occupying all his time and attention, and Pete's listings are probably at the bottom of his priority list.

"It's nice of you to offer, Pete, but I have to be at an appointment in less than fifteen minutes, and I need to put away these groceries before I leave."

"I understand, Megan," he responds. "Is there a convenient time when you'd both be available? I am happy to come back."

"I'm not sure," I answer. "Eric is working all hours on the Saxon Renaud case, and I have no idea when I'll see him again." Pete sighs and frowns, his disappointment obvious. "Why don't you leave the listings with me," I suggest. "I'll be sure Eric gets them, and we'll call you if we have questions."

"That would be great, Megan, thank you." His disappointed facial expression is replaced with a happier one. "Speaking of Saxon's murder," Pete says, "have there been any developments? Is Eric close to making an arrest?"

I'm not sure if Pete is asking out of idle curiosity,

civic concern, or to gauge a timeline for when Eric might be available to look at houses.

"I'm not sure," I reply. "He's confident he'll make an arrest, but I don't know when."

Pete holds out the envelope, not sure where to put it since I'm fresh out of hands. I tilt my head toward the shoulder with my tote bag.

"You can drop it in there," I instruct. Pete delicately opens my tote bag and slips the envelope inside. "Why paper?" I ask. "Why not send the listings in an email? Wouldn't it be easier and save time?"

"Probably," Pete replies. "But I prefer the personal touch of delivering tangible listings. I make a few notes of things for you to consider about each property, and clients like to have somewhere to jot down questions or comments they have."

"Makes sense," I say. "Well, thanks for coming by to drop these off, Pete, but I have to get a wiggle on, or I'll be late for my appointment."

We say goodbye, and while Pete walks across the parking lot and climbs into his pickup truck, I unlock the back door and race upstairs to put the groceries away.

"I'M NOT LATE!" I pant, as I charge into Hairway to Heaven after speed walking down Water Street from Knitorious.

"You're right on time, hun." Kelly smiles and gives me a tight hug.

Have I mentioned that Kelly is beautiful? She bears a strong resemblance to Grace Kelly and has the same refined demeanour.

She's taller than me, most people are, but shorter than April, with a delicate, thin figure. Her blonde hair is always perfectly coiffed, her makeup is on point—neither too heavy, nor too light—and her hands are forever flawlessly manicured. She's a walking testimonial to the services her salon provides.

But Kelly's beauty goes beyond her aesthetic. She's one of those women who is effortlessly elegant. Her movements are so smooth, she appears to almost float. Her voice isn't soft or loud, but confident and warm. Kelly has beautiful taste; her clothes are classically stylish—no trendy fashion fads for her—and her jewelry is understated and chic.

Taking off my coat and hanging it on the coat rack, I'm aware as Kelly takes a step back and appraises my hair situation.

When she crosses her hands in front of her chest, I notice Kelly isn't wearing her wedding ring, and I try not to react. It's been sixteen months since her husband's murder, and this is the first time I've seen Kelly without her wedding ring.

"How are you?" I ask as she guides me to a sink.

"Not as flustered as you seem to be," she replies, smiling.

Kelly drapes a black nylon cape over me and closes the snap at the back of the neck. I cinch the black nylon belt around my waist while she tucks a black towel into the neckband and gestures for me to sit at one of the black enamel sinks. I sit down, and she eases the chair into a reclined position, so my head is in the sink. We're making small talk while Kelly runs the water and tests the temperature with her hand, adjusting the ratio of hot to cold as necessary.

"Oof!" Kelly releases a breathy grunt, and with her lips puckered and her brows knitted together, she turns off the water. "We need to put an OUT OF ORDER sign on this sink," she calls to the employee sitting at the reception desk. She looks down at me and returns my chair to its upright position. "Sorry, hun, we have to move to the next sink. This one's clogged. I called Ryan to fix it, but he's so busy that he had to put me on his waiting list."

"No problem," I say, shuffling sideways to the next chair. "Since Archie retired, Ryan sometimes has more work than he can keep up with."

I'm pleased to report that the next sink is clog-free, and my hair appointment continues as scheduled.

Few things feel as indulgent as someone else washing your hair. I close my eyes and breathe deeply, enjoying the luxurious scalp massage and giving silent thanks to the universe for blessing Kelly with such skilled fingers.

When I'm settled in her stylist chair, I arrange the

excess cape around myself, and Kelly runs her fingers through my hair and assesses what we're dealing with. We decide that Kelly will clean up my split ends and re-establish my layers, then with her comb in one hand and scissors in the other, she gets to work, and bits of my hair rain onto the shiny, white floor.

While Kelly skilfully sections and snips my hair, I tell her how nice it was to see her at the party on Friday night.

"I hope you had fun," I tell her. "When you're ready, you, me, and April should have a girl's night."

"I'd love that," Kelly replies. "I've missed you guys."

We talk a little more, and Kelly asks me about business at Knitorious, which steers the conversation toward knitting. Kelly is a knitter. Activities that require both hands and both sides of the brain are her thing.

"Did I tell you my uncle and his wife bought a hobby farm?" Kelly asks.

"No, you didn't," I reply. "Do they have sheep?"

"Not sheep, but something just as good." She stops snipping and looks at me in the mirror. "Alpacas!" she says wide-eyed and grinning.

"Is your uncle a knitter?" I ask.

Kelly shakes her head and resumes trimming my hair. "No, but his wife is. She also spins and dyes her own yarn."

I'm struck with a sense of déjà vu. Again. This is the

second time I've had déjà vu this week, and it unsettles me. I'm sure I've heard this story before.

"Does she sell it?" I ask, partly out of curiosity and partly on behalf of my yarn store.

"Not yet," Kelly replies. "But I keep telling her she should. Her yarn is beautiful, Megan. She gave me some to give to you."

"I can't wait to see it and squish it," I respond, making a squishing motion with my hands underneath my cape.

"And I can't wait to show it to you." Kelly places her comb and scissors on the counter in front of me and raises her index finger. "I'll be right back." And with that, Kelly disappears into the back room, and I hear her delicate footsteps race up the stairs toward her apartment.

Moments later, Kelly returns carrying three project bags. "First," she says, opening one bag and tilting it so I can see inside, "cat toys. I heard the charity knitters are working on cat toys for the Animal Centre to sell in the gift shop, so I made some with scrap yarn." She holds up a puffy, heart-shaped, stuffed toy and shakes it. The bell she stuffed inside jingles, and she returns it to the project bag, zips it shut, and hands it to me.

I toss the bag of toys toward my tote bag on the empty stylist chair next to me. I miss, and the bag of toys lands on the chair behind my bag. "Thank you," I say. "The charity knitters will love these."

Kelly opens the second project bag and holds up

two skeins of yarn, one is a solid, undyed cream, and the other a variegated black and grey.

I free my hands from under the black nylon cape and reach for the skeins of yarn. They're bulky weight, wonderfully soft, and scrumptiously squishy. They're also familiar in a way that makes me anxious. The more I pet them, the larger the knot in my stomach gets. Yarn *never* makes me anxious; yarn is my happy place, it's where I go to escape anxious feelings. What is it about this yarn that makes me feel this way?

While I continue to pet the skeins of yarn and contemplate my complicated feelings about them, Kelly unzips the third project bag and pulls out her current knitting project. It's a hat. A hat that is an exact match for Sheamus's scarf. Same colours, same stitch pattern, same yarn!

CHAPTER 23

KELLY IS THE "SPECIAL FRIEND" who made Sheamus's favourite scarf? She's the friend who Sheamus said had an aunt who spins and dyes fibre on an alpaca farm. Kelly said her uncle and his wife bought an alpaca farm, and her uncle's wife is a dyer and spinner. Technically, her uncle's wife would be her aunt. Are Sheamus and Kelly dating?

Unable to hide my shocked reaction, Kelly misinterprets my stunned facial expression for admiration.

"I know, it's beautiful right? Kind of leaves you speechless, doesn't it?" she asks.

"It really does," I reply truthfully.

I extend my hand to return the two skeins of yarn I've been petting, and she waves me off.

"Those are for you," Kelly says. "I'm hoping if you knit with them and like them, your feedback might help convince my uncle's wife that her yarn belongs in yarn stores."

"Thank you, Kelly. And please thank your uncle's wife for me." I toss the skeins of yarn on top of my bag.

"That's a beautiful hat," I say, gesturing toward the hat-in-progress in her hand. "Is it for you?"

Kelly looks down at the hat and shoves it back inside the project bag. "No, it's for a friend. It matches a scarf I made him."

I knew it!

How many bulky, alpaca, hand-dyed, slip-stitch patterned scarves can there be in Harmony Lake? Especially ones made with the Ashes to Ashes, Rust to Rust colour? Answer... One, and I've seen it wrapped around Sheamus O'Brien's neck three times in two days.

"The colours kind of remind me of the Irish flag," I observe, watching Kelly's face for a reaction. Nothing.

"That's what I thought too," Kelly agrees. "That's why I chose it. The friend I'm making it for is of Irish heritage."

It's Sheamus; it has to be. I'd bet my yarn stash on it.

"As much as I'd love to sit and talk about yarn all day," Kelly announces, "I better finish cutting your hair before it dries and curls up on us." She zips the project bag and tosses it onto an empty stylist chair.

While Kelly sections and snips, we talk about this and that and share stories about some of our favourite shared customers, but I can't stop thinking about that yarn and about Sheamus's scarf.

Kelly always straightens my hair. First with a big round brush and blow dryer, then with a flat iron. She says it helps her to make sure she cut it evenly because the curls can complicate things, but I secretly think she enjoys the challenge of forcing my rebellious curls into submission. I don't mind. I rarely straighten it myself because of the time commitment, and I'm happy to spend the extra time in Kelly's chair, laughing and chatting with her.

When she pulls the flat iron from its slot, she asks me how Eric is doing. I decide this might be the best opportunity I'll get to steer the conversation toward intimate relationships and ask whether Kelly is involved in one.

"He's great. The chief of police job keeps him busy, but I think it makes him happy," I say in response to her question. "How about you, Kelly? Now that you're starting to socialize, do you think you might start dating soon?"

Her posture becomes more rigid, and the muscles around her eyes and mouth tighten. She looks at me in the mirror and sighs.

"When Paul died, I didn't think I would ever date," Kelly confesses. "I couldn't imagine being with anyone except him, and that was fine with me." She looks down at my hair and runs the flat iron through a long section of it.

Paul is Kelly's late husband.

"That's understandable, Kelly. You don't have to

date. You don't have to do anything that doesn't feel right for you," I assure her. Maybe my instincts are wrong about her and Sheamus. Maybe they're just friends. Friends with chemistry.

She stops ironing again and looks at me in the mirror. "I don't feel that way anymore," she explains. "I don't want to be alone forever, and I don't think Paul would want that for me, either. If I have feelings for someone else, it doesn't mean I didn't love Paul."

"That's right," I agree. "You'll always love Paul, even if you love someone else."

"I realize that now," she says, obliterating another ringlet with her flat iron.

I furrow my brow and squint, looking at her in the mirror. "Kelly, are you seeing someone?" I ask quietly.

She nods and her eyes fill with moisture. Oh, no! What have I done? The last thing I want is to upset my widowed friend and make her cry!

"I'm sorry, Kelly. I shouldn't have asked. Ignore me, I'm being nosy. Please don't cry." I pull some tissues from the box on the counter in front of me and pass them to her behind me.

"Tears of joy," she explains with a shy smile. With her free hand, Kelly fans her damp eyes while she tries to blink the tears away. "I haven't been this happy since before Paul died." She stops waving at her face and rests her hand on my shoulder.

"That's wonderful." I place my hand on top of hers.

"You deserve to be happy. Everyone wants you to be happy."

Smiling and nodding, Kelly resumes sectioning and ironing my hair.

It's obvious Kelly is in a delicate place emotionally. I don't want to make her uncomfortable, but I have a feeling she could help eliminate a suspect in Saxon's murder, so I ask my next question but proceed with extreme caution, asking quietly and gently.

"May I ask who is responsible for your tears of joy?"

"Not yet," she replies, smiling and shaking her head. "I'm not ready to share it yet. I'm still getting used to this new relationship, and we're still getting to know each other. But Megan, he's funny, and sweet, and patient."

"Take your time. No pressure," I say and mean it.

I remember how fragile I felt when I first started dating Eric after my separation. We kept our relationship quiet at first, too, while we got to know each other. The last thing I want to do is scare Kelly back into seclusion, so I'll respect her privacy and won't ask her anything else. Instead, I'll focus on being grateful she's found happiness again, and I'll find another way to get my questions answered.

ME: *Tacos for dinner at my place?*

It's mid-afternoon, and I haven't had lunch yet. My

tummy is rumbling, and my thoughts keep turning to food. I'm standing on the sidewalk outside Hairway to Heaven, debating whether to cross the street to get something to eat at the pub and talk to Sheamus, or skip the pub—and Sheamus—until tomorrow, and give my thoughts about my conversation with Kelly a chance to marinate overnight.

Eric: I wish! I'm working on getting a pile of warrants. It'll be a late night.

Warrants? Arrest warrants or search warrants?

Me: Is the warrant for a person or a thing?

Eric: Yes. For a person who would not submit a thing, and a few other searches.

Time to take this conversation off text. I dial Eric's number.

"Hey, babe! How's your day?"

"Let me guess," I dive right in, ignoring Eric's pleasant greeting, "At least one of your warrants involves Sheamus's inconsistent alibi and his scarf?"

Silence. Brief pause. Sigh. "You're very intuitive," Eric answers my question without actually answering my question.

"Can it wait?" I plead. "Can you move that warrant to the bottom of your pile? I have a hunch, and if I'm right, you won't need to pick up Sheamus."

"When will you know if your hunch is correct?" Eric asks.

"Soon," I assure him. "Today."

"Can you give me a hint?"

"Not until I confirm I'm onto something. If you wait, I promise I'll personally deliver a full explanation and a hot meal," I negotiate.

Monday's special at the pub is Irish stew, and it's one of Eric's favourites.

Another sigh. "Can you deliver both in the next couple of hours?" he asks. "I'm starving."

"Yup!"

I guess I'll talk to Sheamus today.

ASIDE FROM A FEW booths of tourists from the ski resorts, and the regulars who sit at the bar, nursing their beers and watching the giant TV, the pub is empty. I hope Sheamus is here.

"Takeout?" the bartender asks when I approach the cash register at the bar.

"Yes, please." I smile, and she produces a menu from under the bar and hands it to me. I don't need a menu, but I take it and say thank you to be polite. "Is Sheamus around?" I ask.

"He's upstairs in the office," the bartender replies. "Would you like me to call him?"

This conversation will require privacy. "No, thank you, I'll go up and see him." I sense the bartender is about to object because she points to the velvet rope that signifies the stairs are a no-go-zone and opens her mouth as if to speak, but I don't give her the chance.

"Can I have two orders of Irish stew to go, please? With garlic bread." I give back the unopened menu and smile, then turn and walk away, slipping behind one of the silver, ball-top stanchions at the bottom of the stairs.

Sheamus's office door is ajar. I peek inside to make sure he's alone and not on the phone, then tap lightly on the door.

"Megan," Sheamus says when he looks up at me. "I didn't recognize you for a second. You got your hair done." He gestures toward my straightened hair, then closes his laptop and beckons me inside with his hand.

He's wearing the scarf. It's draped over his shoulders.

"Hi, Sheamus." I bend and he gets up, and we meet halfway for a quick hug, then I sit in the chair across from him. "I'm waiting for a takeout order and wanted to talk to you for a minute."

"Irish stew for Eric?" he guesses with a hint of Irish lilt.

"Yes," I confirm. "He's working late and loves your stew." I raise my index finger to my lips. "But don't tell him because it's a surprise," I joke.

"Your secret is safe with me, lass." Sheamus winks.

I'm sure it is. It would seem Sheamus excels at keeping secrets.

"Your hair looks good straight," he comments. "Did Kelly do it?"

"Yes, she's amazing. She makes my hair look better than I can."

"Yup, she's mad talented," he agrees, nodding and with a hint of pride in his voice. "So, what can I do for ya?"

Sheamus's last sentence goes in one ear and out the other because I'm distracted by the corner behind him, remembering the whangee handle umbrella I saw there on Friday night before Adam's victory party. I owe Sheamus an apology for that debacle.

"Earth to Megan."

"Sorry, Sheamus," I say, shaking my head as though it will help me organize my thoughts. I look at him. "I owe you an apology…"

The landline on Sheamus's desk rings, interrupting me mid-sentence.

"One sec." He picks up the receiver, mumbles a few acknowledgements, then moves the phone away from his ear and covers the speaker with his hand. "We ran out of stew at lunch, and the next batch is almost ready. Can you wait about twenty minutes, or do you want to order something else?"

"It'll be worth it," I reply. "I'll wait for fresh stew."

He hangs up, apologizes for the interruption, and says, "What were we talking about?"

"I was about to apologize to you," I remind him. "On Friday night, I saw the umbrella in the corner. I knew the police were looking for a similar umbrella, so I told Eric it was here. Apparently, it wasn't the umbrella they were looking for, and you and one of your employees had to endure being questioned for no reason. I'm sorry."

"Were you snooping around in my office?" he asks rightfully, but with a hint of amusement.

"No. Absolutely not," I insist. "The door was open. Adam and I came in here so he could practice his speech before the party."

"I was joking," Sheamus says. "I know you wouldn't snoop."

Is he joking again? I can't tell. Because I feel like it's common knowledge that I enjoy an occasional snoop.

"I regret that I didn't ask you about the umbrella before I mentioned it to Eric. We're friends, and I shouldn't have gone behind your back."

"*Pshaw*," he says. "You did the right thing, Megan. No need to apologize. Is that what you wanted to talk to me about? Do you want me to have a drink brought up for you while you wait for your order?" He unbuttons his cuffs and rolls up his shirt sleeves, revealing his pale forearms.

I shake my head. "No, thank you, I'm fine." I take a deep breath and prepare to ask him about personal things, things that are none of my business. "Can I ask you something, Sheamus?" I pause, waiting for permission. He nods, and I continue, "Remember when we bumped into each other on Friday, and you told me how Adam's text woke you up and you were half-asleep and confused when you texted him back?"

"I remember," he confirms.

"You told other people that you turned off your phone before you went to bed. How did Adam's text wake you up if your phone wasn't on?"

"Ah, I can see how that would confuse you." He grins and leans forward, putting his muscular forearms on the desk. "I woke up, turned on my phone to check the time, rolled over, and went back to sleep."

"That makes sense," I admit. "Did the text wake up Kelly too?"

CHAPTER 24

I DIDN'T THINK it would be possible for Sheamus's pallor to have less colour than it already has, but his face drains of what little colour it had before my comment, and his clear blue eyes are wide with shock.

"Wh... ho... I... Excuse me?"

"I know about you and Kelly," I say confidently, not feeling at all confident.

He blinks three times in rapid succession with his mouth agape and shakes his head in disbelief. "Megan," he huffs my name. "I'm not sure what you think you know, or who's spreading rumours..."

"I know Kelly is the 'special friend'" who made your scarf," I interrupt him with my circumstantial evidence, and put finger quotes before and after *special friend*.

I don't mention the matching hat she's making, because if it's a surprise, I don't want to spoil it. It's infuriating to spend ten hours of your life knitting a surprise for someone just to have someone else come along and ruin the surprise. I refuse to be that person.

"That doesn't mean we're a couple," he hisses as though there's someone nearby who might hear us. "Friends are allowed to knit scarves for each other."

So, I was right about the scarf.

"Sheamus." I lean forward and put my arms on his desk, mirroring his pose, and place one of my hands gently on his forearm. "I think you left the card game after the fiasco, got in your truck, and searched for Ryan. Then, when you received Archie's text calling off the search, you parked in the lot behind the pub, turned off your phone, and walked across the street to Kelly's apartment where you spent the night. That's why the snow around your house was undisturbed, and the police officer who went to your house and knocked on your door twice on Friday morning said it appeared you hadn't been home. It also explains why you didn't see Adam's car across the street from your house when you looked out your window, because you weren't home to look through your own window."

Sheamus pulls his arm away from my hand, stands up, and walks around the desk. He closes his office door all the way, then returns to the chair behind his desk. He inhales deeply, holds it for a second, then exhales.

"You can't prove it."

"You're right," I acknowledge, "I can't prove where

you were when Saxon Renaud was murdered, but neither can you. Your version of your alibi can't be verified and having an unverifiable alibi is the same as having no alibi at all."

"I didn't kill Saxon Renaud," he exclaims.

"I know," I affirm. "And if you tell the truth about where you were when he died, Kelly can verify it, and eliminate you as a suspect. It'll be over."

He shakes his head. "I refuse to bring her into this, Megan. Do you remember what Kelly went through when Paul was murdered? She was a suspect. The police questioned her relentlessly. She couldn't grieve her husband's death properly because of the investigation. I won't let them re-traumatize her. I won't. If I have to be a murder suspect to protect Kelly, so be it. I'm sure that, eventually, Eric will find the actual killer and exonerate me without having to involve Kelly."

I remember the investigation into Paul's murder vividly because I was a suspect too. It was a traumatic experience that created a bond between Kelly and me that's hard to describe but is only shared between people who have survived a tragic experience together.

"The last thing anyone wants is to hurt Kelly," I remind him. "We all love her. But don't you think it will traumatize her if the investigation into Saxon's murder drags on with you as a suspect? Or if the police charge you because you lied about your alibi, or obstructed the investigation, or something? How will you comfort and protect Kelly if you're defending yourself in court or serving time in prison?"

With tears in his eyes, Sheamus raises his hand to his forehead and rests his elbow on the desk. Great! In the last hour I've made two friends cry. A new personal best.

"Sheamus, I'm sorry, I wasn't trying to upset you…"

He raises his hand in a stop motion. "You're right," he says. "My approach could be worse for Kelly in the long run. And if the tables were turned, and I could help eliminate her as a murder suspect, I'd be angry if she denied me the chance to help."

Huzzah! He gets it! I let out a sigh of relief.

"Is that why you wouldn't give your scarf to the police?" I ask.

He nods and grips one end of the alpaca scarf. "It would lead back to Kelly. They would want to ask her about it."

The landline on his desk rings again, and we pause our conversation while he answers it. He tells the caller we'll be right down and returns the receiver to the base.

"Your order is ready," he says, rising from his chair.

Downstairs, I wait near the bar with my wallet in hand while Sheamus goes into the kitchen to get my order. When he returns, he's carrying an insulated food bag and a paper bag, and wearing his coat. Noticeably absent: his scarf.

As he gets closer, he points to my wallet and says, "Put it away, it's on the house."

"Don't be silly," I argue. "I told you I didn't mind waiting."

He approaches me, and instead of handing me the insulated food bag, he presses his hand into my back and continues walking toward the door. "I insist," he says while we walk. "It's the least I can do."

Outside on the sidewalk, I stop walking. "Where are we going?"

"To drop off Eric's stew," Sheamus replies like it's a foregone conclusion.

"I ordered takeout, not delivery," I remind him.

"We can go together, and while I'm there, I'll amend my statement, give Eric my scarf"—he holds up the paper bag—"then I'll go to the salon and talk to Kelly, so she's not surprised when the police contact her."

"How about this?" I take the insulated food bag and the paper bag from him. "I'll deliver the stew and your scarf. You go to the salon and talk to Kelly *before* you amend your statement, so there's zero chance she'll be unprepared when the police contact her."

"Is that legal?" Sheamus asks as we step off the curb and cross Water Street. "I don't think I'm supposed to talk to Kelly about my statement before I change it."

I shrug. "I don't know, I'm not a cop. You and I talked about your statement, was that wrong?"

Was it? I'm sure if it was, the newly appointed chief of police will educate me when I tell him about it. We're now standing in front of Hairway to Heaven and move next door to Latte Da so Kelly won't see us and come outside to say hi.

"Megan, thank you for helping me see sense," Sheamus says.

"You'd do the same for me." I know this to be true. "I won't tell anyone other than Eric about you and Kelly," I promise. "Kelly doesn't even know I know."

"How is that possible?" he asks.

"I guessed based on some things she said while she was doing my hair," I explain. "She's still fragile, and I didn't want to pressure her, so I went to the pub and pressured you instead."

"And I appreciate it," he says with a chuckle.

We part ways, and while I hustle toward my car in the Knitorious parking lot, I use the remote key chain to start my car so it's warm when I get there. I need to deliver this stew before it gets cold and before Eric files the paperwork for those warrants.

CHAPTER 25

THE FOOD IS in an insulated bag, but I turn on the seat warmer on the passenger seat anyway to ensure the stew stays warm during the short drive to the Harmony Lake Police Station.

Me: I'm here.

Eric: I'll be right out.

"Hi," I say to the familiar-looking, young officer behind the counter in the lobby.

"Hi," he says. "Delivery? You can leave it over there." He points to a chair next to the secure inner door. "Who's it for? I'll page them and let them know it's here."

He thinks I'm a delivery person. I guess I am, sort of.

"Eric," I say through the small round speaker in the bullet-resistant acrylic barrier between us.

"Eric who?" he asks.

"Eric Sloane," I specify. "He's expecting me."

"Hey, you're the lady from the cat house."

A look of recognition flashes across the cop's face at the same moment it flashes across mine; he's the officer who accompanied Rick and me into Saxon's house when Rick rescued Clawdia.

"You're the officer who carried the kitty litter."

He smiles and nods enthusiastically. "Yeah. How's Clawdia doing? Is she happy in her new home?" he asks.

"I don't know yet," I reply. "It's on my to-do list for tomorrow."

Looking slightly confused, probably because I'm still here, he asks me if I'm waiting to be paid for the delivery. I shake my head, and before I can explain that I'm waiting for Eric to come to the lobby and let me in, the secure door opens, and Eric is standing next to me.

"Your hair looks nice," he says, tucking a section of my extra shiny, straight hair behind my ear.

"Thank you," I say, leaning into his touch.

Eric takes the insulated food bag, and when he tries to take the paper bag, I pull my hand back.

"It's a surprise," I say.

"An early anniversary gift?" he asks.

"I guess you could call it that," I reply, shrugging.

Eric takes my free hand in his, and the young officer behind the desk rushes to the locked inner door and opens it for us from the inside.

"You aren't a delivery person, are you?" the young officer asks me quietly.

I shake my head. "Why? Is Eric this friendly with everyone who makes deliveries to the station?" I joke.

He's not amused. In fact, the young man, a rookie cop, looks mortified.

To make up for it, I put in a good word for him.

"This is the officer who helped Rick and me when we picked up Clawdia. He was very helpful and very professional."

Eric looks at the rookie's name tag, then commends, and thanks him.

Eric's police-chief office differs from his detective-sergeant office. His new office is bigger, has nicer furniture, and a window. It's still minimalist, though. Other than two fine art photographs I gave him for his birthday hanging on the wall, and the Newton's cradle on his desk, there are no personal items at all. It's the polar opposite of Adam's office, which has so many photos and knickknacks there's barely enough space on his desk to work.

"What first, stew or this?" I hold up the paper bag and give it a gentle shake.

"Are the contents of the paper bag edible?" he asks.

"Definitely not," I reply, hoping I'm right.

I probably should have opened it to make sure Shea-mus's scarf is actually inside. I'll look pretty dumb if this is a bag of condiments, or napkins, or something.

"Food first," he decides, placing the insulated bag

on his desk and opening it. "Oooh, extra garlic bread." Eric is easily pleased, foodwise.

While we eat, I tell him about my hair appointment and my revelation that Kelly and Sheamus are in a relationship.

"Are you sure?" he asks. "There was no evidence of relationship-type text messages between him and anyone on his phone."

"Did you check his social media accounts?" I ask. "Sometimes people private message each other on social media when they want to keep their relationship secret."

Next, I tell him about my visit to the pub and the enlightening conversation Sheamus and I had.

"Let me make sure I understand," Eric says, soaking up my remaining Irish stew with a piece of garlic bread; the serving sizes at the pub are huge, and I'm rarely able to finish anything. "Sheamus wants to amend his current, inconsistent statement to include a witness who can verify his whereabouts, but you don't want me to talk to the witness who can verify his alibi?"

"Why do you rephrase things to make them sound sketchier than they are?" I ask. "Obviously, Kelly *can* verify the details of Sheamus's alibi, but it would be less stressful for her if she didn't have to."

"I'll see what I can do," he says, stacking the empty takeout containers. "But we'll have to talk to her, and when the time comes, I'll personally take her statement and make it as stress-free as possible."

"Thank you," I say.

"Can I see what's in the bag now?" he asks, rubbing his hands together in anticipation.

"If you want to touch it, you'll need a rubber glove," I warn him.

"Why?" Eric looks concerned. "Is it sharp? Does it bite? It's not alive, is it, babe?"

"No, it's not alive." I laugh.

"Then why do I need gloves?" he asks, pulling a disposable glove from one of his desk drawers.

I shrug. "Because you always wear gloves when you touch evidence, so I assume it's a requirement."

"There's evidence in that bag?" he asks loudly, pointing at the bag like I just told him it's radioactive. "You're just driving around town with murder evidence in your car?"

"How else was I supposed to get it here?" I ask.

"If you called me, I would have had it picked up," Eric replies. "Chain of custody and protection from contamination are important."

"I'm a civilian," I remind him. Sometimes he forgets.

"I know," he says, kissing me. "And you're still a better cop than some real cops I know." With his gloved hand, he opens the paper bag and peers inside. "Is that Sheamus's scarf?" he asks, sounding impressed.

"You're welcome," I say.

"Thank you. You're incredible." After another kiss, he jokingly asks, "Sheamus knows you have it, right?"

"I'm not a thief." I swat his arm playfully. "He wants

his scarf back as soon as possible." Eric nods in acknowledgement. "His revised statement will eliminate Sheamus as a suspect, right?" I ask.

Eric nods. "If his story checks out, and there's no forensic evidence to contradict it, Sheamus is off the suspect list."

"Who else is off the suspect list?" I ask.

"Pete," Eric replies. "His parents verified that he was at their house removing a squirrel from the chimney, and we tracked his cell phone. It was at their house when the anonymous witness called the tip line. Ryan was eliminated because he was on the phone the entire time he was unaccounted for. First, he spoke with his sponsor, then with his dad. I don't see how it would be possible for him to murder Saxon, move his body, run over the body, hide the murder weapon and a penny loafer, then drop off Adam's car at your house, walk back to his own car, and drive home while carrying on an uninterrupted conversation."

"That only leaves Adam and Rick," I conclude. "And I'd bet my life it wasn't Adam."

"We're pursuing other lines of inquiry." Eric rubs my shoulders.

I know he's trying to reassure me, but I hate it when he uses cop speak with me.

"What other lines of inquiry?" I ask.

Eric sighs. "Saxon Renaud had a lot of enemies. Every time we question someone, they lead us to someone else who had a grudge against him."

"Like who?" I ask.

Eric counts on his fingers. "People he owed money to, disgruntled tenants, people he had political differences of opinion with, people he offended…"

"OK, I get it," I interrupt him. "You have a lot of leads."

Eric nods, then there's a knock at the door.

"Come in," Eric says loudly.

The officer who helped Rick and me with Clawdia opens the door halfway. "Sheamus O'Brien is here to see you, Chief. I tried to call you, but your phone is set to DO NOT DISTURB."

"I'll be right there," Eric says, smiling at the rookie.

The rookie closes the office door and returns to his post.

The rookie cop's comment makes me realize that I haven't heard Eric's cell phone make a sound the entire time I've been here.

"Is your cell phone on DO NOT DISTURB too?" I ask.

He nods and opens a desk drawer. "I told you I'm unplugging for at least an hour a day," he reminds me as he takes his cell phone from the drawer and slips it into his pocket.

Eric and I say our goodbyes in the privacy of his office before we walk to the lobby, so he can unlock the secure door to let me out and let Sheamus in.

"Thanks for the stew," he says. "By the time I finish work tonight, most places will be closed, and I haven't had time to pick up groceries. I would've gone home hungry to an empty kitchen."

"No, you wouldn't," I tell him, shaking my head. "I picked up groceries and restocked your fridge and pantry this morning."

"I don't deserve you," he says, hugging me. "Because of you, I won't starve," he jokes.

"Because of me, your kitchen is full of *my* favourite foods," I joke back.

Sheamus and Kelly are in the lobby when we get there. They're sitting side by side, holding hands. So much for Kelly's desire to keep their relationship under wraps. Half of Harmony Lake will know by now, and the other half will know before sunset. I'm not surprised to see her here. I'm sure when Sheamus explained the situation to her, Kelly insisted on accompanying him to the police station to support him.

When Eric gestures for Sheamus to follow him to his office, I remind Sheamus to take his insulated bag with him when he leaves.

"Do you want me to wait with you? I don't mind," I offer, lowering myself into the chair that Sheamus just vacated, next to Kelly.

"Thank you, hun, but I'm OK," Kelly responds. "Can you believe he was willing to be a murder suspect to protect me?"

I nod. "I can," I reply. "Sheamus is a stand-up guy, and he obviously cares about you. A lot. He wants to protect you."

"I know," Kelly says, smiling shyly. "I hope Eric understands, and Sheamus doesn't get into trouble for lying."

"I'm sure it'll be fine," I reassure her. "And I didn't tell Sheamus about the hat, in case it's a surprise."

"Oh, good! Thank you, hun! It *is* a surprise." Kelly reaches into her bag and pulls out the project bag with the hat-in-progress inside. She opens the bag and starts knitting. "You left the bag of cat toys at the salon earlier. I'll bring them by Knitorious tomorrow," she says. "It'll give me an excuse to look at the spring yarn colours."

I offer once more to wait with her, but Kelly shoos me away. "You only have to tell me twice," I tease as I exit the police station.

"Excuse me! Ma'am!"

I'm only a few feet from the door when the rookie cop calls after me.

"Hi." I smile. "Megan Martel," I introduce myself and extend my hand for the rookie cop to shake. "Call me Megan."

"Lucas Butler," he reciprocates. "I'm sorry I didn't know who you were when you got here," he apologizes. "We get a lot of deliveries, and you had a delivery bag, so I assumed you were a delivery person."

"Don't worry about it," I tell him. "It was an honest mistake, and I *was* delivering something. Are you new to the department?"

He nods. "I've only been here a month. I'm still learning who everyone is."

"How do you like it so far?" I ask.

Lucas shrugs. "So far, so good," he replies. "I'm the new guy, so they give me the jobs no one else wants to do, but I don't mind paying my dues."

"You mean jobs like working the front desk and carrying cat litter?" I tease.

"Pretty much." Lucas nods. "But I got to answer a call on the tip line on Friday night. That was exciting. It's the closest I've gotten to a real murder investigation."

Does he mean the call from the witness who said they saw Adam's car leaving the hit-and-run on Lake Access Road?

"The one from the witness who reported the hit and run on Lake Access Road?" I ask.

"That's the one," Lucas replies. "I was working the front desk, so I was responsible for the phones."

"I don't suppose you recognized the caller's voice?" I ask, knowing it's a longshot.

He shakes his head. "No," he replies. "I'm sure it was a man, though. And it echoed like he was in a car. And he was nervous."

"Did he tell you he was nervous, or did he say something that led you to believe he was nervous?" I ask.

"It wasn't what he said, it was how he said it," Lucas explains.

"How?" I ask.

"The caller had a stutter," Lucas reveals. "Some people stutter when they're nervous, right?"

I know at least one person who does.

CHAPTER 26

Tuesday, January 19th

Sophie scurries, losing traction on the wood floor, when she hears the back door thud shut.

"Good morning, Soph," I hear Eric say.

Moments later, he hands me a white chocolate and peppermint latte with extra whipped cream, white chocolate shavings, and a drizzle of chocolate syrup.

"Good morning, handsome." I give him a kiss and relieve him of the coffee cup. "Thank you."

"I'm sorry we didn't see each other last night. I was up to my eyeballs in paperwork, and by the time I left the station, you were asleep."

"Don't worry about it," I insist. "I hope you're getting enough sleep and eating properly."

"I'll catch up on sleep and healthy food when we solve this case," he says. "Taking Sheamus's revised statement and talking to Kelly took longer than I thought."

"I understand," I assure him. "Speaking of the case," I segue, "remember the witness who called the anonymous tip line?" Eric nods, so I proceed. "You didn't mention the caller had a stutter. Is the stutter a holdback?"

The look of confusion on his face tells me this is the first Eric has heard about the caller's alleged stutter.

"Who told you the caller had a stutter?" he asks.

"The officer who answered the call," I reply, hoping I'm not about to get Lucas Butler in trouble.

"The new guy?" Eric asks. "Butler?"

I nod. "We had a brief conversation when I was leaving the station yesterday, and he mentioned he answered the call from the tipster. I asked him if the caller's voice was familiar. He didn't recognize the voice, because he's new in town, but he said the caller's stutter made him sound nervous."

Eric's jaw muscles clench and unclench—something he does when he's angry—and his gaze drifts to his lower left. Something he does when he's thinking.

"Be nice," I say, interrupting both his jaw clenching and his thoughts.

"What do you mean?" he asks. "I'm always nice."

"Don't go charging into the station and yell at Lucas because he didn't mention the stutter before," I explain. "I can tell you're angry."

"I won't yell," he promises, "but I will have to

mention it to him. This is too significant of a detail not to mention it until yesterday."

"Does the call to the tip line coincide with the hole in Rick's alibi that Trudy couldn't verify because she fell asleep?" I ask.

"Yes." Eric nods.

Eric leaves for work, and I resume getting the online orders ready for shipping.

"Good morning, my dear," Connie sings as she enters the store a few minutes after I unlock the door and turn the sign to OPEN.

"Good morning," I respond. "How was your weekend?"

"It was lovely, my dear. How was yours?"

"Busy and informative," I reply.

Connie stops in her tracks and looks at me with one of her eyebrows raised higher than the other. "Hold that thought, my dear, while I make some tea," Connie instructs. "Then I want to hear everything!"

While Connie makes tea, I text April and ask her to come to the store, so I can tell both of them what I've learned, and we can brainstorm what it might mean. Three heads are better than one!

April arrives carrying a white confectionery box.

"What treats did you bring for us?" I ask, sniffing in the direction of the box.

It smells delicious, and I detect a hint of cinnamon, but I can't distinguish what's in the box.

"Apple cider doughnut holes and mini caramel pecan pies with cinnamon roll pie crust," she replies.

I swallow hard because my mouth begins to water.

I take the box from April while she takes off her coat.

"We didn't forget about you, Sophie," April reassures the corgi.

Sophie is already sitting at attention, like a good girl, waiting for her treat. Clearly, I'm not the only one who gets excited when April shows up with a white confectionery box.

April opens the box and removes a small, white, confectionery bag. "Carrot cake dog treats," she says, removing two bone-shaped cookies from inside the bag.

Connie, April, and I settle in the cozy sitting area with our warm drinks, freshly baked treats, and knitting.

Connie and I are Knitters with an uppercase K; we embrace knitting as a lifestyle. April is a knitter with a lowercase k; she knows how to knit, and she knits occasionally, but knitting isn't essential to her everyday life.

Despite being a lower-case k knitter, April has been knitting like a fiend lately. So far, she has made almost a dozen cat toys for the Charity Knitting Guild's cat toy initiative.

"Four more mice," April says, handing me the knitted cat toys from her knitting bag. "These toys have catnip in the stuffing."

"Thank you," I say. "The charity knitters are coming to the store tomorrow to pick them up." I snap my fingers. "That reminds me. Kelly made some toys, too, but I forgot them at the salon yesterday. She said she'd drop them off today." I get up and jot down a quick reminder in my planner to pick up the toys if Kelly doesn't drop them off.

"Speaking of Kelly," April coos coyly, "I hate to say I told you so about her and Sheamus, but I told you so." She smiles smugly.

"Yes, I heard they're seeing each other," Connie interjects. "I can't think of a nicer couple. I think he'll make Kelly very happy, and goodness knows, she deserves some happiness."

I smile and nod.

April narrows her eyes and glares at me. "You aren't surprised," she declares. "You already knew, and didn't tell us, Megnolia?"

"I only found out late yesterday," I state defensively, then look at Connie. "And I agree with Connie, I think they'll be happy together."

"*Hmph*," April grunts under her breath, miffed that I knew but didn't tell her. "I hope it works out for them. This is the happiest we've seen Kelly since Paul died."

"Speaking of secrets," I say, changing the subject, "Saxon Renaud allegedly told someone he had a plan to fix the election so he would win."

Connie drops her knitting in her lap. "Nonsense." She picks up her teacup. "Either your source is lying, or Saxon lied to them."

"Maybe," I reply. "All I know is what I was told. Saxon allegedly told one of his creditors the election would be fixed, and he would be the next mayor. He told them he would reverse the big-box policy, sell his properties, and repay his debts in full."

"If he had a plan, it failed," Connie concludes. "Adam won the election by a landslide."

"How on earth would he fix a municipal election?" April asks. "Especially by himself. I mean he didn't seem to have any friends, and you would need at least one trusted friend to help you pull off something that big."

"Well," Connie says, dipping her chin and looking back and forth between April and me over her reading glasses, "he had one friend."

"One friend who's alibi has a big hole in it," I comment.

"I heard Trudy Nakata is Rick's alibi for the night Saxon died," April says.

"Kind of," I say, giving her a half-smile and making a seesaw motion with my hand.

"Kind of?" Connie asks.

I explain to April and Connie how Trudy fell asleep for an undetermined amount of time while Rick was repairing the holes in her ceiling, after he rescued Cat Benetar.

We discuss how the holes in his alibi, and his relationship with Saxon, make Rick a good suspect for Saxon's murder. I don't mention that the person who called the tip line stuttered because Eric hasn't confirmed it yet.

"I don't know," I admit my misgivings. "Rick and I have spent some time together since Saxon died, and the Rick I know is a nice, funny, caring man. You should see him with Clawdia, he's so sweet. And Trudy always talks about how helpful Rick is and says she doesn't know what she'd do without him."

"Neighbours always say that about serial killers," April reminds me. "They say, 'he was such a good neighbour. He was so quiet. He would do anything for anyone.' It's part of their plan to get people to trust them and not suspect them. They're always the last person anyone suspects."

She's not wrong.

The jingle of the bell over the door interrupts our brainstorming session.

"Good morning, Phillip!" I stand up from my seat at the sofa and leave my knitting on the sofa cushion. "How are you?"

"Frustrated," Phillip replies, holding up half of a key.

"Oh no, Phillip, what happened?" Connie asks.

"My key snapped when I tried to unlock the back door," he explains. "I had to bring in the deliveries through the front door, and I can't get the broken piece of key out of the lock."

"How can we help?" I ask.

It's just gone on 10 a.m., but he's already having a bad day.

Phillip sighs. "Ryan isn't sure he'll have time to fix it today. Can I have my emergency store key? I'll bring it back after I get another one cut."

"This is why you gave me a spare key," I reply, opening the cash register and retrieving Phillip's spare key from under the till. "Here you go." I smile.

Phillip gives me a weak smile. "Thanks." He takes the key.

"Maybe we can fix it," April suggests. "There are loads of YouTube videos showing how to get a broken key out of a lock." She gestures for Phillip to sit next to her, and they search for a video on April's cell phone.

"With Archie retired, Ryan needs to hire a helper," I whisper to Connie.

"Ryan needs to find the time to hire a helper," Connie replies. "I've suggested that Archie help Ryan hire someone, but Ryan wants to do it himself. I'll suggest it again."

Connie and I resume knitting while April and Phillip watch their third or fourth video tutorial about removing broken keys from locks.

"My turn," Connie says, getting up when the bell over the door jingles again. "Hello, Rick. What brings you to Knitorious today?"

My head snaps up from my knitting at the sound of Rick's name. "Hi, Rick," I say, craning my head to see him in the doorway.

"H-hi, Megan," Rick responds, walking toward me.

I gesture for him to sit down. He sits in the over-sized chair at the end of the sofa.

"I was going to text you later today," I tell him, finishing my row and putting down my knitting. "How's Clawdia settling in?"

"I was w-w-walking by your store and came in to g-give you an update," he replies. "She's doing gr-great. Saxon's brother didn't phone or show u-up to get her, but I knew he w-wouldn't."

Rick pulls his cell phone from his coat pocket and opens the photos app on his phone. He shows me several photos he's taken of Clawdia since taking her home on Saturday.

While I scroll through photos of Clawdia on her new scratch post, Clawdia watching the birdfeeder through the window, and Clawdia sleeping on a windowsill, I lean toward Rick and ask quietly, "Do you know if Saxon had a plan to fix the mayoral election so he would win?"

A surprised expression flashes across Rick's face. I'm not sure if he's surprised at Saxon possibly planning to fix the election, or if he's surprised I know about the plan.

"He j-joked about it, but it was j-just a joke," Rick replies. "I'm sure h-he wished he could do it, but he c-couldn't do something like that, especially without help."

"Aren't we the hub of social activity this morning?"

Connie mutters as she once again puts down her knitting and stands up to greet our newest arrival.

"Kelly! It's so nice to see you!" Connie gives Kelly a quick hug.

"Excuse me, Rick." I hand him his phone. "I'll be right back." I stand up but abandon my plan when I realize Kelly is almost right in front of me.

"Hi, Kelly," I say, re-settling into my seat on the sofa.

"Hi, hun. Here are the cat toys you left at the salon yesterday." The small zippered bag jingles and crackles when I take it from her.

"Thank you. The cats will love these," I tell her. "They love the toys with bells and tissue paper inside."

"I know it's a longshot," Kelly says, "but do you have a slitherer I could borrow?"

What's a slitherer? Is it some newfangled knitting tool I've never heard of? I furrow my brow and tilt my head, trying to figure out what she means.

"Can you be more specific?" I ask.

"You know, one of those slithery things?" She puts her hands together in front of her and slithers them toward me. "You shove it down the drain to unclog the sink."

"A snake!" Rick interjects so loudly we all look at him, and April and Phillip even pause the video they're watching.

"Yes! A snake!" Kelly points and hops excitedly when Rick guesses her charade.

"Do you have a c-clog, Kelly?" Rick asks.

Kelly tells Rick about the clogged hair sink at the salon, and Rick tells her he has a snake and can look at the sink for her. She offers to pay him, but he waves away her offer, insisting it will only take a few minutes of his time. She insists on paying him somehow, and after a short, friendly negotiation, it's decided that Rick will unclog the hair sink in exchange for a haircut, which Kelly insists he needs.

"How are you with broken keys?" Phillip asks, holding up his broken key so Rick can see it.

"I'm a trained locksmith," Rick replies. "I have a set of key extractors in my truck." He jerks his thumb behind him, toward Water Street. "I can look at it. It'll only take a few minutes."

Phillip jumps up from the sofa and thanks Rick profusely. April locks her phone screen and drops the device in her knitting bag.

"Are you sure you have time?" Phillip asks. "I don't want to inconvenience you. This is so last minute."

Rick sweeps the suggestion away with his hand. "It's not like I have anything better to do," he says. "I've been at loose ends since my employer died."

And with the mention of Saxon's death, the upbeat mood in Knitorious turns uncomfortable and sullen as we're collectively reminded that his unsolved murder still hangs over our town like a rain cloud.

CHAPTER 27

WEDNESDAY, January 20th

April: Want to come with me to Rick's house?

Me: Why are you going to Rick's house?

April: To drop off treats for him and Clawdia. Rick jump-started T's car yesterday and we want to thank him.

Me: I'm alone at the store until noon, then I have to walk Sophie. 1:00 p.m.?

April: Works for me. I'll pick you up.

Rick Ransan's sudden spate of good deeds are earning him a lot of goodwill among the residents of Harmony Lake. He said he's bored now that he's unemployed, which makes sense, but could there be other reasons for Rick's sudden neighbourliness? Maybe he hopes ingratiating himself with his neighbours will distract everyone from the fact that he's a murder suspect. Maybe he misses his only friend and is trying to keep his mind off his loss. Or maybe Rick has a guilty conscience, and these acts of kindness are his way of making amends.

"IF RICK HADN'T BEEN THERE, T might have waited hours for roadside assistance to show up." April brakes at the stop sign and looks both ways.

Yesterday, when Tamara closed the bakery and left to go home, her car wouldn't start. She'd left the lights on all day, and the battery was drained. April was in Harmony Hills with their teenage son, Zach, attending his hockey game. Thankfully, Harmony Lake's hero-of-the-day, Rick Ransan, was nearby and had his jumper cables in the back of his truck.

"It was lucky timing that Rick parked behind Artsy Tartsy and just happened to return to his truck at the very moment T realized her car battery died," I reply.

"Do I detect a hint of skepticism in your voice, Megapixel?" April taunts. "In case you forget how this works, *I'm* the skeptical friend, and *you're* the optimistic friend."

"Sorry," I apologize. "I forgot." We laugh.

"You don't think it was a coincidence that Rick came along precisely when T needed help?" April asks, sounding as dubious as I do.

I shake my head. "I don't know what to think," I admit. "It seems like Rick is out and about more since

Saxon died, more than he ever was before, and has morphed from an introvert to an extrovert."

April shrugs without taking her hands off the steering wheel. "Maybe without Saxon here to use up Rick's time and energy, Rick can finally be himself. Maybe he was always a friendly, sociable, kind person, but we couldn't see it because Saxon's overbearing, toxic personality overshadowed him."

"You're probably right," I concede. "And if you are, I should encourage Rick to come out of his shell and get involved in the community, instead of doubting his intentions."

April pulls into Rick's driveway and parks alongside his pickup truck. She collects a white confectionery box from the back seat and walks around to the passenger side of the car, where she waits for me to finish signing the *welcome home* greeting card that goes with the knitted mouse toys that I brought for Clawdia.

I made fifteen hand-knit mice for the charity knitting initiative and gave three of them to Clawdia as a housewarming gift. There must be over two hundred hand-knit cat toys for the gift shop at the Animal Centre. I'm sure no one will notice if I give three of the mice that I made to Clawdia.

"Is Rick expecting us, or are we showing up unannounced?" I ask.

"I texted him, and he replied. He knows we're coming," April informs me as we walk up the driveway.

Next door, the curtains in Trudy Nakata's front room twitch. April and I smile and wave at the twitchy curtains.

"Do you think Trudy or Cat Benetar is the curtain twitcher?" April asks.

"Both?" I guess, shrugging one shoulder.

Rick lives in a small, older bungalow. A snow shovel and bag of rock salt lean against the porch wall next to the screen door. I ring the doorbell and we wait. Out of the corner of my eye, I notice Trudy's curtains twitch again.

"Do you think she's spying on us or Rick?" April asks.

"Yes," I reply.

We both cough to suppress our giggles.

Living in a small town where your friends and neighbours watch you more closely than surveillance cameras ever could isn't as annoying as most people think. In fact, it's oddly comforting. I'm grateful I get to live in a community where the residents care about their friends and neighbours so much that they go out of their way to be involved in each other's lives.

To outsiders, we're a community of small-minded, nosy busybodies with too much time on our hands, but that's a misconception; we're actually a close-knit community of friends and neighbours who care deeply about each other and the town we call home.

"H-hi, April." Rick beams. "Oh, and hi t-to you, too, Megan. This is a pleasant surprise, like finding a d-double yolk in your egg when you only expect one yolk."

To the best of my recollection, this is the first time someone has likened April and me to an egg. Rick invites us inside, and next thing we know, April and I are slipping off our winter boots in his foyer.

While April thanks Rick for jump-starting Tamara's car yesterday and gives him a box of snowball cookies and cranberry-orange-banana bread, I glance around Rick's small, cozy home and get a feel for his space.

Rick's home is cozy. It's clean and tidy, yet lived in. His furnishings are neither old nor new, and a few antique collectibles stand out. Family heirlooms, I assume. Judging by the shelf of cookbooks and the extensive herb and spice collection in his kitchen, Rick is a culinary hobbyist. I wonder who he cooks for?

"And we couldn't forget Clawdia," April says, pulling a white confectionery bag from her coat pocket. "Sardine flavoured," she divulges, handing Rick the bag.

Ewww. Sardine cookies sound gross to me, but I'm sure to a cat they sound *pawsitively purrfect.*

"Oh, I brought Clawdia a small housewarming gift too," I add, handing Rick the gift bag of knitted mice.

"Thank you, both!" Rick responds. "Why don't you sit down, and I'll make us some coffee to have with these treats."

We offer to help make the coffee, or plate the sweet treats, but Rick insists he's fine and directs us to the living room. On the sofa, April discreetly nudges my leg with her knee.

"What?" I mouth, looking at her.

She raises her eyebrows and nods toward the dining room. I follow her gaze to a suitcase. It's upright against the wall beside the hutch. There's something on top of the suitcase. I stand up and take two quiet steps toward the dining room to get a better look. It's a passport.

As I take two quiet steps backward toward the sofa, my phone dings. I sink back into the sofa next to April and take my phone out of my bag.

April: Is that a passport? Do you think he's going on the lam?

She's texting me from the next sofa cushion. I turn my head and look at her in disbelief.

"What?" she whispers. "It's not like I could say it out loud."

"I'm not sure how you take your coffee, so I brought everything." Rick places a tray with three mugs of coffee, spoons, and coffee condiments.

"Is Clawdia settled in?" I ask, then sip my coffee.

Rick nods while he chews a snowball cookie.

"Are you getting used to each other?" April adds.

"She's been here less than a week, but it feels like she's always been here," Rick replies. Then he calls for the cat. "Miss Clawdia! Come here, Miss Claaaawdia. Sssspsssssp."

To my surprise, Clawdia bounds into the room from the hall that leads to the bedrooms.

"Here she is," April says, lowering her hand to cat-level and rubbing her fingertips against her thumb, hoping to coax Clawdia to come within stroking distance.

It's hard to believe this is the same small, timid cat Rick and I rescued from Saxon's house. She looks the same, but she acts completely different. This version of Clawdia is friendly and confident. She visits each of us, making certain everyone has a chance to rub her, then jumps onto Rick's lap, puts her front paws on his chest, and headbutts his beard, before coiling herself into a content pile of furry warmth on his lap.

Sophie has taught me that animals have a knack for seeing the essence of who people really are. Animals are neither fooled nor impressed by the facade many people project when they are out in the world. Surely, if Rick were a cold-blooded murderer, Clawdia wouldn't be this comfortable with him. I'm not a cat, but I get a calm, peaceful vibe from Rick too. I just can't believe he's a heartless killer.

"Your hair looks great," I compliment Rick on his new *do*. "Kelly is a great hairdresser, isn't she?"

Rick looks cleaner and more put together with his new style. Before Kelly worked her magic, Rick's head of thick brown curls resembled a curly helmet. Now, the sides and back are super short, and the curls on top of his head are shaped to complement his rugged features. He looks like a different person.

"I hardly recognize myself when I look in the

mirror," Rick responds with a chuckle. "But I expect I'll get used to it." He runs his hand through his curls.

We chat about the weather, the best places to buy pet food and supplies, and other generic topics. I drink my coffee, nibble at my slice of cranberry-orange-banana bread, and wait patiently for an opportunity to ask Rick about the suitcase and passport in the next room.

"Who will take care of Clawdia while you're away?" April asks, as if she can read my mind. Sometimes I swear she has mind- reading powers but won't admit it.

"I'm not going anywhere," Rick replies, looking confused.

"Oh," I interject. "We noticed your suitcase and passport"—I gesture toward them with my almost-empty mug—"and assumed you were going on a trip. Maybe somewhere sunny and warm to escape winter for a few days." I bring the mug to my lips and finish my coffee.

"Oh th-that," Rick replies, turning to look at the suit-case and passport. "I told Trudy I'd drop off the suitcase at the library. It's full of books and clothes and toiletries that someone donated to the book club. The book club collects d-donations for people displaced by natural disasters. They p-put together kits of clothes, toiletries, and books, then send them where they're needed. I think they're currently collecting donations for the hurricane that recently hit the Bahamas, but they take donations all year."

"I can drop off the suitcase at the library," I offer. "I

have to drive past there today, anyway. I'm happy to do it."

"That's nice, Megan, thank you for the offer, but it's heavy. It's full of books. I'd h-hate if you hurt yourself. I don't mind doing it."

"Is the passport part of the donation too?" April asks.

"No," Rick laughs. "The passport is going to the bank. I keep my important papers in a safe deposit box. I renewed my passport, and the new one just arrived in the mail. I need to switch out the new passport with the expired one."

Rick's explanation makes sense, but the suitcase and passport still look suspicious, especially considering Rick is a suspect in a murder investigation.

We thank Rick for the coffee and explain that we have to get back to our respective businesses. We tell him we'll see ourselves out and insist that he not get up because neither of us can bear to disturb Clawdia who is fast asleep and purring on Rick's lap.

"Thanks again, Rick. Bye," I call as I open his front door.

"Wrap up the leftover cake or it'll dry out," April advises. "We'll see you and Clawdia soon."

"Thanks, guys. For everything. Bye," Rick calls from the living room.

"What do you think?" I ask April as we walk to the car.

"I want to believe him about the suitcase and the passport, but I'm not sure I do," she replies.

"Same," I say, nodding. "But he knew we were coming over. If he's planning to go on the run, he would've hidden the suitcase and passport before we arrived, wouldn't he?"

"I don't know," April replies. "But I think we should let the police know, just in case he's planning to skip town."

I nod. "I think you're right."

"Woohoo! Hi, Megan!" Trudy is on her porch, gathering her thick cardigan around her with one hand and waving at me with her other hand over her head.

"Hi, Trudy!" I smile and wave.

"You talk to Trudy, and I'll text Eric to tell him about Rick's suitcase and passport situation," April says. "I never get to tip him off about evidence." She sounds almost excited at the prospect.

"How are you, Trudy?" I ask, trudging across the snowy lawn toward her porch.

"I'm fine, Megan. How are you?"

"I'm well, thank you. We were just next door visiting Rick and Clawdia," I tell her. "I offered to drop off your donation suitcase at the library, but Rick wouldn't have it."

"It's for the best," Trudy says. "That suitcase is much heavier than it looks. I think it might be heavier than me." She laughs. "I couldn't even drag it across the lawn to his house. Rick had to come over here to get it."

"I didn't realize the book club takes donations all year," I say. "I know you do donation drives in response to natural disasters, but I didn't realize it was an ongoing program."

"Oh yes," Trudy responds. "We collect donations all year. The library generously stores them for us until we send them to displaced families."

"If you have a flyer or pamphlet or something to raise awareness about it, I'd be happy to post it on the community bulletin board at Knitorious," I offer.

"That would be wonderful! I have some flyers in the house. I'll get a few for you. I'll be right back." Grinning widely, Trudy holds up her index finger, reminding me to wait here, while she disappears into the house.

"WHAT DID TRUDY WANT?" April asks when I get into her car.

I show her the flyers Trudy gave me and place two of them on the back seat for April to display at Artsy Tartsy.

"It sounds like Rick was telling the truth about the suitcase." April lets out a sigh of relief. "Eric said he'll come to Rick's house and ask about the suitcase and passport. I hope we're not wasting police time and putting Rick through another interview with the police for no reason."

I feel her remorse. I felt the same when I told Eric

about the umbrella in Sheamus's office that turned out to be a false lead.

"We did the right thing by telling the police," I assure her. "It's possible Rick emptied the donated contents from the suitcase and packed it with his own clothes, or mixed evidence to the donated contents to dispose of it."

Maybe Eric will find a missing penny loafer or a few umbrella pieces stuffed in there.

CHAPTER 28

THURSDAY, January 21st

The line of caffeine addicts at Latte Da inches forward, and I inch forward with it because I'm one of the caffeine addicts waiting patiently for my first caffeine fix of the day. My phone vibrates in my pocket, and when I look at the screen, I notice a missed call notification. The call was from Eric. He tried to call me early this morning. Why isn't my phone making its usual ringing and dinging sounds?

April: Did Eric tell you what was in the suitcase?

Me: I haven't talked to him yet. I'll ask him and let you know.

I inspect my mysteriously quiet phone for the cause of its silence. Mystery solved; sometime between last night and this morning, I accidentally hit the silent switch on the side of the phone.

Why did Eric call me so early? Is everything OK?

Maybe there was a break in the case. I'll text him instead of calling him, in case he's in a meeting. Now that he's the police chief, he's in a meeting more often than not.

Me: Good morning! I'm sorry I missed your call. I accidentally turned off the sound on my phone.

Eric: Happy Anniversary!

I'm a bad girlfriend, I totally forgot to wish him happy anniversary. I mean, I *know* it's our anniversary, but I haven't thought about it since waking up. I was caught up in my morning routine.

Me: Happy Anniversary! Are you in a meeting? Can I call you?

Eric: I'm not at the station right now.

Me: Where are you?

"Behind you."

I almost jump out of my skin at the sound of Eric's voice, much to the amusement of my fellow caffeine addicts.

"You scared me." I clutch my chest with one hand and swat him with the other. "Why didn't you tell me you were here?"

"I was about to, but then you texted me," he replies, laughing. "I didn't mean to scare you. I'm sorry." He's laughing so hard, I can barely make out what he's saying.

Eric joins me in line, and we inch forward.

"What are you doing here?" I ask.

"Getting you a coffee," he replies. "I wanted to see

you and say happy anniversary in person."

"Happy anniversary." I stand on my tippy toes and kiss him. "Where are we going tonight?"

"It's a surprise," Eric reminds me.

"If I don't know where we're going, how am I supposed to know what to wear?" I ask.

"You always wear just the right thing," he replies. "It's one of your superpowers."

Coffee in hand, we meander up Water Street toward Knitorious, and I hook my arm through his. "Did you have time to look inside Rick's suitcase?"

"I sure did," Eric exclaims. "Kids clothes, kids shoes, kids boots, kids snowsuit, board books, story books, and a few stuffed animals."

"Oh. Another dead end." My voice sounds as disappointed as I feel.

"I prefer to think of it as eliminating one more line of inquiry."

I guess that is a more positive way to look at it. "What about the rumour that Saxon was planning to fix the election?" I ask. "Did you find any evidence to support it?"

"Nothing," he replies.

Inside Knitorious, I lock the door behind us because the store doesn't open for another fifteen minutes.

Eric and Sophie greet each other, and Eric suggests that we take her for a walk together. I tell him that Sophie and I already had our morning walk, and I need to unlock the door in a few minutes.

"It's kind of Sophie's anniversary too," he reminds me.

"You're right," I admit. "Sophie came to live with me a year ago this month." I crouch down and rub her between the ears. "We've had a big year, haven't we, Soph? Lots of big changes for both of us."

"For the better, I hope?" Eric asks.

"Definitely," I tell him just as my phone dings.

Adam: Can I borrow your escargot dishes?

Me: Sure.

"I didn't know you like escargot," Eric says when I tell him why Adam is texting me.

"I don't," I tell him. "I use escargot dishes when I make baked garlic shrimp or stuffed mushrooms."

Adam: Thanks. Can I please have your baked garlic shrimp recipe? I'm cooking for Jess tonight.

Me: Sure.

Adam: Can I pick them up around 3 p.m.?

Me: I'll be at work, but if you text me when you get to chez Martel, I'll let you in with the app.

Adam: Great! Thanks, Meg!

For the next few minutes, I use my feminine wiles to persuade Eric to tell me where we're going tonight and what my anniversary gift is. Just as my charm is wearing down his resistance, and I'm sure he's about to tell me what I want to know, the thud of the back door closing interrupts us. He's teased me for weeks about this mystery gift, and now that the day is finally here, I want to know what it is.

"Good morning, my dear," Connie sings as she enters the store from the back room. "Good morning, Eric. It's nice to see you. It feels like we haven't seen each other in days." She gives Eric a maternal hug, complete with back rubbing and swaying.

"I haven't been around much because this case takes up most of my time," he explains, sounding apologetic.

"I'm not complaining," Connie clarifies. "Take all the time you need to clear Ryan and Adam's names."

Eric tells us he has to get back to the station, and I offer to walk him to the back door. Connie tells us to take our time, and she'll take care of opening the store. Then she smiles mischievously at us and giggles a very un-Connie-like giggle.

"Thank you for the coffee," I say when we get to the back door.

"Thank you for the happiest year of my life," Eric replies. "I'll pick you up at six o'clock. I love you."

"I'll be ready. I love you too."

I'M HELPING a customer find a wool-free yarn for her project, and she's deep into the story of how she found out she has a wool allergy, when the sound of the bell over the door gets my attention. I know Connie is at the front of the store, so I don't interrupt my customer to turn and greet the new visitor.

Moments later, a tap on my shoulder. "Phillip is here

to see you, Megan," Connie informs me. "Why don't you see what he wants while I show this lovely lady the cotton-silk blend that came in last week."

I excuse myself from my customer, assuring her that Connie is Canada's foremost yarn expert, then thank Connie and leave them to it.

Phillip is fussing with a gorgeous floral arrangement on the coffee table in the cozy seating area. A gorgeous and familiar floral arrangement.

"Hi, Phillip," I say. "Hey! Am I having déjà vu, or I have seen this exact floral arrangement before?" Déjà vu used to be a rare sensation, but this week it's become a regular occurrence.

"It's not déjà vu," Phillip hints. "You've definitely seen this before."

I retrieve my phone from the counter and unlock the screen, then I swipe through the camera roll, stopping to look at each floral arrangement I received last year.

Last January, Eric and I attended a fundraiser together. One of the fundraising events was a silent auction with prizes donated by local businesses. Phillip donated a year's worth of floral arrangements, and Eric had the winning bid. As a result, every month last year I received a gorgeous, seasonal floral arrangement. I took pictures of them. They are truly works of art. Phillip is more than a florist; he's an artist whose medium is flowers.

"Found it!" I declare. "This is identical to the floral arrangement you delivered last January."

"You are a good little sleuth, aren't you?" Phillip teases. "Is there a date on that photo?" he asks, nodding toward my phone.

I bring up the information about the photo. I took this photo one year ago today. "Same floral arrangement on the same date," I observe. "Phillip, my year of floral arrangements ended last month."

"Lance Romance renewed it for another year," he explains. I assume "Lance Romance" is Eric. "You have twelve more arrangements coming to you—well, eleven after today—and he requested that this month's arrangement be identical to last January's arrangement, and that I deliver it on the same day at the same time."

That's a lot of specific requests.

"You remember the *exact time* you delivered flowers a year ago?" I ask, astonished.

He flicks his wrist. "I have no idea. But I try to finish my deliveries before lunch, so I assume it was in the morning. He was fine with that."

"Well, thank you, Phillip. They're just as beautiful this January as they were last January."

I'm not sure Phillip heard me because he's looking past me. I follow his gaze to see what's distracting him and land upon the wool-allergic customer incessantly scratching both of her palms simultaneously.

"What's wrong with Connie's customer?" Phillip whispers.

"She must've come in contact with wool. She has a wool allergy," I whisper.

"Why would she come to a yarn store if she has a wool allergy?" he asks.

"Why do people allergic to chrysanthemums go to Wilde Flowers?" I retort.

"Touché," Phillip replies without taking his eyes off the itchy customer.

Believe it or not, this isn't uncommon. Lots of knitters are allergic to wool or other common knitting fibres. We keep a box of antihistamines under the counter for just such occurrences.

I walk around the counter and dig out the antihistamines to offer them to the itchy knitter.

"While you're near the cash register, here's the spare key for my store." Phillip reaches into his front pocket and produces the familiar, enamel key chain. "I'm glad you had it when I needed it."

I open the till and return the key to its spot under the cash drawer.

"Rick fixed the lock, I assume?"

"Oh yes," Phillip confirms. "It took him less than five minutes, and he made it look so easy! The lock is fine now, and I had another key cut. Who knew Rick Ransan is so handy?"

"Not me," I admit.

"Megan! Thank goodness you're here!" Pete Feeney exclaims before the bell above the door stops jingling.

His outburst gets everyone's attention. Even the itchy knitter stops scratching to see what's going on.

"Pete! What's wrong? Did something happen?"

Phillip demands.

"I'm so glad you're here," Pete says urgently, looking at me and ignoring Phillip's question. "Do you still have the envelope I gave you on Monday? The one with the listings?"

I nod. "Uh-huh. We haven't looked at them yet."

"Have you opened the envelope?" Pete asks.

To be honest, I forgot about the envelope. It's still in my tote bag. I've been carrying it around all week. When I look in my bag to find something, I see the envelope and remind myself to take it out of my bag when I get home, then immediately forget about it again. This doesn't just happen with envelopes; my bag is a black hole of things waiting to be remembered.

I shake my head. "No," I reply. "We haven't touched it." Pete's panicked expression is replaced with relief. "Why?" I ask.

"I gave you the wrong envelope," he explains. "I just realized that I gave your listings to a young couple looking for their first home, and I gave you the envelope with the young couple's mortgage application. It has their private information on it."

"I see," I say.

"That looks uncomfortable," Phillip says to the itchy knitter when she walks in front of him.

"It is," she confirms. "I squooshed the merino roving. I couldn't help myself." She shrugs and looks Phillip in the eye. "It was worth it. I regret nothing."

"It happens to the best of us," I assure her and notice

she's extended her scratching area to include the insides of both her forearms. "Pete, have a seat." I point to the cozy sitting area. "I'll be right back."

Pete opens his mouth to protest, but I pretend not to notice. I hand Connie the box of antihistamines and continue walking to the kitchenette to get our itchy customer a glass of water. Phillip follows me.

"Is it me, or does Pete seem a little too concerned about the envelope he gave you?" Phillip asks.

I'm glad I'm not the only one who thinks Pete's reaction is out of proportion to the issue at hand.

"A little," I agree, "but he has a duty to protect client information. Maybe the house-hunting couple are pressing him to produce their application."

"You're probably right." Phillip shrugs. "I should get back to the shop." We exchange a double cheek kiss. "Enjoy your flowers and enjoy your date tonight." He winks.

"You know where we're going, don't you?" I ask.

Philip pretends to zip his mouth closed with his thumb and forefinger, and before I can ask him anything else, he disappears through the back door.

The itchy knitter accepts the glass of water but declines the antihistamines because she carries a supply in her purse. While Connie rings up her purchase, I join Pete in the cozy sitting area. He stands up anxiously when he sees me approaching him.

"Is the envelope here?" he asks. "I need it."

I shake my head. "It's upstairs in the apartment. I

don't have a key," I lie.

I hate lying; it gives me anxiety, but I sense there's more to this story than Pete has told me so far, and every instinct I have is telling me not to give him the envelope.

"I *really* need that envelope, Megan."

Time to call his bluff.

"OK." I shrug. "Let's call Eric. I'm sure he'll be happy to come home and get the envelope for you." I pull out my phone to show Pete that I'm serious.

"Oh, no," Pete puts out a hand to stop me. "Don't do that." He wipes beads of sweat from his brow, then wipes his palms on his thighs. "I mean, I don't want to interrupt the police chief just for an envelope. Especially not when he has a murder to solve."

I don't know what's in the envelope, but whatever it is, Pete doesn't want Eric to see it.

"Are you sure?" I ask. "What will you tell your clients?"

Pete shifts his weight from one foot to the other, looking rather uncomfortable. "It's fine." He swallows hard. "I'll put them off until tomorrow. If I come back tomorrow, can you have the envelope here?"

"For sure," I assure him.

"Promise you won't open it," he teases, chuckling awkwardly, but I sense he's genuinely concerned I might.

"Promise," I assure him, smiling and crossing my fingers behind my back.

CHAPTER 29

PETE and the itchy knitter leave at the same time. He holds the door for her on their way out, which saves her from having to pause from scratching.

While Connie takes the itchy knitter's water glass to the kitchenette, I text Eric to thank him for the flowers.

Me: Phillip just delivered my gift. They're beautiful. Thank you.

I snap a picture of the floral arrangement and text it to him.

Eric: Glad you like them, but that wasn't your gift.

If a year's supply of floral arrangements isn't my anniversary gift, then what is?

I'm about to text him with more questions, when Connie interrupts me.

"Why did you lie to Pete about having a key to the upstairs apartment? The same key opens the store and the apartment."

"You're right," I admit. "I lied because my gut told me not to give him the envelope. Did you see his reaction when I suggested we call Eric? There's something in that envelope he doesn't want anyone to see, and I'm not sure it's a house hunter's mortgage application."

Connie nods. "I had a feeling he was lying to you too," she admits. "He was more nervous than a long-tailed cat in a room full of rocking chairs."

"The envelope is in my bag," I divulge. "I think we should open it."

"Let's do it!" Connie agrees.

I find the envelope in my bag and meet Connie at the harvest table.

The envelope isn't sealed with glue; it's one of those reusable interoffice envelopes with a string you wind around the button to close it and secure the contents inside. This is a good thing, because if Pete is telling the truth, and the envelope contains a mortgage application with personal information, I'll close it, and Connie and I will pretend we never looked at it.

"Kind of thick for a mortgage application," Connie observes as I pull the stack of papers out of the envelope.

The pile of papers is about a quarter of an inch thick and held together with a binder clip. I sit in the chair next to Connie, and together, we look at the cover sheet. "S R props and comps," we read aloud in unison.

"Is that Pete's handwriting?" I ask.

Connie shrugs. "I assume it is."

We flip through the papers. Listings. Every sheet of paper is information about a property in Harmony Lake.

"Definitely not a mortgage application," I confirm.

"I think these are listings for one of Pete's real estate clients, and comparable listings for comparison," Connie theorizes. "Archie and I must have viewed a dozen properties before we bought the condo, and our agent gave us a listing for each home we viewed, and listings for comparable properties to help us judge whether the property we were viewing was fairly priced."

I flip back to the handwritten cover page. "That explains the 'props and comps,'" I say. "It must be real estate speak for properties and comparables."

"But Pete was insistent this envelope contained a mortgage application." Connie takes the papers and flips through them one by one, looking for misfiled mortgage information, for proof that Pete didn't intentionally lie about the contents of the envelope.

"Don't people complete mortgage applications online nowadays?" I speculate. "Why would he bother printing a copy?"

"I don't know," Connie says. "But most of these listings are for properties owned by Saxon Renaud. And almost all of them have handwritten notes and numbers on them."

"Pete told me he likes to print listings and make notes on them for his clients," I say.

Connie is right. This looks like a package of Saxon's properties, organized by location.

Could this explain the "S R" on the cover page? S R could be Saxon Renaud's initials.

We open the binder clip for better access to the hand-scrawled notes on the listings. Beneath the binder clip, the listings are organized into smaller groupings of three or four properties held together with a staple. My mind flashes back to Sunday brunch when Adam and I discussed strategically purchasing a few of Saxon's properties to make the remaining properties less attractive to developers and investors.

"I think Pete was bundling Saxon's properties and looking for buyers," I say.

"You might be right," Connie agrees. "Look at this." She points to a name and phone number on a listing.

"Reginald White," I mutter. "Reginald White... Why is that name familiar?" I ask.

"Reginald White is the head honcho at Mega Mart," Connie reminds me. "Remember last year when he tried to purchase land from the Animal Centre and part of the Willows's farm for one of his mega stores?"

"Aaah, right," I say, nodding. "But why would Pete be wooing big-box corporations to sell them land in Harmony Lake?" I ask, dumbfounded. "He knows we have a bylaw against it, and his mother spent most of her life advocating to keep big-box stores out of this town."

Connie shrugs. "Maybe Pete was preparing to sell

the properties if Saxon won the mayoral election." Pouting, she shakes her head. "This will break Alice's heart, my dear. It would be best if she doesn't find out."

I nod. "I know, and I'm sure Pete has a perfectly reasonable explanation for this," I say with certainty, not feeling at all certain.

"According to the date on these papers, he printed them before Saxon died. He printed some of them weeks ago," Connie notices.

I wonder if this is the reason Saxon and Pete were having secret FaceTime meetings in the weeks before Saxon's murder.

"You don't think Pete and these listings had anything to do with Saxon's murder, do you, my dear?" Connie asks, her eyebrows pulled tightly together.

"Pete was eliminated as a suspect, remember?" I remind her. "And how would Pete benefit from Saxon's death? Saxon died before we knew the election results. If Saxon won the election, he would have to be alive to take office and reverse the big-box policy. Also, real estate transactions take longer if they involve the owner's estate than if the owner is alive."

If Connie and I are correct, and he was planning to sell Saxon's properties, Pete stood to earn a hefty commission from the transactions. It would be in Pete's best interest for Saxon to be alive.

When the bell above the door jingles, Connie jumps up to greet whoever is here, and I hastily gather up the listings, attach them with the binder clip, and slide them back inside their envelope.

"Hello," I greet the two ladies who are browsing through the shelves of sock yarn.

I walk to the front of the store and nonchalantly return the envelope to my bag.

"THERE YOU GO, SOPH," I say, pulling the purple and white fair-isle dog sweater over her head.

Sophie gives her head, then her body a good shake before she disappears into the store to see what she missed while we were out for our midday walk.

"Marla! What are you doing here?" I ask, fluffing out the curls which were matted down against my head because of my knitted hat. "Today is your day off."

"I came in so you can leave," Marla explains. "Connie and I are sending you home early, so you can get ready for your date tonight."

"That's sweet of you, thank you." I give her a hug. "Where is Connie?" I ask.

"On her break," Marla replies.

I'm about to tell Marla that I'll stay until Connie gets back from her break, when my phone dings.

Adam: *Running early today. Can you let me in?*
Me: *Yup*

I open the app on my phone and unlock the front

door. Adam sends me a thumbs-up emoji to let me know he's inside the house.

Two more customers enter the store, and Marla and I divide and conquer. I'm in the back room looking for a pattern book my customer special-ordered when my phone dings again.

Adam: Where are the escargot dishes?

Me: Dining room hutch, middle door, second shelf.

Adam: Why did you move them?

They've been in the same spot for twenty years, but I don't bother explaining this to Adam.

"Here you go," I say to my customer, holding up the book they ordered.

While I ring up the book, my phone dings. Twice.

"Thanks again. Have a nice day." I smile, handing her the book and receipt.

As soon as she turns to leave, I pull my phone from my pocket.

Adam: Where's your recipe box?

Same place it's been for twenty years, Adam!

Me: Pantry, top shelf, left side.

Adam: thumbs-up emoji

I'm tidying the shelves of sock yarn when it dings again.

Adam: Can't find the recipe box.

Imagine being able to make a brilliant legal argument but being unable to find a recipe box that's been on the same shelf for two decades. Unbelievable.

Me: Look again. It's black. It might be hard to see.

Geez, should I come over later and cook it for you too?

When my phone dings again, I'm tempted to throw the thing across the store.

Adam: You know about the squirrel in the fireplace, right? Also, I still can't find the recipe box.

What squirrel? The fireplace was squirrel-free when I left this morning.

Me: Are you sure?

Adam: About the squirrel or the recipe box?

Me: I'll be home in 10 minutes.

While I grab my bag, I whistle for Sophie to follow me to the back room, then I tell Marla that I have to leave and tend to a potential squirrel situation at home.

SOPHIE TILTS HER HEAD, mesmerized by the muffled scraping sounds coming from inside the wall.

"There's definitely something in there," I say to Adam. He's on his back with a flashlight, looking up the chimney. "Adam, your suit will get covered in soot. Get out of there."

I haven't used the fireplace in years, yet I still get it cleaned every fall. There's no soot to get on Adam's custom-tailored suit, but there's still no need to risk it.

"Keep the flue closed," he instructs, wiping and straightening his suit. We both look at the wall when the scratching gets louder. "Or if you get a pillowcase,

I'll hold it in place and you bang on the wall. Maybe we can knock it into the pillowcase and set it free."

I sigh. "Thanks, but I'll call Ryan. You have to go home and make dinner, and I have to get ready to go out tonight."

I send a quick text to Ryan, asking when he can fit my squirrel problem into his schedule.

"Ryan's rushed off his feet lately, he had to start a waiting list," Adam informs me. "I hope he can fit you in."

Me, too.

While I wait for Ryan to get back to me, I retrieve the recipe box from the top shelf of the pantry. It was in the back, out of view where Adam couldn't find it, despite being almost a foot taller than me and having a better vantage point.

I find the baked garlic shrimp recipe card and slam it triumphantly on the island in the kitchen.

"I swear, Meg, I tore that shelf apart looking, and it wasn't there."

Ding!

"I hope that's Ryan," I say, retrieving my phone from the family room. "He can come by after dinner and liberate the squirrel."

"Aren't you going out tonight?" Adam asks, taking photos of the front and back of the recipe card.

"Yes." I nod. Cancelling this date with Eric isn't an option; he's been planning it for weeks.

I type a response to Ryan, hoping we can figure out a solution.

"Ryan will come by after dinner. He'll text me when he gets here, and I'll use the app to let him in," I tell Adam.

"Perfect!" Adam responds, returning my recipe box to the top shelf of the pantry. "If Ryan has a problem, tell him to text me and I'll come over. It's the least I can do, Meg. You've gone above and beyond your ex-wife duties trying to get me eliminated as a suspect in Saxon's murder."

Trying is the operative word. But try as I might, I've only eliminated one suspect: Sheamus O'Brien. Everyone else has compelling evidence that points to them having motive, means, opportunity, or all of the above. Despite being frustrated at the lack of progress, I feel like the killer is right in front of me, but I can't see who it is. Like the squirrel stuck in my chimney, there's a clue here somewhere; I can't see it, but I know it's there. Also like the squirrel, it wants to be set free.

CHAPTER 30

"You're wearing the same outfit you wore on our first date!" Eric points out when I take off my coat at the restaurant.

"You said wearing just the right thing is one of my superpowers," I remind him, without giving Tamara credit. I don't want to throw her under the bus for giving me a hint.

We're seated in the same booth of the same restaurant where we had our first date one year ago tonight. In very sentimental and Eric-typical fashion, he recreated our first date. I hope he doesn't expect me to order the same meal because I can't remember what I ordered. I only remember being nervous and shocked that this hot guy, for whom I'd harboured a months-long secret infatuation, asked me out.

"How was your day?" he asks, taking my hand.

I tell him about the urgent visit Connie and I had

from Pete Sweeney, and about the contents of the envelope Pete gave me on Monday. Then I tell him about the squirrel situation at chez Martel.

"That's why my phone is on the table." I gesture to my phone. "Ryan said he'll text me to let him into the house."

"Where is the envelope Pete gave you?" Eric asks. "Do you still have it?"

"It's at home," I reply. "Still in my tote bag."

"Mind if I look at it later?" he asks.

"Of course," I reply. "How was your day?"

"We searched two of Saxon Renaud's vacant rental properties today," Eric informs me.

"Find anything useful?" I ask.

"Counterfeit election ballots," Eric replies.

"What?!" I'm gobsmacked. "So, the rumour about Saxon fixing the election was true?"

"He might have *wanted* to fix the election," Eric explains, "but the ballots we found are fakes. His plan was not carried out."

I wonder why it wasn't carried out.

On the surface, this gives Adam even more motive than he already had. But if Adam knew about a plot to manipulate the election results, he would have exposed the plot through appropriate, official channels like the police and the media. Adam has too much respect for the law and for the democratic process to handle it any other way.

The server comes to take our drink order and

deliver our menus. We decide we're not allowed to talk about work, or murder, anymore tonight.

Ironically, I order the same thing for dinner tonight that I ordered on our first date. I only know this because Eric told me after I ordered. He has an exceptionally good memory for details, especially when those details are food related.

After dinner, and before dessert, we exchange gifts. I go first and hand him a gift bag. One by one, he pulls out each item and lays it on the table. Paint swatches, a printout of a sofa, four upholstery samples, and a catalogue from a custom desk and cabinet maker.

"Are these clues?" Eric asks.

"Kind of." I shrug. "I've thought a lot about your suggestion that we renovate chez Martel to make it our home instead of my home, and I want us to do it. I thought we could start by converting the guest bedroom into a home office for you." Picking up the printout of the sofa, I say, "We'll still need your new home office to function as a guest bedroom occasionally, so I thought we could replace the bedroom furniture with a pullout sofa." I pick up the upholstery samples. "We need to choose a fabric for the sofa." I pick up the paint chips. "When we decide on a fabric, we can pick the paint colour, and finally"–I pick up the custom desk catalogue—"I thought we could get built-in cabinetry and a custom desk for you."

"OhMyGod! Are you serious, babe?" Eric asks,

beaming from ear to ear. "Are you sure about this? I wasn't trying to rush you."

I nod, smiling. "Positive. Like you said, we can do it at our own pace."

"This is the best gift you've ever given me! Thank you!" He leans across the table and kisses me. "Your turn." He hands me a small gift bag.

I rummage through the tissue paper until my hand finds an envelope.

I open the envelope and unfold two pieces of paper. Concert tickets. "We're going to see Matchbox Twenty?!" I declare, more loudly than I intend. "I love that band." I rush to his side of the table and throw my arms around his neck. "Thank you!"

I slide into the booth next to him and scan the ticket, looking for the date, and realize this concert isn't anywhere near Harmony Lake. I was expecting it would be Toronto, Ottawa, or maybe Montreal, but this concert is at The Pearl in Las Vegas, Nevada.

"Ummm, the concert venue is in Vegas," I say.

"There's another envelope in the bag," he says.

I pull out the tissue paper and place it on my lap, then I tilt the empty gift bag toward him.

"It must be in the car," Eric says, reaching for his coat. "I'll be right back."

As Eric makes his way to the parking lot, I stuff the tissue paper and other gifts inside their respective bags.

"Good evening, Megan." Out of nowhere, Alice Feeney is standing next to our booth, smiling.

"Hi, Mayor Feeney," I greet her. "It's nice to see you. Is it date night for you and Mr. Feeney?" I ask.

"Heaven's no," she replies, chuckling at the notion. "I'm having dinner with my sister. This is one of our favourite restaurants. I just wanted to tell you I got gauge with the needles you sold me." She winks. "See, I told you I always get gauge."

"I guess getting gauge is your superpower," I joke. "How is your grandson's sweater coming along?" I ask.

"Swimmingly!" Mayor Feeney responds, digging her phone out from her purse. "I have a few photos of it." She hands the phone to me. "See, I finished the yoke and separated for the sleeves. Now I'm working on the body. I might have this sweater finished sometime next week."

"It's beautiful," I say, swiping through the photos, then my phone dings. "Excuse me," I say, handing her phone back to her.

Ryan: I'm here. Can you let me in?

"It's Ryan Wright," I explain to Mayor Feeney.

While I tell her about the squirrel who moved into my chimney this afternoon, and how Ryan is working late to get rid of it for me, I open the app on my phone and unlock the door at my house.

Me: Unlocked

Ryan: I'm in.

"Maybe it's the same squirrel in our chimney last week," Mayor Feeney suggests. "It's possible, we live close enough to each other." She giggles. "Maybe he's moving from chimney to chimney until he finds one where the owners won't evict him."

We laugh. "Well, I hope he doesn't move back to your chimney after Ryan frees him from mine."

"I hope so too," Mrs. Feeney agrees. "But if he does, I won't call my Pete again to get rid of him, I'll call Ryan Wright."

"Why?" I ask. "Pete removed the squirrel on Thursday, didn't he?"

"He certainly did," Mayor Feeney confirms. "But we called him on Wednesday morning. I worried the poor creature would die waiting. I know Pete is busy, between being a full-time firefighter and part-time real estate agent, he's pressed for time most days. I don't want to make extra demands on his time, but if he'd just told me on Wednesday that he couldn't get there until Thursday night—who are we kidding, it was Friday morning—I would have found someone else to take care of it."

"I thought Pete said you texted him in a panic about the squirrel late Thursday night," I say. "I must've misunderstood."

"Or it's more likely he didn't want to admit that it took him a day and a half to take care of it," Mayor Feeney retorts, with a playful huff.

"Didn't you think it was odd when he showed up in the middle of the night to take care of the squirrel in your chimney?" I ask.

She shrugs. "Not really. Firefighting isn't a nine-to-five job. Between my husband and Pete, I'm used to shift workers coming and going at all hours. But it all worked out for the best, because if it weren't for that squirrel, Pete wouldn't have found the crack in our firebox."

"Oh?" I urge. "What does that mean?"

"It means we can't use our fireplace because it's a fire hazard," Mayor Feeney explains. "It must be a hair-line crack, because my husband and I can't see it with our old eyes. But Pete insists it's there, and I believe him. He's a trained fire professional. So, no cozy fires for us until Pete has time to fix it."

"No cozy fires," I agree, distracted by Mayor Feeney's version of events on Friday night. "Better safe than sorry."

The server shows up with our Black Forest cake at the same moment Eric returns from the parking lot. Mrs. Feeney gets up from the booth and greets Eric. She congratulates him on his appointment as police chief, and he congratulates her on her well-deserved retirement.

Mayor Feeney waves toward the door. "Well, I should get going, my sister is getting impatient, waiting to drive me home. Have a lovely evening, you two."

Eric takes off his coat and hands me an envelope. "It was under my seat," he explains, joining me on my side of the table. "That's what took me so long. I had to get the flashlight from my glove box and move the driver's seat to reach it."

I'm only half-listening, because I'm mentally stuck on a few things Mayor Feeney said.

"Babe, open the envelope," Eric says, bringing me back to the here and now.

"Right." I smile. I open the envelope. Two tickets to Las Vegas for the same weekend as the Matchbox twenty concert. "We're going to Las Vegas?" I ask, shocked. "I love Vegas."

"I know," he replies. "It's already arranged with everyone. Connie and Marla will run the store with Sophie, and Adam and April will take turns having Sophie overnight. You won't miss your weekly brunch with Hannah, because you can FaceTime with her and Adam from the hotel."

"Such a thoughtful gift," I say, then kiss him. "Thank you." I wave away the forkful of cake he offers me, and he redirects the fork to his own mouth.

"What's wrong?" Eric asks. "You're distracted. Did Mayor Feeney say something that upset you?"

I shake my head. "No. We talked about knitting and squirrels."

"I know that look," he says, pointing his fork at my face and speaking with food in his mouth. "You figured something out. Whatever Mayor Feeney said or did, it made you figure something out."

"Possibly," I confess.

"Can you tell me?"

"Can we talk about work?" I ask.

"Depends. Is it urgent?"

"I think I know where the murder weapon is."

"Let's talk about work." He puts his fork on the cake plate and pushes the plate away.

I tell Eric about my conversation with Mayor Feeney; a conversation I have a feeling changes everything.

CHAPTER 31

I DRIVE Eric's car home from the restaurant in Harmony Hills while he sends texts, makes phone calls, and organizes his team from the passenger seat.

I'm only privy to one side of the phone conversations, and none of the texts, but it sounds like he assigned officers to track down Pete Feeney and bring him to the station for questioning, and started the process of obtaining a warrant to search Mayor and Mr. Feeney's house.

"Where are we going?" I ask as I exit the highway in Harmony Lake.

"Your house," he replies without looking up from his phone. "I'll drop you off and pick up the envelope Pete gave you."

"Drop me off?" I ask. "Are you going to question Pete?"

Eric shakes his head, hits send, and flips his phone

face down on his lap. "We can't locate Pete," he says with an exasperated sigh. "He's supposed to be on duty at the fire hall tonight, but his shift captain says he left fifteen minutes ago, claiming he didn't feel well. He didn't give any details about his symptoms, and no one knows where he went when he left."

"Is he at home or at his parents' house?" I ask, knowing the police would have already checked there.

"No and no," Eric replies. "I posted officers at each location, in case he shows up."

"Maybe Pete truly is sick," I suggest. "Have you tried the hospital? The urgent care clinic? The pharmacy?"

"We're looking everywhere and anywhere. There's a BOLO on his truck, and every available officer is out looking for him."

"BOLO?" I ask.

"Be. On. The. Lookout," Eric explains.

"Ah," I acknowledge. "I doubt he's avoiding you. I mean, how could he know the police are looking for him unless…"

"Unless what?" Eric demands urgently.

"Unless Pete spoke with his mother, and she told him about our conversation at the restaurant. In that case, he might realize she contradicted parts of his alibi."

"Change of plan," Eric says, pulling himself up to his full-seated height. "Instead of your place, we're going to Mayor Feeney's house."

"Don't you need a warrant?" I ask.

"Not if Mayor or Mr. Feeney give me permission," he explains.

I nod, and Eric phones and texts his colleagues with new instructions.

※

"PULL over here and turn off the lights," Eric instructs.

I do as I'm told and pull over in front of the Henderson house. The Hendersons aren't home to alert the rest of the neighbourhood to our presence outside their house; they're in Winnipeg visiting their daughter and her new husband.

"Now what?" I ask.

We're so far up the street from the Feeney residence that I may as well have parked in my own driveway and walked here. I can't even see their driveway from here.

"Now we wait," he replies.

"For what?"

"For the team to get into position."

"Are the police surrounding the Feeney's house?" I ask. He nods. "Eric, they did nothing wrong. They're harmless octogenarians whose biggest problem right now is the crack in their firebox that's stopping them from enjoying cozy nights by the fire." I glare at him and pause for dramatic effect. "Being raided by a bunch of armed cops could cause them to have a stroke or something."

"We're also waiting for an ambulance," he assures me matter-of-factly. "It should be here any minute. It'll be nearby just in case."

"This seems over the top," I attempt to reason with him. "I'm sure if we knock on the door and calmly explain why we'd like to come in, the Feeney's would cooperate. She was a cop, like you, remember?"

"The Feeneys won't know we surrounded their house. My team is excellent. They're trained professionals." His phone rings, and Eric answers the call. After a few grunts of acknowledgement, he ends the call and unbuckles his seatbelt. "I'll be back in a few minutes with your vest." I doubt I'll need a bullet-resistant vest to protect me from the Feeneys. I open my mouth to protest, but he doesn't give me a chance to argue. "Unless you want to go home and wait there," he says, countering my unspoken protest. I shake my head. "Stay in the car. I won't be far. If you need anything, text me or yell. I'll hear you."

"Be careful," I say, trying to be supportive instead of argumentative. "I love you."

"I love you too." He closes the door softly behind him when he exits the vehicle, and I lock the doors.

The harsh glare of unnatural light reflects off the rearview mirror and into my eyes. I reach up and tilt the mirror to redirect the blinding glare. The headlights are likely from the ambulance that Eric said was en route.

Already jumpy, I flinch when the vehicle with the headlights behind me honks its horn.

"Eric? Megan? Is everything all right? Why are you pulled over?" A familiar voice shouts from the driver's side window.

"Ryan," I mutter to myself, unbuckling my seatbelt. "I better get out and tell him we're fine. Otherwise, he'll honk again or get out of his van and come over here."

"Is everything OK? I thought you guys were in Harmony Hills tonight," Ryan says, lowering his window as I approach his van.

"We were on our way home, and Eric had to stop to visit someone about something." I gesture vaguely to the houses around me, implying he could be in any of them, not necessarily the Feeney's house. "Work stuff." I shrug.

"Does it have to do with Saxon's murder? Is there a break in the case?" Ryan asks.

I tilt my head and scrunch up my mouth. "Maybe," I divulge. "I don't know the details." I resist the urge to tell Ryan how the squirrel he just rescued from my chimney, and his after-hours house call might have helped to crack the case wide open. "But it could be another dead-end."

"Hopefully, it's the real deal, and we can put Saxon's murder behind us," Ryan says, then he tells me he safely removed the squirrel from my chimney. Ryan suspects the critter chewed through the mesh chimney cap his dad installed several years ago—the last time a squirrel tried to set up house in the chimney. "Weather permitting, I'll come by in the next few days and install a new mesh cap. In the meantime, keep the flue closed."

"Thanks, Ryan," I say. "I know you're super busy, so I appreciate you fitting my squirrel into your schedule."

"That's what family is for," Ryan reminds me with a wink.

"I hear you're looking to hire a helper."

"I am," he confirms. "Do you know someone?" he asks with a chuckle.

"Maybe," I reply. "No promises, but I might know a guy. He's a trained locksmith, does basic plumbing, seems to know his way around an engine, and has experience repairing holes in drywall. Give me a few days to find out if he's available. I heard he might be planning to move." By move, I mean go to jail.

Ryan's eyebrows shoot up with interest. "Wow, he sounds great! It's more difficult to find the right person than you'd think," Ryan explains. "Most experienced handymen work for themselves. Less experienced workers need training and supervising, and I don't have time for that right now. If you know someone who would fit the bill, I'd be grateful if you'd give them my contact information."

"Leave it with me," I say.

Ryan smiles, then raises his window, and waves as he pulls away from the curb.

I wrap my arms around myself and shiver. I regret not taking my coat when I left the car. I jog back to the car, and jump inside, turning on the engine and turning up the heat to its highest setting.

Eric: Ryan just drove past the Feeney house. Did he see you?

Me: Yes. He pulled up behind the car and honked. I got out and spoke with him. I'm back in the car now.

Eric: Lock the doors and please stay in the car.

Me: thumbs-up emoji

Still shivering, I reach into the dark backseat for my coat. Instead of my puffy down-filled parka, I feel... hair? Stubble? Skin?

"Hello?" I whisper, my heart pounding so hard I can feel it in my ears.

"Don't scream, Megan."

"Pete?" I ask barely above a whisper.

"Don't scream," he instructs again. "I didn't mean to scare you."

"It's OK, I'm not scared." I'm terrified, but under the circumstances, it's best if we both remain calm. "What are you doing here? How did you get in the backseat?"

My phone is in my hand. I could unlock the screen and phone Eric in less than five seconds, but the glare of the screen would light up the interior of the car, and Pete would know I'm using my phone. Think, Megan, think!

"I was under the Henderson's giant evergreen tree. When you went to talk to Ryan, I waited until you were both distracted, then I hid under the glare of his headlights, army-crawled across the sidewalk, and snuck into the backseat. Thank goodness you left the car unlocked."

"Thank goodness," I agree. Why didn't I lock the car? Argh!!

"I was going to my parents' house," he admits, "but I can't get near it because there are police everywhere."

I can't help but think an innocent person would be concerned about a police tactical unit surrounding their elderly parents' home. If it were me, I'd want proof that my parents were OK. I'd ask if they are injured or in danger. I'd create a dramatic scene and demand answers. Pete isn't doing any of those things because Pete knows the police are here for him. I'll pretend not to know they're looking for him.

"Eric told me to pull over here," I explain. "He said he'll be right back. Something about picking something up for work. He said nothing about you or your parents."

I shouldn't feel guilty about lying, but I do. This is the second time today I've lied to Pete. He lied to me first, but two wrongs don't make a right.

"What did you say to my mother at the restaurant?" Pete asks.

I shrug. "We talked about knitting and squirrels," I reply honestly. "She showed me photos of the sweater she's knitting for your nephew. It was a pleasant and short conversation. Why? Did your mother tell you something different?"

If Eric shows up while Pete is in the backseat, it could get ugly. Pete could take me hostage. Maybe I'm already a hostage. Am I a hostage? Pete hasn't told me I *can't* leave, but I don't feel like I *can* leave, if that makes sense. Is he armed? It doesn't matter; he's bigger and stronger than me. If there was a struggle, I'd do everything in my power to escape. I'm sure I'd put up a better fight than Pete would expect, but in the end I'd lose. Physical strength will not save me from this situation. I need to make sure Eric doesn't come back to the car.

"No, she said the same thing," Pete replies cautiously.

"Pete, do you want me to drive you to your parents' house?"

"No!" he shouts. "Megan, do not start the car. Do you understand?"

"Totally," I say, covertly sliding my phone under my leg. I'm worried if it makes a sound or lights up, Pete will see it and take it.

"Turn off the car. Disengage the engine," he orders.

"OK," I say, disengaging the engine. "Can I please have my coat? It's in the back seat with you. With the heat off, it'll get very cold very quickly."

Pete heaves my coat over the centre console, and I cover my upper body with it as if it were a blanket. Hiding my hands underneath my coat-blanket, I press and hold the side button and the volume button simultaneously on my iPhone. Adam showed Hannah and me how to do this in case we ever need to discreetly call emergency services. Besides calling 9-1-1, it will send a text to my emergency contacts letting them know I'm in trouble and telling them my location. My emergency contacts are Eric and April.

"Thank you," I say to Pete.

Under the guise of adjusting my coat-blanket, I look down at my phone and ensure it's connected to 9-1-1. It is. Without looking, I slide the silent switch on the side of the phone to prevent the phone from making any notification sounds that would remind Pete my phone is here. I grip the phone tightly in my hand, like a lifeline.

"Where's your truck?" I ask, assuming it wasn't under the Henderson's giant evergreen tree with him.

"Why?" he snaps.

"Just curious," I assure him. "Making conversation."

"I didn't mean to snap, I'm sorry. I'm stressed."

"Stressed about what?" I ask.

"Lots of stuff," Pete replies.

"I'd feel stressed too if the police were surrounding my parents' house," I sympathize. "Are your parents OK? Did something happen?" I ask, feigning ignorance.

"The police think I killed Saxon Renaud," he blurts out. "I'm sure they're raiding every place they think I might go to."

I turn my head and crane my neck to look at him in

the back seat. It's dark because we're parked between streetlights, but Pete is lying on the floor. His body is crumpled and bent to squeeze his tall, muscular frame into the too-small space. He must be uncomfortable. Looking at his unnaturally contorted body, I get the urge to straighten my spine.

"Are the police right? Did you kill Saxon?"

CHAPTER 32

I SLIDE my coat-blanket farther down my body to ensure the microphone on my phone picks up his response.

"I didn't kill him on purpose. It was an accident," Pete confesses. "I'm not a killer." He pauses, then adds quietly, "Well, I guess I am a killer, but that's not who I am. It was a one-off. A blip. I'm a firefighter. I save lives, I don't end them."

Out of the corner of my eye, the lower branches of the Henderson's giant evergreen jostle briefly, then stop. Not in a windy way, but in a someone-else-found-Pete's-hiding-spot way. I take a deep breath, feeling slightly more relaxed, knowing help is only metres away. Or maybe it's the squirrel from my chimney taking refuge in the tree's thick branches for the night, who knows, but I choose to believe it's an armed cop.

"Heavy shoulders, long arms," I mumble. "Deep breath, Megan."

"What did you say?" Pete demands urgently. "Who are you talking to?"

"Myself," I reply. Then I explain about my heavy shoulders, long arms mantra, and we do it together a few times.

"Pete, tell me what happened last Thursday night. How did Saxon die?"

"It started long before Thursday night," he says with a sarcastic chuckle. "It started weeks ago when Saxon asked me if I'd be willing to help him sell his properties when he won the election."

"What did you say?" I probe.

"I said yes," Pete replies. "I never thought I'd have to do it. I didn't think he could win. How could the most hated man in town get elected mayor?"

"I hear you," I agree. "But he was so confident. He was convinced he'd win the election and reverse the big-box policy."

"There was a reason for his confidence," Pete informs me. "He had a plan to fix the election."

"How?" I ask.

"One of his shady creditors hooked him up with a counterfeiter who could make fake ballots. Saxon filled them in, voting for himself on most of them to ensure he'd win the election."

"Did he say which creditor hooked him up?" I ask, hoping it's not Jay Singh.

"Some woman in the city," Pete replies, much to my relief. "Saxon said her and the daughter manage the lending side of the business, and the sons manage the collections side. He was terrified of the sons."

"I see," I respond. "How did Saxon pay the counterfeiter? It's common knowledge that he was in a bad way financially."

"He sold everything he could," Pete explains. "His furniture, family heirlooms, electronics, even his car."

This explains the decrepit living situation I saw at Saxon's house when Rick and I rescued Clawdia.

"His plan to fix the election didn't work," I conclude. "Saxon didn't win the election."

"He planned to hire the shady lender's sons to swap out the ballots on election night, but they wouldn't do it without a substantial down payment upfront. He couldn't afford to pay them. That's where I came in."

"Came in how?" I ask.

"Saxon wanted me to start a fire at the town hall while the ballots were being counted. A small fire. Then, when the ballot-counters exited the building, he wanted me to use my mother's keys to sneak into the room where the ballots were being counted and swap the fake ballots with the real ones."

"He wanted to take advantage of your expertise as a firefighter, and your access as the mayor's son," I sum up.

"Exactly," Pete confirms. "But I wouldn't do it. I don't start fires, I put them out, and I don't fix elections. Anyway, I would've done time for either of those crimes."

He'd rather do time for murder than arson and election tampering? Baffling.

"Saxon must've become more desperate as the election got closer," I add, trying to move the conversation forward.

"He harassed me right up until election day. He kept reminding me that if he didn't win, I'd lose out on the commissions from selling his properties. He even had developers contact me to register interest in certain properties."

This explains the notes Pete wrote on the printouts of Saxon's properties.

"Those commissions would have been a lot of money, Pete. Weren't you tempted?"

"No, I wasn't," he insists emphatically, as though the suggestion offends him. "So, after the card game, he changed tactics and came at me from a different angle."

"Tell me about the card game," I say. "If you were the focus of Saxon's attention that night, why did he swap drinks with Ryan? Did Saxon trick Ryan into almost relapsing for his own amusement, or was there another reason?"

"The trick with the lime was a distraction, so Saxon could get me alone. The polls were about to close, and it was now or never for Saxon to implement his ridiculous plan. When Rick backed out of the game to help Trudy with Cat Benetar, Saxon saw an opportunity and seized it. He was desperate, he had nothing to lose. Saxon hoped that after Ryan took a sip of the alcoholic drink, he would rush off to a twelve-step meeting somewhere.

"Sheamus hates to play with less than five players, so the game would end early, and the rest of us would go our separate ways. Saxon could use that opportunity to ask me to drive him home, so he could get me alone. But that didn't happen. First there was a shoving match, then Ryan took off. We were scared Ryan might go somewhere and drink, so instead of going our separate ways, we each picked a direction and searched for him."

I doubt it will make Ryan feel better about what happened when he learns that he was collateral damage in Saxon's larger, twisted plot, but at least he'll have answers as to why Saxon pulled such a nasty stunt.

"Saxon didn't have a car," I point out. "It was snowing hard, and he wasn't dressed for the weather. He must've asked one of you for a lift."

"He was crouched next to my truck when I got there, hiding in the dark. He warned me to let him in or else," Pete admits. "After all, getting me alone so he could blackmail me was the reason he came to the card game."

"He blackmailed you?" Did Saxon Renaud's villainy have any limits? "With what?"

"With proof that I was working with him to reverse the big-box policy and invite huge retailers and restaurants to Harmony Lake.

"But you weren't, right?" I specify.

"Not actively," Pete elaborates. "But I had spoken with representatives from those companies, and Saxon and I had virtual meetings about it. Meetings he said he recorded."

"Those meetings would make Saxon look as guilty as you," I say.

"But Saxon had nothing to lose and didn't care what people thought of him. I have a life here. I have friends and family. If my parents thought I was involved in a scheme to destroy the town they dedicated their lives to serving, it would kill them."

"So, you killed Saxon to prevent him from exposing your role in his plan?" I clarify.

"Megan, he picked up his phone and threatened to call my mother," Pete discloses. "That phone call would have been like a nail in her coffin. It would have killed her. I didn't know what to do. I panicked. I drove around for a while, trying to talk him down, but he wouldn't hear it. Finally, I found a poorly lit side street and pulled over. Then I grabbed Saxon by the collar and dragged him out of my truck. I reached back into the truck and grabbed his stupid umbrella. I was going to drive off, leaving him and his umbrella on the side of the road. But he said if I didn't switch those ballots immediately, he would phone my mother, then post everything on social media for the entire town to see."

"What did you do?" I ask.

"I grabbed that stupid umbrella with both hands and used it to pin him against my truck by the throat."

I gasp audibly and bring my hand to my throat, which suddenly feels quite dry and constricted. "Oh, Pete."

"It was surreal. Time sped up and slowed down simultaneously. It felt like I watched his eyes for hours, waiting for the life to drain out of them. Yet, it also felt like he was gone seconds after I pinned him by the throat." Pete sits up and looks at me, placing his hand on the console between the front and back seats. "I didn't realize I was killing him. Believe me, Megan, it wasn't until I looked down and saw Saxon's feet dangling above the ground that I realized how much strength I used. And by then it was too late."

"I believe you," I assure him, gently placing my hand on top of his. I'm not sure how much of Pete's story I believe, but if he's capable of strangling a grown man with almost his bare hands, I want him to think I'm sympathetic and on his side. "Why did you take him to Lake Access Road in Adam's car? And how did you get Adam's keys?"

"I didn't plan any of this," Pete attests. "When I realized Saxon was dead, I knew I had to get rid of his body. I thought I could make it look like an accident. Visibility was awful that night because of the blizzard, and it would be easy for a driver to lose traction in the snow and accidentally veer off the road. I wasn't wearing my gloves, and my hands were cold. I lowered Saxon to the ground and leaned him against the tire of the truck. It looked like he was sitting. He didn't look dead. I shoved my hands in my coat pockets to get my gloves, and found two things, my cell phone, which I turned off, and Adam's keys. I don't know how Adam's keys got there. I suspect they fell out of his coat pocket when the coats fell on the floor during the shoving match. When Sheamus and I picked up the mess, Sheamus must've picked up Adam's keys and put them in the wrong coat. Our coats are almost identical, except Adam's is dark blue and mine is black."

This makes sense, and Adam's keys getting lost in the commotion is one theory Eric, Adam, and I considered from the beginning.

"So, when you saw the keys, you saw an opportunity to frame someone else for Saxon's murder?" I speculate.

"No," Pete shakes his head. "It wasn't like that. I wasn't thinking that far ahead. My pickup truck is big. I'm a muscular guy, but it wouldn't be easy to hoist Saxon's dead body into the back of my truck. Or into the front. My truck is just too high off the ground. Besides, I couldn't bear the thought of driving with a corpse in the passenger seat."

"Adam's car was more efficient, and less likely to injure your back," I say, finding it harder and harder to disguise my contempt.

"Pretty much," Pete responds, shrugging. "So, I shoved Saxon's body in a snowbank and used the shovel I keep in my truck to make sure the snow completely covered him. Then I turned my phone on and drove to my parent's place and parked in their driveway. I set my phone to silent and left it in my truck. Then I walked to Sheamus's house, hoping Adam's car would still be there."

This all sounds very premeditated for something that Pete insists he didn't plan. Remembering to turn off your cell phone so your whereabouts can't be traced, then turning it on again when it can give you an alibi, doesn't sound like the actions of someone in shock because they just spontaneously committed murder.

"You recovered Saxon and his umbrella from the snowbank and put him in Adam's trunk," I suggest.

"How did you know that?" Pete asks, looking confused.

"There was forensic evidence that Saxon was in the trunk," I reply.

Pete shakes his head. "I didn't think to clean the trunk. I only cleaned the parts of the car that I touched."

"You did a good job," I tell him. "They found none of your DNA or fingerprints in the car."

The corners of Pete's mouth quirk downward smugly, as if he's pleased to hear he did a good job eliminating the evidence.

"I took back roads to and from Lake Access Road, so no one would see me driving around in Adam's car."

"Smart." I almost choke on the compliment but force it out, anyway.

"I was going to leave his umbrella with him, but when I used it to pin him against the truck, I wasn't wearing gloves. I'm sure it would've led the police straight to me. I put the umbrella in the trunk, so if I got pulled over or something, it wouldn't be visible. Thank goodness I did that, because if I didn't, I wouldn't have noticed that one of Saxon's shoes came off when I lifted him out of the trunk and was still there."

Pete must've taken the umbrella and penny loafer out of Adam's trunk in my driveway, and that's when the lucky penny fell out of the penny loafer and onto the bumper of the car.

"Why did you call the tip line after you abandoned Saxon's body?" I ask. "If you hadn't called, he probably wouldn't have been found until spring. By then, any evidence on his body probably would've been destroyed by the elements."

"I didn't want an innocent person, or even a kid, to find the body. And I knew without a body Saxon wouldn't be declared dead right away, he'd only be a missing person. His estate would be in limbo. His executors will need to sell his properties to pay off his debts. I didn't want to delay that."

It's more likely Pete was hoping to be the real estate agent who would sell Saxon's properties and didn't want to delay his commission payments.

"And the stutter you pretended to have when you called the tip line was to frame Rick Ransan for Saxon's murder?" I hypothesize.

"Look, Rick would be a suspect anyway because he and Saxon spent so much time together, and everyone knows Saxon bullied him. The stutter was less about pointing the finger at Rick and more about leading the police away from me."

"Why did you leave Adam's car at my house?" I ask. "You could've left it anywhere."

"Do you want the honest answer?" Pete asks.

Of course, I want the honest answer! Hasn't he been honest so far?

"Yes." I nod.

"I was tired," he confesses. "The whole experience left me physically and emotionally exhausted. You live around the corner from my parents' house. It's a short walk from your house to theirs. Also, I know how much Adam loves his car, and I knew he would freak out when it wasn't where he left it the night before." Pete shrugs. "I figured you'd find it when you woke up, and Adam's panic would be short-lived."

"Adam's car has a sophisticated GPS tracking system. His panic would've been short-lived, anyway."

Even in the dimly lit interior of the car, I see Pete's jaw drop, and his eyes widen with worry.

"Then why didn't he use it to track me down that night?" Pete asks.

"His phone died," I reply. "He drained the battery using the flashlight on his phone to search through the snow for his missing keys."

"That was lucky," Pete says.

"So, you walked from my house to your parents' house and disturbed your parents, so they could verify your alibi?" I presume. "Did you actually remove a squirrel from their chimney?"

"I walked from your house to my parents' house and got my phone out of my truck. I missed a group text from Archie telling us we could stop searching because Ryan was safe. I responded and told them I was glad Ryan was OK, and that I already abandoned the search because my parents were having a critter crisis." He shrugs. "It wasn't a lie. I did abandon the search, and my parents did have a critter crisis." He pauses briefly, then adds, "I really removed the squirrel. You can ask my mother, she saw it."

"When you shoved Saxon's umbrella up your parents' chimney, did you lie to them about the cracked firebox to make sure they wouldn't open the flue to start a cozy fire and watch the umbrella fall into the fireplace?"

"I shoved the umbrella and penny loafer up there first, then I shoved a pillow up there last, so if someone opened the flue, nothing would fall out," Pete replies matter-of-factly. "How did you figure out that's where I hid the umbrella and shoe?"

The missing umbrella and penny loafer were hold-backs. Only the killer or someone with intimate knowledge of the crime would know about them. Same for Saxon's cause of death. Everyone believes he was run down by Adam's car. They don't know he was already dead when the car ran over him.

"I didn't mention the shoe, you did," I inform him.

"Mayor Feeney said you found a hairline crack in the firebox when you removed the squirrel. She said that she and your dad looked for it but couldn't see it." Should I make him feel guilty for lying to his parents? He seems to have more remorse about how all of this affects them, than about taking a fellow human's life. "She blamed it on their ageing eyesight, you know. She trusts you so much that it didn't occur to her you might be lying or mistaken about the crack."

"This will break her heart, Megan. You can't tell her."

"I won't," I assure him. "The police will. They even have an ambulance on standby in case your parents need medical assistance when they find out."

"It'll be your word against mine," Pete warns.

"No, it won't." I shake my head. "My phone has been connected to 9-1-1 the entire time we've been talking."

I hope it's connected to 9-1-1. I was so caught up in Pete's confession, that I haven't checked it in a while. I can't check it now, because I sense that Pete might attack if I dare move a muscle. He has nothing left to lose, he's desperate, and desperate people do desperate things.

"You're bluffing," he challenges. His eyes narrow, and his jaw muscles clench and unclench.

"Why do you think Eric didn't come back to the car?" I ask, hoping it's because he's been listening to our conversation remotely.

"Hand me your phone, Megan," Pete commands.

"Pete, I'm getting out of the car now."

Slowly, and without breaking eye contact with him, I move my hand out from under my coat-blanket so I can open the door.

Sensing that Pete is about to lurch forward, I brace myself and swallow hard. Suddenly, his chest and forehead light up with half a dozen tiny red dots. We notice them at the same time and look at his chest. Aim points. There are at least half-dozen guns aimed at him.

"They're on your forehead too," I whisper. "Are they on my forehead?"

Slightly unnerved at the thought of so many guns in such close proximity to me, I glance down and scan my own chest for tiny red dots. Nothing. Phew.

Pete swallows loudly and shakes his head. "No dots on your head." He raises his hands to his shoulders, palms out, in a surrender gesture. In the dim light of night, beads of sweat glisten across his brow. "Tell them not to shoot," he pleads.

Without taking my eyes off him, I slowly reach for the door handle, planning to step out of the vehicle slowly and carefully while keeping an eye on Pete. I don't know what I'll do after that, but running toward the Henderson's giant evergreen and taking shelter behind its thick trunk and dense branches is a possibility. So far, so good. Gently, I tug the handle and unlatch the door. It immediately flies open, and hands grab me by the arm and waist, yanking me out of the car.

CHAPTER 33

I CAN'T TELL if I'm walking or being swept along, but it feels like I'm calmly floating through the chaos.

The loud, frenzied scene outside the car is a stark contrast to the dark, quiet scene inside the car. A cacophony of voices, crackling radios, flashing lights, and out-of-sync boots thudding on the ground are almost loud enough to compete with the sound of my heart pounding throughout my entire body.

The officer's left arm is around my waist, and my right wrist is in his right hand. He says reassuring, comforting things, but I'm too overstimulated to process his words and respond.

Behind us, the commotion grows louder, even though we're moving farther away from it. I turn my head, but everything is a blur because we're moving too fast. The scuffling intensifies, and desperate to see what's happening, I try to break free from my unchosen chaperone. He contains me, but not before I glimpse a pile of officers cuffing and searching Pete Feeney, who is face down on the frozen asphalt.

His parents must know by now that something is happening. His poor parents! I hope someone is with them. I hope they're OK.

We continue moving forward while I crane my neck and struggle to look back.

"You're OK, Megan. You're safe now."

"Officer Butler?" I snap my head to the right.

"Call me Lucas." He halts abruptly, then helps me stop when I keep going forward because of the momentum we built up. "Everything about that was amazing. You have mad interrogation skills."

"Thank you?" I respond, hoping it was a compliment.

Lucas's enthusiasm for Pete's arrest is palpable. He's so proud and excited. I remind myself he's a rookie, and this might be his first time attending the takedown of a murder suspect.

"I've never heard a live interrogation before." Lucas shakes his head. "The way he just opened up and told you everything... The way you encouraged him to keep talking... How did you stay so calm? It was sick!"

The English language has evolved a lot in my lifetime, and I'm fairly confident the young people have redefined "sick" as a good thing. I've heard my daughter use it with friends and in social media posts. But to be sure, I better ask.

"Is 'sick' good or bad?"

"It's *good*," Lucas confirms. "It's like saying something is cool or groovy."

"Right," I acknowledge. "Thank you for pulling me from the car, Lucas. You were great." I smile.

In our previous conversation, Lucas hinted he hasn't attended many crime scenes. I want to assure him he's doing a good job.

"The chief trusted me to take care of you, and I won't let him down," he says proudly.

He guides me to a gurney, and I realize we're standing next to an ambulance. Lucas positions me in front of the gurney and applies gentle pressure to my shoulder encouraging me to sit down.

He's so young; everything about him is youthful and full of potential. He reminds me of my daughter, idealistic and determined to make the world a better place. Lucas is only three or four years older than Hannah—too young to be taking down cold-blooded murderers and seeing the worst humanity has to offer. Something about him triggers my maternal instincts. I want to ask him if he's cold and suggest he put on his gloves, and I want to make sure he had dinner, but I don't. I resist my maternal urges.

Lucas moves aside, and an EMT swoops in, fussing over me and asking me questions about my breathing, chest pain, and any injuries I might have.

"I'm fine," I assure her. "Honestly. If anything changes, I promise to seek medical attention."

"Humour me and let me check your vitals, please."
She has a calming presence and a pleasant bedside
manner.

She's doing her job, and I don't want to be difficult. So, I sit still, answering questions when asked,
and cooperating when she tells me to take a deep
breath, then let it out. I zone out, watching the red
gauge wiggle back and forth on the blood pressure
cuff, my mind spinning with everything Pete told me
in the car.

"Megpie! Over here!"

The sound of my best friend's voice brings me back
to the present.

"Thank you," I say when the EMT releases me from
the cuff.

I jump off the gurney and race toward April with
my arms open.

"Where are you going?" Lucas calls after me.
"Megan! Hold up!" His boots thump behind me when
he gives chase.

April is standing behind a barricade; she's too far
away.

We wrap our arms around each other tightly,
squeezing the barricade between us.

"I'm so happy to see you," I say, tearing up. "What
are you doing here?"

"Your phone sent me a text with your location when
you called 9-1-1," she explains. "What the heck
happened? Why were you sitting on a gurney?" She

pulls away and grips my shoulders. She scans me from head to toe, then back again, looking for injuries.

"I'm fine," I assure her. "They're being overly cautious."

April and I move to the end of the barricade, away from the crowd. Lucas moves with us, staying a few feet behind me. I can't see him, but I can sense his hovering.

Whispering in her ear, I give April the abridged version of everything that happened tonight, starting with the conversation Mayor Feeney and I had at the restaurant.

"Wow. I'm speechless," April says when I finish filling her in. "Thank goodness you're OK." She hugs me tightly and rubs my back. "You're shivering. Where's your coat?" she asks.

"Backseat of Eric's car," I reply. "I feel and see myself shivering, but physically, I don't feel cold." Actually, I feel kind of warm, like I was running or something.

"Adrenaline," April diagnoses. "When it wears off, you'll feel cold. Let's go over to the ambulance and borrow a blanket, then we'll ask if you can have your coat."

April's impossibly long legs step gracefully over the barricade.

"Ma'am, you can't do that. Get back behind the barricade. That's why it's there." The officer points from April to the barricade, like he's ordering a rebellious teenager to her room.

"She's fine, she's allowed to be here," Eric says, jogging toward us, taking off his coat. "There you are. I told Butler to keep you at the ambulance," he says, draping his coat over my shoulders.

"It's not Lucas's fault," I defend the rookie, shaking my head. "I ignored him and ran away." Eric wraps his arms around me and kisses the top of my head. "Lucas did a great job."

He tells me he loves me under his breath. Three times. His hug grows progressively tighter until I have to gasp for air.

"Sorry," he says, letting go and taking a step back to appraise me from head to toe like April did.

The EMT should hand out stickers that say NOT INJURED, so I can stop insisting I'm fine; it would save time.

"I'm not hurt," I assure him.

"I know," Eric says, "If you were, Pete Feeney would be full of bullet holes."

"You're trembling," he observes, drawing his eyebrows together. "Are you cold, or is it adrenaline?"

I nod, because at this point, I'm not sure.

April taps my shoulder. "Megastar, if you need me, I'll be over here." She jerks her thumb over her shoulder. "My phone is blowing up. Everyone is worried, and I need to let them know what's happening."

"Thank you," I respond. "You're the best. Tell them I'm not ignoring them. I left my phone in the car." It fell out of my hand when Lucas yanked me, but I don't say this out loud because he's within earshot, and I don't want him to feel bad.

"Butler," Eric calls the rookie, and he rushes over. "Can you please retrieve Megan's coat and phone from my car? Thank you." He smiles.

Eric takes me by the hand and leads me between two houses. It's pitch black, and we're standing in about a foot of snow. He hugs me again, but his body is more relaxed this time. His heart rate is slower, and he doesn't try to squeeze the air out of my lungs.

I pull away first this time. "It's all on tape, right? The entire 9-1-1 call was recorded? It's a good confession?"

I don't mean good as in well done or critically acclaimed. Eric distinguishes between good and bad evidence. Good evidence is evidence that will hold up in court. Bad evidence isn't admissible but helps the investigation along and usually leads to good evidence.

"It's a beautiful confession." He smiles. "It's so good, a couple of cops want the transcript to study it."

"Consider the confession part of your anniversary gift," I tease smugly.

"As great as the confession is, an even better gift would be not almost having a heart attack when your phone texted me to tell me you were in trouble, then a 9-1-1 dispatcher calling me so I could listen to you and Pete."

"I'm sorry you were scared."

"I was terrified, babe." He exhales loudly, and his eyes fill with moisture that twinkles in the moonlight. "I feel like I aged ten years in the fifteen minutes you were in the car with him."

"I didn't know what else to do," I confess. "I was afraid if you or someone else approached the car, it might push him over the edge. I felt like I could manage the situation if it was just me and him."

"You did the right thing," Eric insists. "And we had the car surrounded immediately. Pete wouldn't have been able to hurt you if he tried." I nod. "Trust me, if he tried, he would be dead. It took all my willpower not to get you out of there."

"I half-expected you would," I admit. "Why didn't you?"

"Three reasons. First, we didn't know if Pete was armed. Second, I had faith you would save yourself. It's one of your superpowers. Third, I knew he'd confess for you. You have a way of getting people to talk. If I had burst in there before Pete confessed, you might have never talked to me again."

He's right. As soon as Pete started talking, I had a feeling he would confess, and if Eric stormed in and prevented the confession, neither of us would be happy.

"Was Pete armed?" I ask.

He shakes his head. "No, thank goodness."

Eric's phone dings. "Butler. He has your coat and your phone." I nod again, and my teeth chatter. "Are you starting to feel cold?"

"Uh-huh," I reply, thinking about how nice the heated seats in the car will feel.

"The adrenaline is wearing off. Let's get your stuff and get you home. I started the car, so it'll be nice and toasty." Eric takes my hand and leads us back into public view. "We'll take your statement tomorrow."

"April can drive me home," I suggest.

"I'll drive you," Eric responds. "April can meet us there. She can stay with you while I come back to talk to Mayor and Mr. Feeney."

"How are they?" I ask. "Do they know Pete killed Saxon?"

"I'm not sure," he replies. "Two of their children are with them, and their daughter is worried about Mr. Feeney's heart. She asked us to wait and talk to them with medical assistance nearby. Obviously, we're honouring that request. Now that the medics have checked you and Pete, we'll send them to the Feeney house, and I'll meet them there."

"I can come with you," I offer. "If you think it would help."

"It would help if you were safe and sound at home."

"I bet this will be our most memorable anniversary ever," I point out.

"I hope so," Eric responds. "I don't think my heart can handle an anniversary more exciting than this one."

CHAPTER 34

WEDNESDAY, March 3rd

It's unseasonably warm for early March, and the cloudless, sunny sky makes it feel downright spring-like. Spring doesn't officially arrive for two more weeks, but today Mother Nature is teasing us with a sneak peek of the warm days ahead.

To take advantage of the unseasonably warm day, we walked to Harmony Lake Town Hall this morning to attend Mayor Feeney's community spirit award ceremony.

The community spirit award is one of our town's highest honours and recognizes the contribution Mayor Feeney has made to the quality of life and community spirit of Harmony Lake.

It was a lovely celebration, with several residents sharing funny and touching anecdotes about her and paying tribute to her long history of civic pride and contributions to our community.

Besides a plaque, Mayor Feeney's name will be engraved on the wall of fame at the town hall alongside the previous award winners, and the town council voted to rename the waterfront playground, Alice Feeney Park.

Most of the businesses on Water Street closed, so the owners and employees could attend the ceremony. A group of us are heading back to our respective businesses, walking as leisurely as possible to maximize our time outside.

"Mayor and Mr. Feeney seemed in good spirits," April comments. "It's nice to see them out and about again and not worried that the media will ambush them."

"I know," I agree. "It almost feels like the town is back to normal."

The story about Saxon Renaud's murder, his attempt to fix the election, and Pete's arrest was picked up by a regional news outlet. They spun it like some kind of Murder She Wrote, small-town mystery, and it drew attention from other media outlets who wanted to report the story.

Pete agreed to accept a plea deal and avoid a long, drawn out trial when his siblings convinced him that the unwanted attention and stress of a trial would harm their parents' health.

In exchange for some concessions in his plea deal,

Pete provided information that helped Eric track down the shady lender who hooked up Saxon with the counterfeiter. The lender was more than happy to point Eric toward the counterfeiter, for Eric not tipping off her local police department about her quasi-legal lending operation.

"Bon voyage," April says as we pass Artsy Tartsy, and she and Tamara stop to go inside.

"I'll text you," I promise, then hug them because this is the last time I'll see them until Eric and I get home from Las Vegas.

"I spoke with Phillip and gave him a key," Eric says. "He said he's fine to let the cabinet makers in and out of the house while we're away."

"Great," I say, taking his hand. "Thank you for looking after that."

The guest room renovations are underway, and by the time we get home next week, Eric should have a fully functioning home office.

"Are we property owners yet?" Connie asks as she unlocks the door at Knitorious.

"I don't think so," I reply. "Adam said we probably won't hear anything for a couple of weeks."

"It's so exciting!" Connie says. "I hope they accept our offer."

After Saxon's murder was solved, and Adam and Ryan's names were cleared, Adam and I called a family meeting and told everyone about his idea to purchase a few of Saxon's properties. We showed everyone our research and our projections. There was more interest than we expected, and now Eric, Adam, Connie, Archie, Ryan, April, Tamara, and I have formed a property management company called Oppidum Group. Oppidum is Latin for *small town*. We submitted an offer on a few properties, and Saxon's estate is considering it. Some members of our corporation are more impatient than others.

"Hey, Soph! Did you miss us?" I crouch down and rub her. She's not used to being alone at the store during the day. I felt guilty leaving her here, but the only dogs allowed at the town hall are service dogs.

"I'm going to change out of this suit and get my luggage," Eric says. "I'll be down in a few minutes. We need to leave by noon if we're going to get to Toronto in time for dinner with Hannah."

"My luggage is already in the car." I smile.

One of the few downsides to living in a remote town is the five-hour drive to the airport. Our flight to Vegas is tomorrow, but we're driving to Toronto today and staying in a hotel tonight. Having dinner with Hannah the night before we leave, and the night we get back, is a bonus.

Sophie goes into greeter mode when the bell over the door jingles.

"Hey, Rick! How are you?"

"I'm good, Megan. How are you?" He greets Sophie then walks over to the counter.

"I take it you aren't here to buy yarn?" Connie jokes.

"No, but I have a question about knitting," he replies.

"I'm intrigued," I say. "What can I help you with?"

"Clawdia loves the knitted mice you made for her. Especially the one filled with catnip. I want to get a few more, but they're sold out at the Animal Centre. Do you sell them here?"

"I don't," I reply. "But I have ten hours' worth of car rides and ten hours' worth of flights in the next week, and I'm sure I can use that time to make a few more mice for Clawdia," I offer.

"That would be great! Thank you," Rick responds. "I'll pay you for them, of course."

"No, you won't," I correct him. "If you want to pay it forward, make a donation to the Animal Centre."

"I can do that," Rick says. "Ryan and I are doing some roof repair work there next week. I'll knock a little off their bill. It's the least I can do after you set me up with Ryan."

The Charity Knitting Guild's cat toy drive was an enormous success. Between in-person sales at the gift shop, and on-line sales through their website, they sold out of toys within a week. I think the charity knitters are planning toy drives regularly. I've already started knitting mice for the next one.

Rick and Ryan work together now. I suggested it to both of them as soon as Rick was cleared as a suspect in Saxon's murder. They have complementary skill sets, and Ryan was exhausted from all the hours he was working. For the first month, Rick was Ryan's employee, but then they became partners. Instead of calling themselves, The Wright Men For The Job, which was the name of the company when Archie and Ryan worked together, they're now called, R & R Handymen. Their tagline is: We repair & renovate while you rest & relax.

Ryan is working normal hours and taking two days off each week. He and his partner, Lin, could book a last-minute getaway a few weeks ago and spend some time together enjoying the sun and the beach. Rick is more outgoing every time I see him. He's getting to know people in the community, and they're getting to know him. He started seeing a speech therapist, and I can't remember the last time I heard him stutter.

Rick opens the door to leave and holds it for Sheamus and Kelly, who are on their way in.

"Ya still in for poker tomorrow night, fella?" Sheamus asks Rick.

"Wouldn't miss it," Rick replies, then says goodbye to everyone and leaves.

"Why, Sheamus O'Brien, I don't think we've ever had the honour of your presence at Knitorious," Connie declares.

I think she's right. I can't remember Sheamus ever being here.

"Well, my girlfriend's a knitter, so you might wanna get used to me stopping by," he retorts proudly.

"Kelly, I'm glad you're here. I want to show you the

hat I made with the alpaca yarn you gave me." I rummage around under the counter and pull out the hat.

"It's beautiful," Kelly compliments. "What do you think of the yarn? Did you like it?"

"I loved it," I reply. "I gave half of each skein to Connie, so she could take it for a test drive too."

"And?" Kelly asks anxiously, looking at Connie.

"It might be the nicest bulky alpaca I've ever had the pleasure to knit with," Connie says.

Kelly claps her hands in front of her chin. "I can't wait to phone my uncle's wife and give her your feedback. She'll be so happy." I wonder if she'll be as happy as Kelly appears to be.

I'm not sure if it's the positive yarn review or Sheamus that's making Kelly downright giddy. I don't care, it's just nice to see her thrive again.

"When you talk to her, tell her I would be honoured if Knitorious was the first yarn store to carry her line of alpaca yarn."

"Really?" Kelly asks, wide-eyed and grinning. "Thank you, hun! I'll phone her as soon as I get back to the salon!"

The bell above the door jingles, and Jess and Sophie make a beeline for each other. Jess loves dogs, but two of her kids have allergies, so she hasn't had a pet since she was a child. Adam is taking Sophie home with him tonight, and Jess can't wait to pretend she has a dog. From the look of it, Sophie can't wait either.

"Hey, fella, I thought you were still schmoozing and being all political at the town hall," Sheamus says to Adam.

"I've completed my mayoral duties for today," Adam says. "After lunch, I have to put in a few hours at my law practice."

"I sent you and April a copy of Sophie's schedule," I say to Adam. "Did you get it?"

"It wasn't a schedule, it was a complicated spread-sheet," Adam replies.

At least he looked at it; otherwise, he wouldn't know it's a spreadsheet.

"Do you have questions about it?" I ask. "Sophie is routine driven. She likes to know what to expect and when to expect it."

"The dog will be fine, Meg." I sense frustration in Adam's voice. "You trusted me to take care of our child, remember? And she's still alive."

"Point made," I agree.

"Is Sophie's stuff by the back door?" Adam asks. "I'll put it in the car before I forget."

I nod. "It's piled up on the counter."

"I have a copy of the spreadsheet, too, Megan," Jess reassures me from the sofa in the cozy sitting area. "Don't worry, it's under control."

"Thank you," I mouth to her.

I'm doing a mental inventory of Sophie's stuff to make sure I didn't forget to include anything when Kelly's phone rings.

"It's her!" she declares excitedly. She answers the call, then places it on hold and looks at Sheamus. "I can't wait to tell her what Megan and Connie said about her yarn. I'll just be a minute. I'll step outside."

"Take your time, a ghrá," he says as she walks toward the door, already talking on the phone.

"A ghrá?" I ask, having never heard the word before,

"It's Gaelic," he explains. "It means, my love."

"It sounds beautiful," I respond.

Sheamus joins Jess and Connie in the cozy sitting area, and they ask him to say other terms of endearment in Gaelic.

"Are you ready for your trip, Meg?" Adam asks, returning from the parking lot and leaning on the counter next to me.

I nod. "I'm looking forward to it. Thank you for taking care of Sophie."

"I don't mind," he says, "and look how happy it makes Jess." Adam straightens up and looks toward the back room, smiling.

"Hey, Adam," Eric says, approaching the counter.

"Hey, man. We'll miss you at poker tomorrow night."

"Hello, everyone," Eric smiles at Connie, Jess, Kelly, and Sheamus.

Kelly finished her phone call and came back in when I was talking to Adam.

"Are we ready to go?" I ask, leaning into Eric.

"We can leave whenever. My suitcase is in the car."

"I know Adam and I can't take Sophie home until tonight, but would it be OK if I took her for a walk?" Jess asks.

"Sophie would love that," I reply. "I'll go in the back and get her leash."

"Actually, Meg, I think I put the leash in my car." Adam pulls his keys out of his pocket and hands them to Jess. "It's in the trunk."

"Uh-uh," she protests, giving him back his keys. "No way. I'm not going anywhere near that trunk. It's creepy."

It is creepy. The corpse of a murder victim rode around inside that trunk. I'm not sure I'd go near it either.

The insurance company repaired the damage to Adam's car and had it detailed. He seems just as attached to it as ever, but some of the locals have developed a morbid fascination with it. It's not uncommon for people to ask Adam if they can look inside his trunk or even touch it.

"Come by the station when Megan and I get back. I'll bring out the cadaver dog, and we can see if he signals on your trunk," Eric suggests to Adam.

"Yes!" Adam points to Eric and laughs. "Let's do it. I bet he'll still smell it."

"You two are twisted," I say.

"I'll fetch the dog's leash for ya, Jess," Sheamus offers, probably to escape this macabre conversation.

He takes the keys from Adam and walks toward the back door. As soon as Sheamus crosses the threshold from the store to the back room, Kelly jumps up from the sofa.

"We only have a minute," she declares. "Phones out everybody and calendars open."

Not used to Kelly being this demanding, we do as we're told.

"Why do we need our calendars?" Connie asks.

"I'm planning a surprise birthday party for Sheamus," she explains. "Does Saturday April 10th work for everyone?"

We all nod and murmur out of sync.

"It doesn't interfere with Easter or with the Between The Covers Book Fair," Kelly informs us. She looks at me. "This date doesn't conflict with your dad's visit, does it, hun?"

I shake my head. "He's not scheduled to arrive until the following week. He's coming for the book fair."

"Perfect," Kelly says. "Save the date, everybody. I'll be in touch soon with the details."

"Here he comes," Connie says when the back door thuds shut.

"OK, well I should get back to the salon," Kelly announces. "Are you ready to go, sweetie?"

Sheamus nods.

"And Sophie and I will be across the street at the park for a few minutes if anyone needs us," Jess says.

"Jess, would you mind some company on your

walk?" Connie asks. "I want to enjoy as much of this rare warm day as possible before it disappears."

"I would love some company." Jess smiles.

Eric and I hug each of them goodbye, and they wish us a good trip.

"Why didn't you tell me Mitchell is coming to town?" Adam demands as soon as the door closes behind everyone.

"It's in the family calendar," I inform him.

"I don't look that far ahead in the family calendar," he says as though it's a previously established fact. "You know I need lots of time to brace myself before your father comes to town."

"Wait." Eric holds up his hand. "Why are you so freaked out about Megan's dad coming for a visit? Don't you get along?"

"Mitchell *hates* me," Adam explains. "He's hated me since the day we met, and every time we see each other, he hates me even more. And it's not just me, he hated his other sons-in-law too. But he hates me the most."

"Other sons-in-law?" Eric asks, looking both confused and concerned.

"My sister's current and ex-husbands," I clarify, so he doesn't think I have skeletons in my closet that might be the remains of husbands-past I haven't told him about.

"Do you think your dad will hate me, babe?"

"*Will* hate you?" Adam asks. "You haven't met

Mitchell yet?" Adam looks at me, then Eric. "How have you avoided meeting Mitchell?"

"I had a series of court dates in the city last time he was in town," Eric explains with a half-shrug. "I stayed over."

"That was lucky," Adam says. "If I were you, I'd book more court dates for the second week of April," he mutters.

"Stop trying to scare Eric," I chide Adam.

"He should be scared, Meg," Adam insists. "Every time your father comes to town, he brings trouble with him, and each incident is worse than the one before. It wouldn't surprise me if someone dropped dead during one of his visits."

"He's exaggerating," I reassure Eric.

At least I hope it's an exaggeration.

KEEP READING for a sneak peek of Sins & Needles: A Knitorious Murder Mystery book 7.

CLICK HERE to read an exclusive bonus scene from Crime Skein.

SINS & NEEDLES: A KNITORIOUS MURDER MYSTERY BOOK 7

CHAPTER 1

WEDNESDAY, April 14th

"I can't believe Claire Rivera will be here, in person! At our humble, little yarn store!" Marla claps her hands in front of her chin in delight. Her short, spikey pixie cut and brilliant blue eyes remind me of an excited elf.

My corgi, Sophie, jolts awake at the sound of Marla's clap, then realizing there's nothing to see here, lowers her head and resumes her nap.

Marla works part-time at my yarn store, Knitorious. Claire Rivera is her favourite author. Besides being the world-famous author of the hugely popular Familia series of books, Claire is also an avid needle felter and fellow fibre enthusiast. She's in town this week to attend Harmony Lake's annual Between the Covers Book Fair.

In honour of Claire's attendance at the book fair, our

local Charity Knitting Guild needle felted miniature versions of the characters and settings from Claire's famous book series. They're selling the miniatures during the book fair and donating the proceeds to ABC Life Literacy Canada, a nonprofit organization that supports community-based literacy programs.

Claire learned about the charity knitters' initiative when an anonymous fan—me! I'm the anonymous fan—sent her a link to an article on The Front Page, Harmony Lake's online newspaper. She emailed me, asking if she could visit Knitorious after-hours to view the display in person. I replied, telling her I'm closing the store early today for a special reveal for the charity knitters who crafted the display, and suggested that she would be welcome to attend. She accepted my invitation. To protect her privacy, and prevent mass disappointment if she doesn't show up, I haven't told the charity knitters that Claire is attending. The only people who know are me, Connie, Marla, my best friend, April, and my boyfriend, Eric.

"How's that?" I ask, after placing the last character into the display.

"Oh, Megan, it's perfect!" Marla replies, her blue eyes sparkling. "Claire Rivera will love it!"

Until this week, I never noticed how often we refer to famous people by their first and last names as if it's one name.

"I certainly hope so," Connie interjects. "As a needle

felter, Claire Rivera should appreciate the time and effort that went into this exhibit."

Needle felting is the process of repeatedly stabbing animal fibre with a barbed needle to manipulate the fibre into 3D sculptures. Each miniature character and object in our display took hours of work and thousands of stabs.

Connie is my other part-time employee and surrogate mother. Connie and I met when Adam, Hannah, and I first moved to Harmony Lake almost seventeen years ago. We became instant friends, and soon after, we became family. I lost my mum just after Hannah's first birthday, and Hannah was born when I was just twenty-one. So, when Connie and I met, I was a young, recently married, new mum who was grieving. I'd wandered into Knitorious to buy yarn because I had knitted through my entire yarn stash while knitting through my grief during Hannah's naps. Connie welcomed us, nurtured us, and filled the mother and grandmother-shaped holes in our hearts. At almost seventy-one years young, she's the most beautiful, smart, and sophisticated woman I know. Connie is the original owner of Knitorious. I started working for her part-time about six years ago. Last year, she decided it was time to retire and move out of the apartment above the store. She moved into a new condo with her boyfriend, Archie, and I took over as owner of Knitorious. So, now I own Knitorious, and Connie works for me part-time. We've come full circle.

"According to the Harmony Lake rumour mill, Claire Rivera has been in town for over a week already," Marla informs us, smoothing her salt-and-pepper pixie cut. "Rumour has it she and her assistant are staying in a rental cottage on the lake, and she's writing the next *Familia* book."

Most of that is probably true. The Harmony Lake rumour mill's remarkable accuracy rate is matched only by their speed and dedication.

"Has anyone seen her around town?" I ask.

"Not that I've heard," Marla responds, "but apparently, she's reclusive when she's working."

"Claire Rivera isn't the only celebrity in Harmony Lake this week," Connie reminds us. "I heard that Jules Janssen and her entourage booked an entire floor at King of the Hill."

Jules Janssen is an award-winning, A-list Hollywood actor. She's attending the Between the Covers Book Fair to sign copies of her autobiography, *Pretending to be Real: My Life as an Optical Delusion.*

King of the Hill is one of the two ski resorts in the Harmony Hills mountains. The mountains border our cozy town to the north, and the lake borders us to the south. Harmony Lake is a tiny patch of small-town paradise nestled snugly between a lake and a mountain range. The mountains keep us busy with tourists during the winter months, and the lake ensures we're overrun with tourists in the summer months.

"Why would she need an entire floor?" I wonder out loud.

Marla counts on her fingers and replies, "Her manager, her agent, her publicist, her security team, her glam squad…"

"I get it," I say, nodding. "It takes a team of people for Jules Janssen to go anywhere." Great, now I'm referring to people by their first and last names too.

"This will be our biggest, most successful book fair ever. We've never had three celebrities before," Marla observes. "And none of them would be here if it weren't for you, Megan. I can't tell you how thankful the book club is."

"It was nothing," I reply. "I just made one phone call."

The book club worried the annual book fair would be a bust because Harmony Lake has had some less-than-positive publicity over the past year, thanks to a sudden surge in mysterious deaths. It scared the organizers that book lovers might skip Between the Covers in favour of book fairs hosted by towns with lower murder rates.

The organizing committee embraced the negative publicity and made murder mysteries and crime thrillers this year's book fair theme. To help make the book fair a success, I asked my father, famous mystery author Mitchell Monroe, to attend as a guest author and maybe do a reading and sign some books. My father, who loves to be the centre of attention everywhere he goes, graciously accepted the invitation. He and my stepmother, Zoe, are scheduled to arrive in Harmony Lake tomorrow.

I doubt he'll be as excited as Marla about two other celebrities; Mitchell likes to be the most famous person in whatever room he occupies.

"Well, because of your phone call, the other two celebrities came to us!" Marla sounds amazed. "First, Claire Rivera contacted us because she heard we scheduled Mitchell Monroe to attend, then Jules Janssen contacted us and asked if we could fit her in as a guest author. Can you imagine? A celebrity worried *we* might turn *them* away!"

"I'm looking forward to seeing Mitchell and Zoe again," Connie says, changing the subject. "I hope we're able to spend some quality time together between book fair engagements."

"We're having a family dinner on Saturday night," I remind her. "And I'm sure Mitchell and Zoe will make time for you. I think they come to Harmony Lake as much to visit you and Archie as they do to visit me and Hannah."

Hannah is my daughter. She's nineteen years old and attends university four and a half hours away in Toronto. Mitchell and Zoe are stopping in Toronto to visit Hannah on their way here. They're staying in Toronto overnight, then driving to Harmony Lake tomorrow morning.

"Well, I'm carrying around a few copies of the

celebrity authors' books and a pen, so if I bump into them around town, I can ask them to sign them for me."

"That sounds heavy," I respond. "If I bump into one of them, I guess I'll have to ask them to sign my e-reader," I joke.

While we tidy the store to prepare for the big needle-felting-reveal party and celebrity-author guest star, we gossip about the rumoured plot of Claire Rivera's next *Familia* book and the outlandish tabloid magazine stories about Jules Janssen's love life. Our conversation ends when the bell over the door jingles, and a customer enters the store.

"Hi, there," I greet the customer, smiling.

She acknowledges me with a tight-lipped smile. Sophie rushes from her bed to the door to greet the new arrival, but the customer either ignores or doesn't notice the corgi pacing at her feet trying to get her attention. Sophie finally gives up and jumps on the sofa in the cozy knitting area to lick her wounded pride.

She doesn't look familiar. But with her dark sunglasses and baseball cap pulled down over her eyes, it's hard to tell. She might be a tourist in town for the book fair.

I busy myself pushing a broom around the back half of the store, aware of the mystery shopper lingering nearby. She sneaks glances at me as she slowly wanders toward me. When I feel her gaze on me, I turn and she looks away. She pets the yarn like she's shopping for canned goods, not squishy, fluffy yarn. I don't think she's a fibre artist.

"Can I help you find anything?" I ask when she's about a metre away from me.

"Are you Megan Monroe?" The mystery shopper asks.

"I was. Once upon a time," I reply. "No one has called me that for over twenty years. Do we know each other?"

"I'm sorry." The mystery shopper shakes her head. "I wasn't sure. I couldn't find any information about you online. You're Mitchell Monroe's daughter, right?"

Great. She's a Mitchell Monroe fan. I bet she's here to ask me to help her meet my dad.

"Yes, Mitchell Monroe is my dad, but my name is Megan Martel," I explain. "Listen, if you're hoping to meet Mitchell, he's scheduled to read from his latest book…"

The mystery shopper waves her hands, interrupting me mid-sentence. "I'm not a fan," she elaborates. Then she chuckles. "I'm sorry, that sounded rude. I mean, I *am* a fan, I've read several of your father's books, but that's not why I'm here. I'm here to ask you a favour."

This piques my interest.

"What kind of favour?" I ask.

The mystery shopper takes off her sunglasses and baseball cap. She shakes out her thick, glossy, auburn hair and flashes me an impossibly white, toothy smile.

"You're Jules Janssen," I say, shocked and maybe a bit starstruck.

She nods. "Is there somewhere private where we can talk?" she asks, checking behind both shoulders for potential interlopers.

Why would an A-list celebrity look for information about me online? What kind of favour could she possibly want me to do for her? There's only one way to find out.

"Sure," I reply, "follow me." I jerk my head toward the back room.

CHAPTER 2

I GESTURE for Jules to go first, and as she steps in front of me, a finger taps my shoulder.

"Is that Jules Janssen?" Connie mouths, exaggerating her silent words to ensure I understand her.

"Yes," I mouth, nodding.

"What does she want?" Connie mouths, concern creasing her forehead and the corners of her blue eyes.

I shrug. "I don't know," I mouth. Then in my normal volume, I add, "Why don't you join us? I'm sure Marla can cope by herself for a few minutes."

Connie nods in agreement and slips past me into the back room.

Marla is busy making adjustments to the front

display window and didn't seem to notice our incognito guest. I guess Jules's disguise works. I tell Marla that Connie and I will be back in a few minutes, and tell her to holler if she needs us.

Jules introduces herself to Connie, and I invite them to have a seat at the table in the kitchenette area. I offer Jules a tea or coffee, which she declines, and join them at the small table.

"I understand Claire Rivera is planning to visit your store this evening," Jules says.

"Where did you hear that?" I ask, neither confirming nor denying her statement.

"Irrelevant," Jules responds, waving away my comment. "I've been trying to meet with Claire for months. She won't take my calls or answer my emails. She's a hard person to get in touch with. I've resorted to following her to book fairs and book signings to get some face time with her."

"OK," I acknowledge with a one-shoulder shrug. "What does it have to do with me?"

"I'm hoping you'll give Claire a gift for me," Jules explains, unzipping her backpack and pulling out a gift bag with tissue paper artfully sticking out of the top.

"What is it?" I ask.

Jules Janssen might be famous, but I don't know her, and I'm not comfortable acting as a liaison between her and Claire. Especially if Claire has made it clear that she doesn't want to talk to Jules, and if I don't know what I'm passing along to Claire on Jules's behalf.

"Just a few small tokens," Jules replies. "I'll show you." She pulls the tissue paper out of the bag and places it on the table. "A copy of my autobiography, signed of course." She places the book on top of the tissue paper, flattening it, then she pulls out another book. "A popular needle felting book, signed by the author, with a personal inscription for Claire." She places the needle-felting book on top of her autobiography. "I had to pull a few strings to get this," she says, smiling and tapping the felting book. Jules reaches into the bag once more and pulls out a small felted sheep. "I needle felted this sheep myself. I learned how to needle felt to show Claire that I'm the perfect actor to play Mama in the film adaptations of the Familia book series."

The Familia book series tells the story of a modern-day organized crime family and their matriarch, Mama. Mama is a complex, interesting character. She's a loving mother, PTA member, and moral compass, but she's also a ruthless mob boss who will stop at nothing to protect her family and their interests. She's also a needle felter, and her needle felting acts as a plot device to show the reader how Mama feels; the more aggressively she stabs her current project, the angrier she is.

"I wasn't aware the Familia series is being made into a film," Connie says, excited at the prospect.

"It's not," Jules confirms, looking at Connie, "but I plan to change that." Claire turns to look at me. "I was born to play Mama," Jules insists. "I know Claire has said publicly that she'll never allow the books to be made into movies, but I know if I talk to her, I could change her mind."

"And you're hoping these gifts will convince her to talk to you?" I deduce.

Jules nods enthusiastically. "Exactly!" Her smile shows more teeth than I think I have in my entire mouth. "When she reads my autobiography, and this note I wrote to her,"—Jules opens the cover of the needle-felting book to reveal an envelope addressed to Claire in cursive handwriting—"I know she'll see I can help her bring *Familia* to life and introduce the series to a whole new audience."

I feel like she's trying to sell me something. This is definitely a practiced sales pitch.

I sigh. "If I see her," I disclaim, "I'll give Claire the gift bag, but I can't guarantee she'll contact you, or that she'll even open it."

"That's all I ask," Jules says, then she places her hand on top of mine. "Thank you, Megan! I appreciate it."

"No worries." I smile and drag my hand out from under hers.

"Also," Jules adds, lowering her chin and looking up at me coyly from beneath her long, well-maintained lash extensions. "I was hoping you could put in a kind word for me. Maybe you could say something like, I think Jules would be perfect for the role of Mama."

I don't like being manipulated.

"Jules," I say, sitting up a little straighter in my chair, "I'm happy to give the gift bag to Claire on your behalf, *if* I see her, but that's all I can do. Besides, I don't even know Claire, so my opinion won't mean anything to her."

"That's not what I hear," Jules responds matter-of-factly. "I'm told Claire and your father used to be very close. I'm sure it's not a coincidence that she's attending this book fair and visiting your store. I mean, you must be friends, otherwise why would an author as famous as Claire Rivera attend a book fair in this hick little town?" She chuckles, ignorant to the casual insult she just made.

I'm offended, and judging by the way Connie is smoothing her silver, chin-length bob with her chin held high, I'm not the only one.

Connie opens her mouth to speak, but I speak first, hoping to stop her from saying something she might regret. Connie is fiercely protective of the people she loves and of our sweet, tight-knit community. I think Jules Janssen just lost a fan.

"Like I said," I stand up, "I'll pass along the gift to Claire if I see her. If not, I'll leave it at the front desk at your hotel." Following my lead, Connie and Jules also stand up.

Connie opens the door that separates the back room from the store. "It was lovely to meet you, Ms. Janssen. I hope you enjoy your stay in our hick little town," she says in an over-the-top, saccharine-like voice with a fake smile plastered on her face.

"It was lovely to meet you, too, Connie," Jules responds, seemingly oblivious to Connie's intended sarcasm. "Here," she says, thrusting a business card at me. "This is my private number. Call or text me if Claire says anything at all about my gift, a potential movie, anything."

I take the card and smile. Jules gathers her auburn tresses and twists them into a bun, which she covers with her baseball cap. Then she dons her sunglasses and tugs the brim of the cap to shield her face. She hoists her backpack onto her shoulders.

"Have a nice day," I say.

Jules walks briskly toward the front of the store with her head down.

I gesture for Connie to exit the back room ahead of me, but she closes the door, places her hands on her slim hips, and quirks an eyebrow.

"Claire Rivera used to be close to your father?" Connie asks. "Neither you nor Mitchell have mentioned this before."

"Actually," I say, securing Jules's business card to the side of the fridge with a magnet, "we told you. We just didn't use Claire's name." I resume my seat at the table in the kitchenette.

"I'm listening, my dear," Connie says, taking the seat across from me.

"Remember about ten years ago when my dad's

author assistant resigned out of nowhere, then became an overnight sensation with a book series that my dad swears was his idea?"

Connie nods, then gasps when the realization hits her. "You don't mean Claire Rivera is the assistant who stole Mitchell's idea?"

I nod. "That's what my dad says. He swears the *Familia* series was his idea. He hadn't written any books, but the series was in the development stage, and he had made extensive notes when Claire quit. Then less than a year later, out of nowhere, she hit the best-seller lists with the first *Familia* book."

"Why didn't Mitchell do something?" Connie asks. "Couldn't he have sued her or something?"

"He considered it," I admit, "but he didn't want to give her any more oxygen, as he likes to say. He believes there's no such thing as bad publicity, and he didn't want to help make Claire's series more popular than it already was. Also, he didn't want to appear bitter, like he resented his former assistant's success. He confronted her privately, but she denied it. So, he did nothing. He kept writing his books and moved on with his life."

"Does Claire know you own Knitorious?" Connie asks. "Is she coming tonight intentionally to see you, or will she be shocked you're here?"

I shrug and shake my head. "I don't know. I've been asking myself the same questions. She emailed me at the store email address, but when I replied, I signed the email, Megan Martel. She knows my dad is attending the book fair. Back in the day, before my father accused her of plagiarism, she knew I lived in Harmony Lake. Claire and I were never close, but we were friendly. We haven't spoken since she resigned as my dad's author assistant."

"It sounds like tonight might be more interesting than we were expecting," Connie observes.

We stop talking when someone knocks on the door. Marla opens the door enough to peek her head in.

"I'm sorry to interrupt, ladies."

"You're not interrupting anything, Marla," I assure her.

"Megan and I were just talking about the book fair," Connie adds.

"Would one of you mind standing on the sidewalk and telling me if the book fair banner in the display window is straight and centred?" Marla asks.

"Of course," I reply, standing up.

"Megan, you take the sidewalk, and I'll help Marla in the window," Connie instructs.

Stepping onto the sidewalk, I squint into the midday sun. I should've grabbed my sunglasses. I position myself on the curb and use one hand as a visor to keep the sun out of my eyes as I squint at the store window.

I use my free hand to point to my left. "To the left," I shout, even though they can't hear me.

Marla and Connie nod, then move the banner to the left.

"Stop," I shout, holding up my hand in a stop motion. They stop, and I give them a thumbs-up.

I point to the right, then jerk my thumb upward. The right side needs to move up a little. Marla complies, and I wave when she raises it enough. Then I give them another thumbs-up.

I'm about to go inside when something catches my eye. In the blur of my peripheral vision, something moves around the corner, in the laneway that leads to the parking lot, behind the store. I check for traffic, then step backward, off the curb, and onto Water Street. I crane my neck and squint, trying to peek around the corner. It's Jules Janssen. The back of her baseball cap and backpack are facing me. She's not alone. A younger, well-dressed, bald man stands in front of her. They're stance is intimate and friendly, and they're in each other's personal space. He's smiling and laughing. He's handsome. His hand moves to her butt, further convincing me they're more than friends. He stoops down and kisses her. Yup, definitely more than friends.

If someone told me this morning that I'd catch A-list celebrity Jules Janssen canoodling with a tall, handsome stranger in the alley beside my store, I would have said they were crazy, but here we are.

CLICK HERE to read the rest of Sins & Neeldles: A Knitorious murder mystery book 7.

ABOUT THE AUTHOR

Reagan Davis is a pen name for the real author who lives in the suburbs of Toronto with her husband, two kids, and a menagerie of pets.

When she's not planning the perfect murder, she enjoys knitting, reading, eating too much chocolate, and drinking too much Diet Coke. The author is an established knitwear designer who has contributed to many knitting books and magazines. I'd tell you her real name, but then I'd have to kill you. (Just kidding! Sort of.)

http://www.ReaganDavis.com/

ACKNOWLEDGMENTS

I owe the biggest thanks you, dear reader. Your love and enthusiasm for the first three books in the series gives me the determination and inspiration to the series.

Thank you to Kim of Kim's Covers for another perfect cover.

Thank you to Chris and Sherry at The Editing Hall for correcting all my misplace punctuation and making the story readable.

Eternal love and gratitude to the Husbeast and Kidlets for everything.

Made in the USA
Columbia, SC
10 April 2023